T0165391

Triple Six Fix

The Journey of An Unlikely Guru

Stephen Brown

iUniverse, Inc.
New York   Bloomington

Triple Six Fix
The Journey of An Unlikely Guru

iUniverse books may be ordered through booksellers or by contacting:

iUniverse
1663 Liberty Drive
Bloomington, IN 47403
www.iuniverse.com
1-800-Authors (1-800-288-4677)

ISBN: 978-1-4502-2990-6 (sc)
ISBN: 978-1-4502-2991-3 (ebk)

Printed in the United States of America

iUniverse rev. date: 5/22/2010

Chapter One

(Late July, 2010)

Leo Ciampi stood in his barber shop in downtown Norton, some thirty-five miles northwest of Boston on an unseasonably cool, just slightly overcast day. Norton was a small old mill city on the wrong side of prosperity. Once vital to Massachusetts and home to many mills during the Industrial Revolution, Norton, like many such small mill cities, fell on hard times after the Second World War.

Leo's shop had stood downtown for decades, since 1908, with Leo himself standing there seemingly the entire time. He was sixty-five years old, so it was only an illusion that he'd been standing in place at the barbershop since it opened. Leo's shop was situated on Merrimack Street, the main thoroughfare in Norton, a busy street that led right to City Hall at the end of its reach. In front of Norton's City Hall was a monument to what the city claimed were the very first two casualties of the Civil War and another recognizing the struggles of the early mill workers. The monuments to bygone eras seemed to suggest there would be little to celebrate in the future. Norton seemed to have nothing left but memories of a glorious past.

Like the city itself, Leo's barbershop seemed unchanged through time, except for wear, tear and decay. The shop was long and narrow and nestled between other store fronts. The chairs had been bought in 1947, reupholstered in 1976 and not touched again except for repairs, when the occasional swathe of duct tape was placed on rips in the vinyl seats. The floor was well worn from years of traffic and neglect and groaned in an ancient tongue of protest when walked upon. The door was old and creaky and hung wearily on the hinges. On the walls were framed *Sports Illustrated* magazine covers from many years before, each giving mute testimony to golden ages now gone. There was a little TV on a homemade shelf quietly broadcasting the local twenty-four hour news channel, but hardly anyone who happened to be in the shop paid any attention to its unobtrusive pronouncements.

The shop—and by extension, the city of Norton— was old, beaten down and worn out. The entire town seemed to creak like Leo's fatigued floor and appeared to be made of the same ancient, crumbling brick as his tired, old building.

True to the unchanging nature of the town, Leo's shop had always remained a barbershop as the decades slid by, even as other businesses around it occasionally came and went. The shop was almost as much of an unchanging monument as any Civil War memorial, and had served as a witness to much of the little old mill city's changing fortunes. Locals had come to downtown Norton for haircuts at the shop's location for ages. It was touch-and-go for a while in the early '70s, when men weren't getting a haircut every two weeks like they'd done in the '50s, but the shop's proprietors had seen that tough period through, just as the barbershop had weathered all the other calamities Fate had thrown at the town.

Wars and social upheaval couldn't destroy Leo's barbershop, but now the barbershop's, and the city's, latest concern—the eroding, remorseless tide of an ever deteriorating economy—seemed to be history's most relentless and most lethal of challenges. Survived, Norton always had, but just a bit weaker after every epidemic, always not quite able to totally recover, just a bit more worn and faded after every battering.

Just as the city itself seemed helpless and flummoxed by the hammer-blows of changing epochs, so too did Leo himself seem hopelessly out of step, like something left over from another time, an anachronism given human form. He was paunchy in the face, and like most good barbers, almost totally bald. He wore an old-fashioned white coat when he worked, which he felt gave him a look of legitimacy and class. He respected tradition and felt *olde timey* wearing the white coat. It was as if he were showing his solidarity with the Good Ol' Days, which seemed so under siege these days, as they do in all days. In part, it was the history of the old mill town and of his shop and his personal belief in the superior status of all things long gone that weighed on Leo this particular afternoon.

"Fucking hippies," he cursed quietly to himself, his mind wandering.

Leo busied himself with empty tasks in his empty shop, putting scissors in jars of bactericide water and then sweeping the already clean floor upon finding no other busy-work to do.

"Fucking goddamned hippies," he softly repeated out loud, momentarily stopping his sweeping to provide enough silent space for his thoughts to be appreciated, unchallenged by distracting sounds.

Leo had his back turned toward the entrance when the venerable old bells that had hung in front of the shop's door since an earlier, more prosperous, time rang out, announcing somebody had stepped through the entranceway. Leo turned around expectantly. Business had been slow for a long, long time and any customer was good news. He was, however, disappointed to see the man who came through the doorway.

The man was thin—thinner than he used to be, in fact—and bearded. More bearded than he used to be, as well.

"Another one of those fucking visiting hippies," Leo thought to himself, though of course he did not voice any of the displeasure or reflexive dislike he felt towards his new customer. Their money was green too, after all.

"Can I help you?" Leo asked, a note of hostility and unfriendliness involuntarily creeping into his voice.

"Yeah," said the man softly and a bit wearily as he stood surveying the shop. The man was fully bearded, but otherwise generally kempt. His hair was long, but not wildly so. He moved slowly, as if aching from a long journey, and he coaxed himself toward the chair behind which Leo was standing. "Just a trim," he said, almost apologetically, as he sat down.

Wordlessly, like a priest performing an ancient rite, Leo started the process of unfolding an apron to place over the man, who, he realized, was older than the other hippies who had come to town recently. The man, as it turned out, was thirty-seven years old, though Leo couldn't have guessed the age exactly, as his beard obscured much of his face and appearance.

As Leo took out the various instruments of his trade, he took an optimistic turn after his initial, particularly dark, appraisal of the man and the hairy growth covering his face.

"Shave the beard?" Leo asked with a sudden lilt in his voice. Shaving off that hippie beard would perhaps be the highlight of a not undistinguished barbering career.

"No thanks," said the customer plainly and distantly, not anxious to open a discussion on the subject.

Leo frowned. He hated fucking hippies.

There was a period of silence as Leo started grappling with the task of trimming the man's hair. Unable to bite his tongue with the bearded stranger any longer, Leo finally spoke up.

"You must be one of them Earth people who've come to town the past week," Leo said almost in accusation, unable to entirely mask his aversion. Leo was incorrect about this man being a hippie, of course. "Hippies" were a phenomenon related to the late 1960s. There hadn't been real hippies around in almost forty years. But Leo's view of the world changed only slowly.

"Huh?" asked the bearded man with sudden animation. "What do you mean?"

"The hippies, the Earth people. What do they call themselves?" Leo pondered, momentarily stopping his fine shearing. "Earthbums? What is it? Oh, I know—Earthpeace! They call the group Earthpeace! That's it." He said the name merrily at first, happy that he'd remembered the name, then with the final words, his tone descended rapidly to reflect his disapproval once he'd remembered the wretchedness of those about whom he was speaking.

"Earthpeace?" parroted the bearded man in response. "No, I don't know 'em. Never heard of 'em." He then lapped back into silence, giving every indication he could that the topic—and conversation in general—were of no interest to him, though Leo steamrolled any such hint that stood in his way.

"Yeah, you know who they are—they go around causin' trouble, savin' baby seals, stoppin' the Japs from killin' whales, stoppin' drillin' for oil, stoppin' this, stoppin' that," said Leo with disgust. He wanted to give every one of them a military-issue buzz cut, an 'I Like Ike' pin and a draft notice. "That's all they do, bitch about America and stop stuff."

"Uh-huh," said the bearded man with a perfunctory grunt, entirely disinterested.

"You never heard of Earthpeace? They're invading the whole fucking town. Bunch of damned, dirty hippies, they are."

"Oh, yeah," said the bearded man laconically, "I remember them now—vaguely," he added quickly, hoping his slight recollection of the non-profit environmental activist outfit would stifle the old barber. He'd noticed a few young, grungy kids around town in his travels. Earthpeace must be the explanation for their presence, he realized.

Leo examined the man as he continued to give him a trim.

"Sure you don't want me to get rid of this undergrowth?" he asked, waving his scissors around the area of the customer's beard as if performing an exorcism ritual.

"No. Thanks."

Leo sullenly went back to trimming and only the occasional snapping of scissors broke the silence. He took stock of his customer. He truly didn't seem to know anything about Earthpeace. Then why the beard? Leo examined his customer more closely. Though bearded and longish of hair, he was otherwise neat, more so than he'd realized when the man came in. Maybe he wasn't a complete bum; maybe he just went for the hippie look, with the beard and all. Leo's views of the man softened a bit—but only just a bit. No reason he couldn't talk to the guy a bit, no reason he couldn't at least feel him out….

"When I saw you, with the beard, plaid shirt and jeans and longish hair and all, I figured for sure you was one of them Earthpeace hippie kids. Sorry 'bout that," Leo said with a satisfied chuckle, trying to look at the man as a friend and ally.

"Don't worry about it," said the customer, exhibiting no interest in his social standing with the old barber.

"It's just that they're up and down this damned street all day, you see?"

"They are?"

"Oh, yeah."

"Why would Earthpeace descend on an old mill city like Norton?" the bearded man asked, immediately regretting opening up an extra conversational can of worms with the suddenly chatty old barber. Sitting in a barber shop by yourself all day must make you desperate for human contact, the bearded customer surmised.

"Ah, just sticking their nose where it don't belong," snarled Leo. "They rented a first-floor office downtown, just up the street from here on Merrimack Street. Downtown's so dead these days, even they could afford rentin' out a place. Rented it out for a few months to be their hippie headquarters for their protestin' and trouble-makin' and petition signin'. They'll be in town for a few months, from what I hear. It's about the airport expansion project. You know about the airport expansion, don't you?"

"Airport expansion? You mean Slocumb Airport? The little airport outside of town?" the bearded man asked, surprise evident in his voice.

Slocumb Airport was indeed the small, semi-private airport right outside town. Slocumb wasn't big and had no commercial flights to speak of. There was a very small, very relaxed and very casual Air Force base that supported research and electronic systems instead of hosting military aircraft—no fighter jets or anything sexy like that at Slocumb—and the other half of the airfield was used as a private airport for shipping companies like UPS and private airplanes. In fact, Slocumb had no Air Force planes based there at all. It did not have its own runways; it used the runways of the civilian airport adjacent to the Air Force Base, and less than one percent of the airplanes that landed on the runways of Slocumb Field were military. But the fact there were any Air Force facilities on the premises made the government a closer partner than it would have been otherwise.

"Yeah, that's it, Slocumb Airbase," said Leo, using the old name 'Airbase' that the place used to go by when first built. "Anyway, they're going to expand it and these Earthpeace hippies are all upset. They're saying it's going to disrupt a lot of wildlife and migration around Winslow Woods, where that guy Emerson Thorston wrote that nature book in the 1800s," said Leo with disgust. "Stupid hippie bible," he added in the way of an editorial comment.

"And that's why the Earthpeace people are coming to Norton?"

"Ahhh, they're trying to 'rally' the citizens," explained Leo with mocking overtones and a dismissive wave of his hand. "The State House and state Senate gave their approval to the airport expansion and the state representative and the mayor of Norton didn't hardly say a peep, and now Earthpeace is trying to stop it. They say with the airport expansion, the flight traffic is going to destroy Norton. There's going to be tons of air traffic going overhead after the expansion, where there wasn't before, plus all that stuff about destroying the wildlife of Winslow Woods. They're right about the air traffic," lamented Leo. "It's gonna be terrible. They could have expanded that Avery Airport down on the Cape, but all the rich people live down there, so you know that wasn't gonna happen."

Just then, serendipitously, a loud rumble practically rattled the windows, startling the bearded man enough that he flinched and almost ducked by instinct.

"There's a damned big plane flying overhead, now," said Leo. "Never flew 'em that big over the town until about twenty years ago. By law, we get only one of them a day. Once the airport expansion goes through, we'll get 'em flying overhead all day long," he complained mournfully.

"So you don't want the airport traffic destroying the city of Norton either? Then why do you hate these Earthpeace people being in town so much?" the bearded man asked quizzically, turning his head around to look up at Leo.

Leo stopped, lowered his instruments and looked at him nonplussed for a moment.

"Because I hate fucking hippies," he said plainly, as if the answer were painfully obvious.

"I see," said the bearded man, turning back around in the chair and emotionally removing himself from the conversation.

Leo sensed this and once again a pre-rapprochement silence took hold.

His unhappiness at being met with silence caused Leo to once again return to his dark musings on the bearded man.

"Don't suppose you follow sports, young fella?" Leo asked skeptically, eventually breaking the quietude.

"Sure I do," said the bearded man confidently.

"Really? You're a sports fan?"

"Sure I'm a sports fan. Why wouldn't I be?"

"Oh, I don't know, I just thought you wouldn't care about sports," lied Leo, for he had a fully formed opinion about the nature of the bearded fellow's tastes. Males with beards, even older ones like this guy, were more interested in smoking wacky marijuana than wholesome pursuits like tackling players and hitting balls. Grass was to be run on, not smoked, that was Leo's philosophy—and he wasn't shy about sayin' it, either. "See that ball game last night? Boy, did that reliever ever blow it with that curveball!"

"It was a slider," said the Bearded One with casual self-assurance.

"No, no, it was a curve," said Leo, vacillating once more and suddenly developing a slight grudging respect for his bearded customer, who was at least man enough to know different types of pitches. Maybe he really wasn't a secret sissy after all.

"It was a slider," the bearded customer said with an unruffled confidence that rattled Leo.

"No, Varitek," he said, referring to the catcher for the Red Sox, "put down two fingers—for the curve," Leo said with finality.

"There was a man on second base. They changed the signs. They switch up the signs with a runner on second and I was watching the catcher give the signs. The ball broke down into the lefthander's batter's box. Trust me," the bearded man said, finally bothering to make eye contact with Leo by turning half around and looking directly at him, "it was slider."

The Bearded One was right, thought Leo, there *was* a man on second. The man was so authoritative that Leo conceded in his mind—if not in the conversation—that the bearded man must be right.

"You watch a lot of sports, then, fella?" Leo asked.

"Used to," said the customer curtly, again returning to his old taciturn self, looking straight ahead, trying to give every indication he didn't want to talk about himself.

Leo went on for a while talking about local sports teams, every once in a while the Bearded One almost reflexively correcting him on small details here and there. *How does this hippie-looking guy know all this stuff?* Leo asked himself in consternation.

Then he had a stunning revelation.

"Hey," said Leo, his eyes widening suddenly in awed recognition, stopping his work and lowering his scissors in disbelief. "I know who you are!"

"Do you?" said the bearded man defensively. "Tell me, where are you from?" he asked, anxious to cut Leo off at the pass and turn the question around before the barber could pose it at him.

"Yeah, I know you," said Leo, ignoring the question and tapping his scissors in the air in the direction of the bearded man sitting in his chair. "You're that guy who used to do sports on TV! On Channel Six!"

"Sorry," said the customer flatly, almost with hostility, "you've got the wrong guy."

"Yeah, yeah, what used to be your name?" Leo mused, ignoring his denials.

"*Used to be* my name?"

"Sorry—you know what I mean," apologized Leo humbly, for he loved fame and celebrity as much as anybody else. "What's your name?" he said to himself, closing one eye in concentration.

The bearded guy said nothing and looked sternly straight ahead.

"Come on," said Leo, mumbling to himself, "what was it now?" He looked up to the ceiling. "I'll be forgetting my own name next…. I've got it! Jack! Jack Webster! That's who you are! You're Jack Webster, you used to be the sports anchor on WKTD, Channel Six!"

"Sorry, I don't think so."

"Gosh, yes! I used to watch you all the time!" gushed Leo with enthusiasm. "I used to love your Sunday night weekly wrap-up show, too! What was it? *Sports Finale*, it was called! That was a great show!" Leo gushed, gripping the chair with excitement. "And you used to be the voice of the Boston Bruins during the hockey season! Boy, I used to love your work. And you also used to—" Leo suddenly stopped short. There was another TV show Jack Webster used to host, one that brought him into more homes than all his other work combined, but it brought him infamy as well, and when Leo suddenly realized where he was going with his sentence, he stopped in his tracks and feigned that he'd forgotten what he was going to say. "Yup, you were something else," Leo said.

The bearded man in the chair glanced quickly at the old barber blackly. He knew to what the barber was referring.

"I'm flattered, but I think you've got the wrong guy."

"Yeah, why I remember one time," said Leo, again pausing his hair clipping duties and continuing to ignore any denials, "I remember you were big buddies—drinking buddies and skirt-chasing buddies if rumors are to be believed—with that star center the Bruins had back then, Kelleher was his name." Leo was looking up, trying to recall all the details of the story. "You were interviewing him one night on your Sunday late show, *Sports Finale*. Anyway, you were interviewing your hockey star buddy from the Bruins—everybody knew you guys ran on the town together—at the fancy bar across the street from where the Bruins played." Leo broke into a big smile, recalling the story. "And you'd both had a couple of drinks—everybody could tell you'd both had a couple just by lookin' at the two of you—and you said something as a joke, but your buddy didn't take it that way and got ticked off and said something kind of insulting to you, so you gave it right back to him. Then he up and slugged ya!" Leo exclaimed with enthusiasm as he started laughing.

The bearded man smiled at the memory. Luckily for him, he could hold back his grin enough that his beard hid any display of emotion.

"Yup, then you hopped up off the floor and tackled him and started throwin' punches! That was a real brawl, too! Boy was that ever something!" Leo again cackled with joy. "Boy, that's all everybody was talking about for a week!" he said with admiration.

"That *was* something," the bearded man conceded.

"I remember the next week, everybody in the whole damned state tuned in to your *Sports Finale* show Sunday night to see what would happen! That was *real* appointment TV, I'll tell ya that. Everybody wanted to see if Jack Webster was going to go at it with his buddy from the Bruins again! Then you made up—made up like men," added Leo approvingly with a brief, stern nod. "Shook hands, had a laugh." Leo chuckled. "Boy, was that ever somethin'...."

The man sat still in the chair, trying hard not to show any emotion, but he was smiling behind his beard. "Good times," he thought to himself.

Leo, who was now done with the haircut, started brushing off the bearded customer with a small, talcum-laden whisk broom and slowly removed the apron that was covering his customer.

"Boy, that was a long time ago," commented Leo. "I haven't seen you on TV since—" Leo again caught himself and stopped short, in mid-sentence. "Well, anyway, that *Sports Finale* show really misses you on Sunday nights, I'll tell you that. It's gone down the drain since you left. Hell that whole damned station misses you real bad on the evening news and on everything else you used to do, too. They could use you back on TV there, that's for sure." Leo paused and the words hung heavily in the air. "So, anyway, what brings you back to a little old mill city like Norton?" he asked the bearded customer eagerly. All the cities and towns within seventy miles of Boston watched the Boston TV stations, but even though Norton might watch Boston stations and certainly followed Boston sports teams, in just about every other respect it was a world away, and nobody would expect to see a former television star hanging around Norton.

"Actually...I'm *from* Norton originally," said the Bearded One slowly and drawn out, as if admitting to an embarrassing rumor.

"No kidding! I never knew the great Jack Webster was from Norton," Leo said proudly. "Not that somebody's gonna brag about being from this old town," he conceded. "Aw, see that, Jack?" complained the barber, as he happened to look out his window. "There go a bunch of those smelly Earthpeace hippies now."

Jack looked outside the window and a bunch of young people, mostly with a practiced semi-disheveled and pseudo-hippie appearance, were streaming by the window. "Looks like they're headin' up to City Hall, up the street there. Probably going to protest the airport expansion and throw eggs at veterans while burnin' flags," Leo lamented improbably.

"Yeah… anyway," the customer said as he gingerly got out of the chair, again being as stoic and silent as possible, not admitting to any name as he watched the young people walk by. "What do I owe you for the haircut?" he asked, reaching for his wallet.

"*You*? You don't owe me nothin'," said Leo, prideful that such an important local celebrity would come into his barbershop. "Your money's no good here, Jack," he asserted strongly, putting his hands up to refuse payment, renouncing a few dollars he could ill-afford to pass up.

His customer nodded, half thankful, half ashamed.

"Thanks," he said wearily, then he slowly and apologetically walked out. The bells above the door jingled merrily as he left, oblivious to his solemn countenance as he passed underneath. As soon as the man was gone, Leo rushed over the phone and called up an old buddy.

"Hey, Tom, it's Leo," he said after his friend picked up on the other end. "You'll never guess who just came into my shop for a haircut! Jack Webster! Yeah, that's right, the guy from TV! He's got a *beard* now! And kinda long hair! Trying to keep a low profile now after what happened a few years ago, I guess. Yeah, I'm sure it was him, I'm positive! Yes, that Jack Webster—the guy who was involved in that huge scandal a couple of years ago! Can you believe it? I thought he was still away, too. Oh, yeah, it was him, I'd know him anywhere. I'm sure it was him. No, I don't know why he's in town now. Well, if he comes back, I'm gonna take a picture and put it on the wall! I can't believe it! Right here in my shop, *Jack Webster*.…"

Chapter Two

(Four Years Previous, Early August, 2006)

The quiet, darkened television studio was suddenly jolted alive with blaring lights and thundering, brassy theme music.

"Good evening everybody, and welcome to *Daily Number Live!* here on WKTD TV, Channel Six!" declared Jack Webster buoyantly, staring right into the camera, a broad, unctuous smile reaching from ear to ear, one hand pointing triumphantly at the camera, the other hand holding a microphone to his mouth. His tailored suit straining to hold back his athletic build, his hair perfectly manicured short and neat, Jack cut a confident figure, a man at the top of his game and the star of the show. The lights, cameras and a million eyeballs were all focused on him. And he ate it up.

To the viewers watching their televisions at home, the scene was a familiar one, a nightly one, an exciting one. After Jack energetically rolled out the show's introduction, a disembodied voice declared enthusiastically to the television viewers at home, "It's time for the live, daily drawing of the Massachusetts Lottery! Today's daily drawing is for August 9th, 2006! Now, let's play the Daily Number... with your host... Jack Webster!" boomed the voice as the *Daily Number Live!* theme song victoriously paraded in the aural background. The scene on the television screen was stock footage of a jumble of numbered ping-pong balls bouncing and jostling, followed by a happy montage of winners scarcely able to believe their luck. It was a standard opening with brash, vaguely big band-sounding theme music playing behind the announcer's voice, announcing a triumph that in fact had not yet materialized.

Despite all the horn sounds and enthusiastic voice-overs, the state lottery drawing was not, in truth, a dramatic and exhilarating event when viewed in person on the WKTD soundstage. The set was quite thin and plain when seen up close. The backdrop was simple and looked like it could have been thrown together by a high school drama club. Despite the modest production value of the set, the daily drawing show was always hugely watched. People enjoyed the lottery. They enjoyed playing it, they enjoyed watching it. And they very much enjoyed Jack Webster hosting it.

Jack Webster, as he stood, smiling and looking directly at the audience at home behind the camera, said "Hi, everyone, I just want to remind you that starting tomorrow, the new 'Fortune's Wheel' lottery tickets are going on sale, so stock up now so we can make some millionaires out there. The lottery drawings are audited by Burke-Holtzman, CPA, an independent accounting firm, and the official overseeing the drawing from Lottery Security is Bill Hillgrove," Jack announced rapidly, for no one cared about such trivialities and formalities. They were watching to see the selection of the magic, life-giving numbers. "Tonight's senior citizen witness is Alfred Woodhouse! A reminder, the guaranteed annuity of the Daily Pick Three drawing tonight is at least one *million* dollars!"

Jack's appearance was entirely different than it would be just a few years later. He looked stylish and magnificent, his athletic frame and powerful yet taut torso the result of years of gym memberships and a life on the athletic playing fields of educational institutions and a dutiful, dedicated avoidance of libraries and study halls. His good looks and designer suits landed him on many a "Best Dressed" list around town, on a few local magazine covers and more than a few gossip pages. He was an ex-jock and still had the football running back's physique he had in college, even though he was now thirty-three and long past his collegiate playing days as a star in the backfield of a local Division Two powerhouse.

His athletic background and charismatic personality led him to a much desired position: sports broadcaster on the local news in a sports-crazed city that he always called home. In his ten years on air, he'd become easily the most popular sports broadcaster on the local TV news scene. Jack's good looks and confidence made him popular with women and his earthy jock-oriented personality made him a hit with male viewers.

So popular was he, in fact, that in addition to his sports anchor duties, his radio job with the local professional hockey team and his Sunday night sports show, the station's management wanted Jack to get more face-time and asked him to host the extremely popular *Daily Number Live!* show at 7:05. The Massachusetts lottery did not have its own facilities to televise the lottery drawing, so its partner, WKTD, supplied the set at the station's studios downtown. It was a great paying gig—*Daily Number Live!* was the most watched local show on television—and Jack had quickly accepted the offer.

"There are three sets of ping-pong balls, numbered zero through nine," Jack explained to the television audience rapidly from his familiar spot on the set. The crew, just a few dozen steps away, focused on him, though Jack spoke only to the audience. There were never many new viewers to *Daily Number Live!* on any given night, but the explanation of the drawing process was a formality that was required by rule to be done at the beginning of every drawing.

"The drawing begins when the balls are released and then mixed into the machine," said Jack. The "machine" was in fact a clear, large Plexiglas box. It looked not unlike a large fish tank. The box sat on a table with "Massachusetts Lottery" on a banner on the front of the table that concealed the lower half of anybody standing behind it.

If one looked at it from the front, the box, or fish tank, had three transparent tubes leading into its side, at a ten o'clock angle, each tube being filled with its own set of ping-pong balls numbered zero through nine waiting to be released. At the time of the actual drawing, Jack would go over and lift a stopper that released the balls from the first tube into the box, then the second, then the third. The final piece of the mechanism was an air pressure device under the table (which was erroneously called a vacuum device) connected to the fish tank box in which the numbers rested.

Once the three sets of balls were dropped into the fish tank, a button was pressed on the side of the table, then the air pressure device was activated and the balls started bouncing and dancing inside the box. At the top of the box there was a second group of three clear tubes going straight up, each about six inches apart. The balls would go up the tubes into a tiny, clear holding box where they could be seen by the viewer once selected. This was a standard sort of machine used by many state lotteries across the country, each built to look slightly different, but each working on the same principles. The entire box and device were clear and transparent, except for the vacuum machine device hidden below, of course. People loved to watch the light ping-pong balls flutter and dance around and then rapidly zoom up the tubes to reward the faithful partisans of each number.

Jack looked into the camera with the confident smile of a publicly popular people-person and declared, "We'll be right back in a minute after this message to see who is going to win some money!" putting a jocular arm around senior citizen witness Alfred Woodhouse. That's what

Jack was known for, being the popular guy you knew in school that was so likeable you could not even begrudge him his success. This sort of popularity was difficult to pull off, but Jack did it effortlessly. He was probably the most popular figure on Boston television and was always the most popular person in any room, maybe the most popular person in the city and the most popular and envied person you ever met. If there was a happier-seeming person on planet Earth than Jack Webster, you'd have been hard-pressed to name him.

Then the red light above the camera went out, indicating the camera had gone off and they were in commercial. Jack's entire countenance changed. The friendly, confident face dropped and his eyes dulled. His microphone, which he had been holding at rapt attention, went limp and drooped down in his hand as his arms fell to his sides. Where before he had seemed to engage the entire room, he now withdrew into himself.

A short, mostly bald, sad-faced, older man with wild white hair on the sides of his head rumbled over to Jack. He wore a dusty, black, cloth apron with deep pockets around his waist, a loose, ragged shirt and baggy pants, which he tugged at with stubby fingers. His face was haggard and seemed to droop at every opportunity, suggesting a careworn basset hound. He spoke with a pronounced Russian accent.

"Georgi," Jack said as the man came toward him, for that was the Russian's name, Georgi Sholokhov, "has the problem with 'the box' been fixed?"

"Yes," said the old man, sounding exhausted, as if afflicted by a long, dreary Russian winter. "I fixed it yesterday. I ran several tests on it last night. Late last night, after everyone else had left."

"You did? Nobody told me."

"Yes, I fixed it," said the older man in a pendulous, sing-song cadence, as if persecuted and hounded yet again. "I did it late, I was here alone. Everybody else had of course gone home."

Georgi was the assistant stage producer and art director, but those were just wordy titles. Georgi was really Mr. Fix-It. Anytime WKTD Channel Six needed a backdrop built, Georgi was the one to do it. He was a legendary handyman around the station, which is why he always wore an apron the likes of which you'd expect to see on a woodworker or craftsman, which is what he really was. Georgi had, in fact, built the *Daily Number Live!* set himself. He also attended odd production issues when called upon in his role of jack-of-all-trades, which is why he said, "Jack, the sponsor tonight is Okee-Dokey Supermarkets."

"The sponsor is what?" asked Jack, thinking he misunderstood the man due to his accent.

"Ohhh…keee-Dooo…key," Georgi slowly enunciated, frustrated that his accent had gotten in the way again. "The supermarket company. They are the sponsor tonight."

"Ah, yeah, OK, I know what you mean now."

"Make sure you work in their name when we come back from break," Georgi said as he shuffled off to his position behind the camera, mumbling something grousingly to himself in Russian as he scurried away.

By chance, Bill Hillgrove, the lottery official who was in theory auditing the drawing, wandered by.

"Hey, Jack, how's it going?" he asked with unwarranted enthusiasm. Hillgrove was a heavy-set accountant from the suburbs, and his slight association with Jack Webster was one of the very few thrills he had ever known in a life designed mostly to avoid excitement as well as hardship. Supposedly there to oversee the drawing process for the state's Lottery Office, mostly Hillgrove just wandered around the set aimlessly, stealthily stalking the food cart or secretly lusting after the college girls who worked as interns with a shameful flame that smoldered but dared not ignite.

"Hey, Bill," said Jack with as much interest as he could muster for the heavyset man. "Say, Bill, we're going to start the cameras in a second," Jack hinted leadingly with a half-truth designed to coax the compliant auditor away to a safe zone where he wouldn't bore the star of the show or otherwise be underfoot.

"Huh? Oh! Sure!" said Hillgrove cooperatively and without complaint, just happy to be on the team. Taking the insinuation in the manner it was intended, he chugged off into the dark recesses of the set, out of sight, just where Jack preferred him to be.

Alfred Woodhouse, the senior citizen witness, had been off to the side, watching with interest the exchange between Georgi and Jack about the "fish tank" repairs. Like so many other people, he'd always watched the popular lottery show and was interested in the goings-on around the drawing, but he found the excitement less than he'd anticipated and, much to his disappointment, discovered he was a bit bored. Jack noticed him watching out of the corner of his eye, but ignored him.

"Was the fish tank box broken, Mr. Webster?" the elderly man asked gently. It was unusual for someone to address Jack as "Mr. Webster." Jack was such a beloved public figure in the matey world of sports that strangers almost always called him "Jack," even when first meeting him.

"Humm? Oh, no, not broken, really. It just had something a little wrong with it. The balls weren't flying up quickly enough because some air was escaping. There was a crack in one of the tubes or something and Georgi—the prop man I was just talking to—sealed it with super glue or something."

"I see. Say, Mr. Webster," the senior citizen inquired, "How *does* that box work?"

Jack looked at the box. "Well, see on the left of the box here, there are these three tubes filled with the numbered balls. Each tube has a set of numbered balls, zero through nine. I press the button and they all dump into the clear, main big box, which we sometimes call 'the fish tank.' Then—and this is where you come in—you do your job as the night's senior citizen witness by pressing this button on the other side. That turns on the wind, which tumbles the balls in the tank. It doesn't take much air flow to float a ping-pong ball—in fact, even a hairdryer can easily float a ping-pong ball. See, we call it a vacuum, but what really happens is, the clear main box gets filled up with air pressure and that's why the balls dance around, because they have no place to go, and the air currents jumble them around. People really like watching the balls jump around on TV. We used to have just a tumbler that mixed up the balls like a spinning laundry dryer, but it didn't have much of a dramatic impact on the viewers, not like the fish tank does."

The old man looked at the other three tubes going straight up, like the pipes of an old church organ, each about six inches apart and a foot and a half long, from the top of the transparent fish tank box, where many times before he'd seen the balls fly up into the little holding box at the end of the "church organ" tubes. A ball that went up to the top of the tube into the holding box was a winning ball. The main fish tank box was about three feet long and two feet high and sat on the table, which itself was a few feet high. The final resting place of the winning numbered ball was almost eye level, which was by design for benefit of the television cameras.

"How do the winning balls fly up the tubes to the top? There isn't a vacuum pulling them up."

"No, there isn't" said Jack engagingly, for he was always a good host when the occasion called for it, "but the effect is exactly the same as if there *was* a vacuum attached to the top. See, what happens is, at the top of the tube where the winning balls go, I press the button on the side of one of the receiving tubes, and that creates an opening on the tube, leaving a place for the air to go. The air from box below rushes up and out the opening. It's like having a hole in a garden hose. Because of the air pressure in the fish tank, once you give a place for the air to go, the air rushes up there, taking a ball with it. Imagine filling your cheeks with air, like a jazz trumpeter, then you part your lips a bit and the air rushes out your lips. If there was a ball in your cheeks, it would be carried out, right? Same thing here. Sometimes the air current takes two balls at the same time, but only one ball fits in the receiving box.

Once one ball flies up into the little holding box, I merely let go of the button and re-seal the tube and move on to the next tube to draw the next winning number. Do that three times and you have your three winning numbers."

Alfred, the senior citizen witness, studied the device for a moment. It was a simple device. Numbered balls dumped into a main, transparent box, the main box then filled with air pressure and air currents from below the table on which it sat, then a button was pressed that let air escape a tube going straight up from the top of the main, air-filled box to select one of the numbered balls. Do this with all three tubes and you have the Daily "Pick Three" Number and a million viewers every night as well.

"Simple, eh?" asked Jack rhetorically with a cocky jocularity.

"Yes, it is," responded the old man ponderously, sizing up the device for a moment. "Sure seems like it would be easy to fix, though."

Jack was stunned. His face went blank and his entire mind stopped. He looked at the empty main box.

Sure seems like it would be easy to fix.

"3...2...1...," said the disembodied voice of Linda, the director and stage manager, from off in the darkness behind the cameras and lights, announcing the commercial was ending and rousing Jack back into action.

Jack was uncharacteristically distracted, almost shaken. Always in charge, he stammered and talked distractedly, with none of his easy confidence on display.

"Uh, welcome—welcome back! Welcome back to *Daily Number Live!* here on Channel Six." He moved with an awkward shuffle to get into position next to the fish tank. "Now, here with us for the, uh, that is to say, acting as the senior citizen witness, is Alfred Woodhouse. Now, Alfred, if you'll release the balls into the chamber...."

Alfred pressed the button and released three sets of simple ping-pong balls, each numbered zero through nine, into the main chamber. "Alfred has released the numbered balls into the chamber," Jack informed the listeners with a mumble. He stole a sudden, intense, purposeful look around. Bill Hillgrove, the lottery official required to be present at all drawings, was—as always—wandering off, nowhere to be seen, likely lecherously following around a young female intern at a safe distance, or gluttonously attacking the commissary's cart of pastries with abandon and without conscience.

"I'll now just press the button to start the chamber," said Jack, and after he'd done so, air pressure filled the main fish tank chamber. The balls started jumping and jumbling around. *Sure seems like it would be easy to fix.* The words silently echoed in Jack's mind with a new, curious fascination. He watched the balls dance, each carrying with it a piece of a fortune, each ball a piece of puzzle that, when put together created a picture of wealth—easy, free, effortless wealth.

Mesmerized, Jack watched the balls dance. It was as if he were watching the workings of the universe itself. It was beautiful...entrancing. It was a dazzling dance of energies, combinations and possibilities coming into fruition, then fading and repeating again. The energies of the world were taking shape, falling apart and taking shape again, all in the blink of an eye. He felt he could watch it for hours....

Jack snapped back as he remembered his duties. "For the first number," he said into the microphone. He pressed the button on the first receiving tube to begin selecting the winning numbers. A ping-pong ball immediately flew up from the fish tank, up the tube and into the little holding box to become the first winning number of the drawing.

"Eight," announced Jack plainly.

He pressed the button on the second tube and another ball flew up the second tube.

"Five," he said.

He took another step, pressed the third button and the third ball few up the third and final tube.

"Four," Jack said. "The Daily 'Pick Three' Number for today is eight, five, four." He sounded a bit spacey and provided none of his usual banter. "Come back tomorrow and we'll be making more millionaires, see you then everybody."

The red light on the camera went out. Alfred Woodhouse, seeing Jack staring off into space and realizing there would be no magic bonding moment with the famous and gregarious Jack Webster, simply wandered off in disappointment, his role played and his services no longer needed.

Jack dropped his microphone from his grasp and held on to it by the wire as it dangled languidly a foot above the floor, and stared off, lost in thought.

Georgi Sholokhov, ever vigilant in his duties, determinedly scuffled over.

"Jack! You did not mention Okee-Dokey Supermarkets! And I told you about it just before we went back on the air! They are going to give the boss hell because you did not mention them!"

"Billy Bowman," said Jack, coming to life and slapping Georgi on the back and referring to the WKTD station manager who was technically in charge of *Daily Number Live!* but who was never around the stage at the time of the actually drawing, "has the smooth tongue and big paycheck to deal with it, I say. He can handle it. Sponsors always bitch. Tell them I'll make it up to them for sure," Jack promised vaguely. He wasn't going to get in trouble. Jack Webster was everybody's Favorite Son, and always *was* everybody's Favorite Son, whether it was his high school history teacher who couldn't bring himself to force the academically mediocre youngster Jack into line with a failing grade, or his college football coach who loved Jack's determination and charisma and thus could overlook his zeal in pursuing an active and vibrant social life around campus. And now, even though they were about the same age, he was Billy Bowman's Favorite Son for his roguish magnetism, high ratings and behind-the-scenes stories of the town's most important athletes that just couldn't be told on-air. Jack wouldn't really be in trouble. He never was.

"I'm sure Billy will be all right," agreed a disarmed Georgi noncommittally. Jack was Georgi's Favorite Son as well. He looked at Jack as sort of a member of the family. Georgi didn't have a large extended family in America, as most of his relatives were still residing outside Moscow, and therefore he was even more eager to have Jack in the fold.

The lights went down in the studio and the crew quickly started packing up. It was the same crew that had earlier done the news at six o'clock and they were anxious to go home. The news was broadcast on the stage in the next room over. Soon this sound stage would be empty.

Georgi, in pursuance of his duties, unlocked the main chamber of the lottery machine and rounded up all thirty balls that were used daily for the Pick Three lottery. He used a black leather bag to transport them.

Jack watched him closely.

"Say, Georgi, you're the only one who handles the lottery balls, aren't you?"

"Yes," Georgi Sholokhov confirmed disgruntledly.

"So if something went wrong with the balls, you'd be the only one who deals with them?"

"Yes, Jack," Georgi said wearily, as a good Russian should. "I am the only one who handles them. I am the only one who handles any problems around here. I am the only one who does *anything* manual around here."

"Interesting."

Georgi, feeling the topic had run its course, then turned to Jack as his eyes lit up. "Tell me, Jack, are you going to see Aleksandra tonight?"

"Yeah. She should be here soon, actually."

There was a particular reason Georgi thought of Jack like family. Aleksandra was his niece and one of Georgi's few relatives in the entire country. Aleksandra was his sister's daughter and he'd put her up when she came to this country years ago as a youngster. He thought of Aleksandra as a sort of substitute daughter, and he was delighted when the twenty-seven-year-old Aleksandra started a passionate romance with Jack. Georgi—like everyone else—felt Jack was a great catch, he being a handsome, locally famous TV personality and the leader of the pack wherever he went. Georgi beamed with pride at the relationship.

Right on cue, a solid door with a push-bar handle opened from the hallway off in the distance, letting in light from the hallway, illuminating the darkening, empty studio. In sauntered Aleksandra, a fashionable jacket slung over her shoulder, accenting an expensive and stylish ensemble. She was momentarily silhouetted like a *femme fatale* in a dramatic scene from an old *film noir*. At five foot six with a model's figure, she confidentially strode onto the scene—any scene—befitting a woman who knew she was wanted wherever she happened to find herself. Her hair was red-rust in color, shoulder length. Her lanky, toned frame made an observer comment that she looked like honey being poured seductively from a squeeze bottle as she oozed supinely from place to place. She had a confident smile and wore glasses to read— which she tried to do only rarely. She did not like wearing her glasses, feeling they distracted from her spectacularly angular face and cheekbones. She and Jack, with his cocky manner and athlete's physique, cut a dashing couple on the occasions they were seen together out on the town.

"Ah," she said, coming to Jack and Georgi, purring with a slight accent, "my two favorite men!" She embraced her uncle. She only came to the *Daily Number Live!* set after hours and did not often get to see Jack and her uncle together. "Uncle Georgi," she said, breaking her embrace of him, "are you keeping my man out of trouble?" she asked.

"Trouble? Ah! Well, no, not tonight. But he will be fine. They need him here! He is the big man around here!"

said Georgi proudly, his accent much more pronounced than hers. Jack watched with a crooked smile.

"And you," Aleksandra said, coyly tugging on Jack's tie, "I've missed you." She embraced Jack and kissed him with a passion that should have made on-lookers and relatives uncomfortable, but Georgi radiated pride and approval as he looked on. To see his own blood at the top of the heap in his adopted country made him proud, and he was old enough that the physical workings of romance left no trace of embarrassment.

Jack, equally at home with all things physical, was not shy about expressing himself with Aleksandra as well. Such inhibitions and modesty were for insignificant people, the losers of the world. In high school, Jack had been the popular star athlete dating the head cheerleader, openly French-kissing in the hallways, heading up a spectacularly advanced sexual Manhattan Project, unlocking the secrets of the atom while the lesser lights of his peers lived in caves, covering themselves in goat hides and jabbing each other with pointy sticks. Some things, it seemed to him, never changed. He seemed destined to be a Winner forever.

"Did you have a good show?" Aleksandra asked, provocatively running her fingers inside his lapels.

"Yeah, it was OK," said Jack, evasively. "My sports segment on the six o'clock evening news was better."

There was an awkward pause.

"I should leave you two alone," said Uncle Georgi approvingly in his gravely Russian voice. "I will go and attend to my duties and get ready to close up the studio. Jack, I will shut everything off here, just go when you are done here."

The WKTD studio where *Daily Number Live!* was filmed was located on a small part of a larger studio complex. One could access the other sets, such as the one where the news was done and the set where a couple of local news discussion shows were filmed, by ducking into the hallway and going down a door or two. Because the *Daily Number Live!* set was small and relatively undemanding, the cavernous area off-camera was sometimes used for storage and miscellaneous demands.

"Now, Jack," Aleksandra asserted, rubbing her hand inside his jacket, "we are alone. Are we going out to dinner tonight?" she asked with a purr tinged with an exotic Russian accent. A lesser man would have melted, but Jack was not a lesser man. He was where he belonged. This was his station in life.

"I can come over tonight, yeah," he said with resignation, because he anticipated an issue. "But I can't stay over."

Aleksandra frowned with an exaggerated pout and pulled her hands off of him.

"Aleksandra," he started. He never called her "Alex" as others did. He liked saying her full name. He felt it was sophisticated, and he liked feeling sophisticated. "You know I can't stay over."

"Why?"

"You know I can pretty much only stay over when the Red Sox or Bruins or somebody are on the road, and they just came back from a road trip. This weekend should work out, though, this weekend should be OK."

Aleksandra pouted some more. Jack put his arms around her.

"I know, I know. I don't like it, either." He kissed her reassuringly on the forehead. "Don't worry, this won't go on forever." He hugged her close to him. "You know I love you, but you know I need to work on some issues first. It won't always be this way."

"I'm not going to play this game forever, you know," she warned, separating herself from him. "I'm not going waste the best years of my life and wait around until you grow tired of me."

"Don't worry, I don't want that, either," said Jack. He mused on the nebulous idea that had just recently come into his head. Aleksandra lately seemed to be throwing down the gauntlet in demanding more of a commitment, indicating he would need to provide something more than vague words at some point, so he decided to give her an insight into this thinking. Jack gently grabbed both of her arms firmly and stared at her. "I want to be with you, and… just now, I was actually thinking of something. It's something that can help me—help both of us—to get where we want to be."

"What is it?"

"I'm not sure. I'm not exactly sure right now, anyway. Let me think about it, because it's only just come to me. I need to think about it a little bit first." He kissed her warmly, as much a partner as a lover, for he spoke truthfully to her about what he wanted. "I just need to think about it first…."

Chapter Three

(Late July, 2010)

Jack left the old barbershop in downtown Norton on Merrimack Street after his haircut and went outside. By the time Leo the barber had gotten around to letting Jack off the hook for the bill for the trim, the group of young Earthpeace people who had irritated the old barber by walking past his window had moved on up the street.

Having nowhere to go, Jack stood there on the sidewalk and did nothing. His hands were in his pockets, but he was otherwise at a loss as to what to do next. It was at times like this that he wished he smoked. It would have been the perfect time to linger on the sidewalk and nonchalantly light up a cigarette.

Jack calculated that the old barber was undoubtedly correct when he'd guessed that the young people from Earthpeace streaming past his shop window had been heading off to a protest of some sort. The young would-be rabble-rousers were almost certainly off to congregate at City Hall, located, as it was, right up the street. Jack scratched his bearded chin. A couple of Earthpeace people continued to straggle by.

The barber had also been correct in guessing his identity, of course. He was indeed Jack Webster, formerly the brightest star in the constellation of local television. But that was almost four years ago. Four years since the firmament of his celebrity lit up the night, four years since he'd been on top of the world. In some ways, it seemed a much longer time than that. In other ways, it seemed merely an instant ago.

Now he was a guy who had a new, lousy job (coordinated by the state) delivering carpets to business and industrial locations as part of a work-release arrangement. It was decided by the authorities that inmates got acclimated back into society better if they had work when they got out, and though Jack was not a large threat for recidivism no matter what his immediate employment status, this menial job had been arranged for him as part of his 'rehabilitation' back into society. At the present moment, his modest re-acclimation efforts consisted of passively watching a bunch of Earthpeace hippie-wanna-be kids passing by.

Of course, these young people—mostly college aged and just-out-of-college-aged—were not really hippies. These were Earthpeace activists. They were protesters, yes, and they practiced a studied unkemptness when compared to the rest of society, but hippies belonged to another generation. Nor were they, in general, the inheritors of the mantle from the anarchists and other agitators who had caused the infamous riots at the 1999 World Trade Organization meeting in Seattle and elsewhere. While the Earthpeace kids might have sympathy for the aims of the WTO protesters who rioted all across the globe, this group was, in reality, just a local chapter of environmental activists, not wild-eyed extremists. Their radical sympathies were mostly reserved for a world of fantastical daydreams and coffeehouse conversation. They might have romantic visions of an Anti-Globalization style of protest, but their numbers were small and they were not, by and large, rioters by nature.

Sadly for the protesters gathered in the little city of Norton, the interest level in what they were doing was nothing on the scale of a WTO protest, either. Earthpeace was in it for the long haul, raising awareness, usually acting locally (as they were here in Norton) against things that threatened the environment. A few of their number wanted to express their idealism by throwing trash-cans through police cruiser windshields, but mostly the group was just out to hold signs and change minds.

Bored, Jack, stopped one of the Earthpeace youngsters.

"Hey, what's going on?" he asked. "What are you guys doing?" He need ask no more. Earthpeace types were never hesitant to tell an interested party what they were up to.

"We're going off to City Hall to protest the airport expansion," the kid replied happily with upwardly-mobile enthusiasm.

Jack looked at the kid—plaid shirt, jeans, weak beard, messy hair, but unmistakably a middle-class college kid. The group's young people were idealistic—annoyingly so, in Jack's estimation. They pretty much all looked like this kid, even the ones who where older. A few older, veteran protesters—legitimate hippie leftovers—were there, and there were even a couple of clean-cut local residents who shared Leo's social outlook and thus were embarrassed to be in the company of such rabble as the Earthpeacers, but who were motivated out of self-interest to engage in a marriage of convenience to stop the airport from flying large airplanes over their homes. Looking at the scruffy protesters, Jack realized he pretty much looked like one of the Earthpeace people himself and realized why Leo the barber had mistaken him for one of their congregation.

Then, as Jack's mind was wandering over the suddenly smooth terrain of this realization, he saw her.

She was one of the Earthpeace people, tiny, with long, straight, light brown hair. She looked to Jack to be a vision of young life itself—idealistic, perky, vibrant and physically vigorous. Jack reversed his previous cynicism on the protesters' idealism and was immediately captivated. In the work of an instant, he was determined to meet her. She was probably a lot younger than he was, maybe by ten years, but he didn't care. Jack had always done well with the ladies and considered age difference to be little in terms of an obstacle. His eyes followed this young woman walking off ahead of where he was standing.

Jack had always been a killer with the ladies, and he'd longed for their company greatly after his long absence. He had been out a few months and was anxious to return to a life of romance. Jack had good tastes, and his recent encounters with women—being fresh out of the state's custody, with virtually no money and all—had left much to be desired. But despite his current sullen, stunted and withdrawn disposition, deep down he was still confident in himself. Jack was sure the old skill lingered.

Then Jack got an unexpected opportunity. The Earthpeace kid to whom he'd aimed his inquiry was still talking, and asked him a question, "So, you're here to hook up with Earthpeace, aren't you?"

The kid, like Leo the barber, saw Jack's appearance and assumed he was in town to join the protest. There is a tide in the affairs of man (Jack recalled somebody saying to him once) which when taken at the flood, lead to fortune, and Jack was all about seizing opportunities in his affairs; he always had been. And so he seized now.

"Yeah," answered Jack, suddenly inspired. "Yeah, I am."

"Great!" said the kid. "Thanks for caring!"

Jack, standing there, quickly melded into the group of Earthpeacers who were straggling by and simply started walking along with them, carried away by the current. The girl he wanted to meet was with Earthpeace, so he'd go along with Earthpeace. He had no interest in perpetrating a charade beyond how it served his purpose of meeting this young woman, but he could afford a few hours of his time….

Jack walked along with the others, quickly passing them in his efforts to catch up with the young woman he'd seen.

The kid to whom Jack had initially spoken was apparently something of a follower by nature and seemed to attach himself to Jack, keeping pace with him as he moved rapidly along the sidewalk. The kid introduced himself as Phil as they walked.

"So, Phil" said Jack to the kid, trying to bring himself up to speed on the topic that brought Earthpeace to town, "what's this airport expansion all about? Why does it have you up in arms?"

"Man, they want to expand the airport—"

"Who does?" interrupted Jack, his old television sports reporter's nose demanding the Who, What, When and Wheres of the situation.

"The state's Department of Transportation has ownership of the airport."

"I see. And they want to expand the airport?"

"Yeah."

"And you don't like that?"

"No way, man," said the kid as they walked down Merrimack Street towards City Hall, past the shops and the storefronts, an uncomfortable number of which were empty. "See, the expansion project threatens Winslow Woods, the woods that are the very birthplace of the environmental movement! It's going to screw up the migration of twelve separate bird species and increase traffic through the national park next door. The noise pollution alone would drive off half the birds, given the side of the airport they're building on! The nesting area of the Blue-Bottled Finch is going to be destroyed," the kid said with rising indignation.

He went on a bit more about the negative impact of the airport expansion on the city of Norton, but Jack quickly grew bored and tuned him out. He looked up, and just ahead, going into a convenience store, was the girl he was so anxious to meet.

"I'll talk to you later," Jack told Phil, unceremoniously dumping him on the spot, leaving the kid behind, grasping at air with a puzzled, confused look on his face.

Jack hurried a bit and went inside the store, grabbed a bottle of water and stood in line next to her and made it seem like happenstance that he pulled up alongside the young woman.

"Hey, how you doing?" said Jack confidently, extending a hand to the tiny girl. "My name's Jack."

"Hi!" said the young woman with the perkiness Jack was hoping he'd find. "I'm Ava."

"Ava?" asked Jack. "Haven't I seen you before?"

"I don't think so, have you?"

"Maybe. Going downtown?" She answered that she was. "Great, I'm going too. I'll join you," Jack said with a casual assumption of authority that he'd found women always appreciated. They went outside and started walking.

"Where would you have seen me?" Ava asked.

"Not sure. I'm guessing you were too young to be at the WTO protests in Seattle in 1999, right?" Jack continued, casually integrating the information Phil had accidentally fed him.

"Yeah, I was only, like, sixteen years old back then, just in high school."

"Oh, yeah, that's what I figured," said Jack. So, she was twenty-six. He was thirty-seven. He could overcome that spread of years. As he chatted with the young woman, he was pleased to find she was perfectly friendly with him. He was regretful that he had this ridiculous beard and lost all that weight from his heyday on television, back when he still had a powerfully built physique and had not yet hidden his leading-man looks behind an outburst of facial hair, but he was very pleased with the girl at least. She was tiny, maybe a little more than five feet tall, a petite frame to her. Ava's hair was light brown with blond streaks, and the corner of her mouth formed a very distinctive smile, her wonderfully feminine features combining to burn an image into Jack's mind. He was immediately taken by her youthful energy and optimism. He hadn't encountered that sort of positive, can-do outlook for ages. He was entirely smitten.

"I haven't seen you at the meetings," she said, presumably referring to Earthpeace, "are you new around here?" she asked with a friendly openness Jack found irresistible.

"Oh, well, I'm originally from these parts, but I've been away for a while," he said, smirking and congratulating himself for his inside joke.

"Oh, great!" Ava said. What was supposedly great about his statement, Jack could not say.

"Yeah, I haven't set foot in this town for years and years and I'm trying to re-acclimate myself to what's going on."

"Good for you!" Ava said with the hopefulness one only finds in young people.

"Yeah, well, I love the birds—especially the Blue-Bottled Finch—and I just can't stand the thought of those little fuckers losing their nests, you know?"

Ava stopped in her tracks.

"You love the BB Finch, too?" she asked with wide-eyed disbelief.

Jack, stopping as well, produced a practiced startled, amazed looked and said, "Don't tell me you do, *too*?"

"Yes," she said in astonishment at the serendipitous meeting of a kindred spirit. "Back in my junior year, when I was going to be an environmental biologist, I did a whole big field study on them."

"What a small world!" said Jack, making a mental note to research all he could on the Blue-Bottled Finch before she started quizzing him about their habits and hobbies. "Ava," he said, "I'm very glad I met you."

They continued walking to City Hall, exchanging views on the villainy of the airport expansion project and the poor slobs of Norton who were having it forced down their throats, all the while two souls in perfect harmony.

Jack didn't care about pollution or birds or any of those things, but he was glad to have some talking points with the girl, who he now knew as Ava. When he'd been walking with him, the kid Phil had gone on a while about various environmental impacts the airport expansion would have, but Jack just concentrated on remembering the name of the bird Ava had mentioned. He'd come to love the Blue-Bottled Finch in the last few moments and its future was very near to his heart. He just had to remember the name.

"So why are they expanding Slocumb Airport, anyway?" asked Jack, his curiosity oddly and suddenly piqued. The little city of Norton seemed like an odd place to put more air traffic. Slocumb was just a small airport precisely *because* of its location.

"Well, they were looking at expanding Logan International Airport in Boston," explained Ava, "but it was too crowded, and anyway, that's a major international airport. What the Department of Transportation is trying to do is expand air space for private jets and business flights for goods and shipments for carriers like DHL and UPS and FedEx and stuff, so they wanted to expand a small airport outside of the city. Now, you're probably wondering, why don't they expand Avery Airport down on Cape Cod, right?"

"Exactly," said Jack, who was wondering no such thing. In his head, he was already moving on, his tide of intellectual curiosity quickly receding.

"Well, the answer is simple: Senator Shea's family lives near where they'd have to expand Avery Airport. So what it came down to was, either the rich people like Senator Shea and his wealthy neighbors near Avery Airport got inconvenienced, or the working class nobodies of Norton—a poor, little, rundown old mill city—got screwed. Not hard to figure out how that was going end, was it?" she asked in quixotic disgust.

"No, not at all," said Jack, who had run with an important set of people in downtown Boston and hadn't given a crap about his hometown of Norton since he'd left it in the 7th grade. He thought it a good thing that these working-class nobodies weren't taken into consideration.

"What's your last name, Ava?"

"Basri. Ava Basri."

"Basri?" asked Jack. "Nice Italian name, right?"

"Nope. Iraqi."

"It's an Iraqi name?" asked Jack with surprise. The young woman before him was tiny, slightly dark skinned, as if well-tanned, but with long dirty brown/blond hair to her shoulders. She didn't look like what he'd expect someone of Iraqi descent to look like.

"Actually, my parents were Iraqi Jews. They left Iraq a long, long time ago when it started to feel unfriendly. And they came here. They actually didn't meet back there, they met in this country, among a little community here. I've never been over there myself!"

"You're probably not missing much these days. So what are you doing now? Aside from working for Earthpeace, that is."

"I'm actually a graduate student."

"No kidding!"

"Yup. Art major. I work in metals. Sculpting, blow torch, hammer, the whole thing. I went to California last year on the invitation of a guy I met here in school. I stayed with him and his wife." Jack raised his eyebrows. "No, no! Nothing like that. He's over sixty! He helped me a lot, put me in touch with people. I'm actually putting together a show of some work I've done. It's a first for me. I'm nervous, but very excited."

"I'd like to see that," said Jack enthusiastically. He knew nothing about art, except that he knew what he liked—which was also nothing. To him, artistry was a majestic home run, a bone-crunching hit on a defenseless quarterback or a slap shot from the blue line that whizzed pass the goalie and lit the lamp, but if this girl was an artist, he was on board with an enthusiasm to rival that of the most dedicated blue-blooded Back Bay Brahmin patron. She was going on and on about her sculpting, but the words and phrases meant nothing to him, yet he managed to nod at the right time and occasionally ask a question that gave the impression of being semi-informed.

She was very lively as they talked, so Jack figured he was pulling it off and pulling her in.

"So you've never even been to Iraq, where are you from?" he asked.

"The South Shore," she said. He wanted to know if she was from the area. Being from south of Boston, she'd probably recognize who he was once he revealed himself from behind the cover of his beard, or she would know people who did, once she eventually got to know him well enough to sleep over. It was something he'd have to deal with eventually.

"So, you're from Norton?" Ava asked Jack.

"Huh? Uh, yeah. Well, that is to say, I moved back here recently," Jack answered evasively. He'd ended up back in Norton by a judge's decree. Part of his deal for his release from state custody was that he be placed in a halfway house of the judge's discretion. The judge placed him in a location he thought would be good for Jack: his old hometown of Norton, and that's how he landed in such a bleak purgatory.

Jack was actually pleased with the location despite the fact he considered Norton a backwater shithole of the lowest order. He didn't want to go back to live in Boston, that was for certain. There were far, far too many people there who knew him—actually, just about *everybody* in the city knew him—and after his shameful incarceration, that was the last thing he wanted, to be spotted and gawked at everywhere he went.

He'd been a very big local celebrity during his time on television doing sports in a sports-crazed city, and he could barely go anywhere without being spotted. And when he was living high on the hog, he loved the attention. He practically never bought a drink for himself, barely ever paid for a meal and most importantly, found plenty of women anxious for his company. Now that he was in disgrace, he wanted desperately to be unseen, which is why he grew a full beard, to hide his face, and by extension, his humiliation. Behind his full beard, people almost never recognized him, except when they got a long, close-up look at his face—like a sports fan barber might, for example. He hated and loathed his gruesome beard, but it gave him the anonymity he needed. He figured it would be easier to hide behind his beard, in the middle of nowhere, in Norton, where people wouldn't expect to see him. He could be camouflaged, invisible....

"Cool," said Earthpeace Ava, seemingly happy at the news Jack had returned to his hometown. "We wanted to protest at Senator Shea's mansion, but the thing's a compound. We set up a demonstration there, but the cops escorted us off and ran us out of there," she concluded sadly. "That's why we came here to Ground Zero, to Norton. We thought if we could bring attention to the city, people would take notice," she said optimistically, oblivious to reality. Nobody cared about a little rundown old mill city like Norton.

They walked in silence for a moment. Then Jack, again uncharacteristically interested and musing on the situation, spoke up.

"So if the airport expansion is going to destroy the leafy splendor of Winslow Woods, what's a little city like Norton got to do with anything? The Woods aren't *that* close to Norton."

"Well, the airport itself is going to wreck the woods, but the air traffic is going to all be directed overhead. Both will be impacted. The woods are far enough from Norton, but the planes themselves are going to buzz right overhead, about a thousand feet, as they come in."

"So I've heard. Didn't the city of Norton say anything about this?"

"Are you kidding? Mayor Ryan is totally in debt to the Shea family—like every other politician in the state. Ryan is totally in Shea's pocket."

"So the citizens of Norton are against it?"

"They all are. Well, those who are informed are, anyway. A lot of people aren't even aware what's going on. The city isn't getting anything from the airport expansion, not even barely any tax money at all. It's going to be a disaster for the city of Norton, and they can't even fight back. They're just a bunch of broke, working-class families with no connections, especially not when compared to the Shea family. No politician in this state wants to cross the Shea family. Nobody can overcome the Shea family in this state."

Just then, they arrived at the City Hall protest site. Jack looked up and took notice. He was singularly unimpressed with the Earthpeace gathering. There were about three or four dozen uninspired Earthpeace people there, milling around, with seemingly nobody directing them on what to do. Had the protest even started? Jack couldn't tell.

"What's going on?" he asked Ava.

"We're protesting. I guess they already started," she commented.

Jack turned and looked back at the group again. Several of the people were off in separate clumps, talking socially, saying things to bewildered pedestrians as they passed by. A group of about six were walking in a circle and chanting something as they held signs. It certainly wasn't the Seattle '99 World Trade Organization protests.

"Is this *it*?" Jack asked, perplexed. One tall, larger kid was shouting something into a microphone to nobody in particular. The whole city seemed united in ignoring the big kid. It was as if he were uniquely invisible to the entire population of Norton.

"Yeah," said Ava, "just about." She seemed concerned. "What do you mean?"

"Well, it's just that... I don't know, this looks pretty unimpressive."

"Really?" she asked, worried.

"No, I mean, I'm sure it's fine," Jack assured her. He didn't give a crap about what these kids were doing or if they succeeded in whatever it was they were hoping to accomplish, he was only there to chat up the girl.

Jack made pleasant conversation with Ava as they did people-watching together, making her laugh with observations about disinterested passers-by and the two bored cops who had been assigned to "keep the peace" at the pathetic protest.

The kid with whom Jack had initially spoken came over, full of optimism.

"Hey, Ava," he said to her.

"Hi, Phil," she answered.

Phil, that was the kid's name, noted Jack. He'd forgotten it already.

"Things are going well," Phil said happily, bobbing his head in approval.

"Jack here seems to think it's a little disappointing."

"Well," said Phil, "it'll be better once the media gets here."

"Media?" asked Jack, suddenly concerned himself.

"Yeah," said Ava, "we alerted a bunch of media outlets. We need publicity to wage a public-information campaign."

Jack was going to point out that wars got waged, public-information campaigns got...run, at best. But he was too concerned about the arrival of the media to dispute the grandiose wordage.

"Who's coming?" Jack asked.

"Oh, everybody," said Ava. "We contacted *The Boston Globe*, *The Norton Times* and all the TV stations."

"Really?"

"Yup."

"TV stations? Like which ones?"

"Channels Four, Five, Six and Seven and the local cable news station, too."

Jack knew that meant WKTD, Channel Six, could be coming by. The very last thing in the world he wanted was to be discovered or filmed by his old TV station.

Jack took stock. There were about forty Earthpeace people milling around.

It was unlikely they'd get much—if any—media attention or publicity. Indeed there wasn't yet a media member on site at all. But they'd been alerted. They *could* come. If any of his old colleagues recognized him, they'd have a story worth reporting. After what had happened four years before, what Jack Webster was up to nowadays would still be news. Jack couldn't take the chance he'd be spotted. Public humiliation wasn't his gig.

"Hey, I'll be back in a minute," he said to Ava. With that, he went over to a clump of the protesters and said something of no consequence, keeping an eye on Ava and Phil. After a second, when he was sure they weren't noticing him, he slipped on around the corner and down the street.

Luckily for him, his one-room apartment was nearby. Or, to look at it another way, unluckily for him, as the neighborhood was downtown, but also rundown. It wasn't crime-ridden, but it was decidedly working-class, to say the least. He hadn't been there long, but he knew there was an old bar nearby. He proceeded to duck into the place before heading home, feeling a need to drown his sorrows and maybe feel a little bad for himself.

The tavern was called The Worthy House. To call it old hardly did it justice. If Leo's barbershop downtown seemed old, this place looked like it had its origins in the mists of antiquity. Built in 1832, it didn't look to have changed a bit since the doors had first opened. In fact, it hadn't seemed to have been cleaned since it opened, and as he looked around, Jack thought perhaps even some of the patrons hadn't left since opening night, either. The bar dated back to when Norton was a booming mill town, back when America started manufacturing things in the 19th century and before Norton stopped manufacturing things in the 1970s.

Jack had gone by The Worthy House several times but hadn't gone in before. Now that he was inside, he congratulated himself on his previous wisdom. The place, which made the dubious claim that Poe drank there, was a dive. It was a very narrow place, but long, going north to south. The ceiling was dark, but partially painted pink (now a dingy and dirty pink) with dark brown joints running across and with ancient, creaky, rotating fans overhead. There was a long bar running the entire length of the place with a mirror behind it, like one would see in a Wild West movie. There were steep, narrow stairs leading up to God-knows-where. The lighting was dim, for which Jack was grateful, as he did not wish to see the place, or its customers, in any greater detail than necessary.

Jack went in and sat down at one of the rickety tables along the wall opposite the bar, toward the back. After a bit, when nobody came over to volunteer to serve him a drink, he got up and went to the bar and bought himself a cheap pitcher of beer. Money was tight, so bottled imports were out of the question and Jack resigned himself to the questionable output from the domestic drafts. He sat down and tasted his drink, and discovered it to be as awful as he'd feared it would be. He wondered if the place had ever cleaned the taps since the days Poe had been there cruising for chicks.

Sitting down, feeling very blue and looking for something to distract himself from his mediocre beer and his situation as well as the disappointment of having to desert Ava just as they were enjoying a feast of reason and a twining of souls, Jack looked around and took stock of the beer-soaked denizens.

It was afternoon, so the place wasn't too crowded, but it was plenty crowded enough considering the time of day.

One guy at the bar wore a tank-top shirt and a greasy green baseball cap of unknown parentage. He was slumped over his glass—and not his first glass by a long shot, judging by his posture and glassy eyes. There was another guy three bar stools down, an old guy who looked seventy but was probably aged twenty years by hanging around this place every day, Jack surmised.

There was an old rummy woman with a small glass of brown liquor and a large glass of ice next to it, going on and on about her dog at home to the lady working behind the bar, who was hanging on her every word. There were two guys coming down the steep stairs who looked slightly buzzed, talking loudly about having played pool upstairs.

Jack could look no further. He was disgusted. Losers, all of them, he decided. Forget building the airport expansion next to Norton, he felt. They should tear down the mill city and build it *on* Norton.

Soon enough, Jack was sitting down to his third pitcher of watered-down beer to drown his sorrows, vowing to switch to bottled beer next time—cost be damned—and taking stock. He was feeling a bit sorry for himself, and not without cause, if one looked at it from his angle. He wondered, How had he come to this? He used to run in the most glamorous circles in Boston. Late nights, bright lights... good times. Now, instead of working on Ava, he was stuck in a dark, dirty, little working-class dive drinking hideous draft beer because he had to hide from public view. He was disgusted with it all.

Just then the door of The Worthy House opened, letting in a poisonous natural sunlight. All the denizens of the place turned towards the invading brightness and squinted at the antagonistic violation of luminosity emanating from the outside world.

Jack immediately recognized the lightness-bringing intruders to this world of dank nihilism as a group of Earthpeace hippie kids. Wearily, Jack sighed. This was probably the sight he wanted least of all. Tragically, that kid Phil was with them, and worse yet, he'd recognized Jack and waved a happy, jaunty hello.

Phil and two others, one a larger, angry-looking younger kid came over and Phil merrily pulled chairs out and joined Jack.

"Hey, Jack!" Phil said happily, glad to meet a friendly face. "Fancy bumping into you here!"

Jack had ducked the 'protest' about an hour before and had been planning to leave The Worthy House as soon as he was motivated enough to do so. Sitting among plentiful alcohol, the motivation had so far eluded him, but the upbeat presence of the kid Phil might well prove inspiration enough.

"Hey, Phil," said Jack flatly and without much enthusiasm. Phil still looked tickled to see him, however.

It was all well and good for the kid to be upbeat and optimistic in this grim tavern, Jack sourly consoled himself. After all, Phil and the Earthpeace kids weren't sentenced for a stretch here like he was; they were just visitors, slumming a bit, playing hippie for a while before they'd continue along off to law school or whatever bright future they had meticulously laid out before them by their upper-middle-class parents. Jack, on the other hand, was at The Worthy House tavern as sort of a continued jail sentence, a purgatory, a prison which kept prisoners behind bars of a different kind. Jack wasn't sure what the future held for him, what with his record of the past few years. It was possible he'd be stuck in Norton and The Worthy House forever—a thought that horrified him.

The woman who worked there came out from behind the bar, apparently figuring three new customers were worth the effort, whereas a solitary Jack had done nothing to incite her into action, and soon the four of them were sitting in front of beers.

The three young guys all had their drinks and Jack sat broodingly. He hadn't wanted their company and resented it in a low-key way, so he ignored their conversation with each other for awhile as they talked amongst themselves. But he couldn't be overlooked forever.

"So, Jack, what did you think of the protest?" asked Phil eagerly, his head bobbing up and down as it always did.

Jack began to languidly open his mouth, but before he could say anything, the big kid jumped in.

"It was fucking pathetic!" he declared.

"Why do you say that, Greg?" the third Earthpeace kid asked meekly.

"It was a freaking joke!" Greg answered angrily. Jack recognized Greg: he was the kid who'd been impotently haranguing nobody in particular with a megaphone out in front of City Hall. It was possible he was angry because his efforts had been for naught and he'd been ignored, but Jack didn't think so. He cast Greg as a Militant, always angry in a righteous way about something.

Greg was a big kid, a few inches taller than Jack and wearing the Earthpeace standard-issue pencil-thin facial hair as a beard. He reminded Jack of a young 1960s Bill Walton, except beefy and with a perpetual angry scowl.

"This isn't like Cancun," complained Greg. Greg then went on an earnest monologue about how he'd gone to Cancun, Mexico in 2005 on the guise of going on spring break, only to join the World Trade Organization protests there. Clearly he was implying this group's dedication to the cause was not up to snuff, not up to the standards to which he was accustomed. Jack tuned him out, however. Greg's bona fides as a battle-tested tree-hugger and Earth-saver interested Jack not in the least. He was thirsty and ordered a water—bottled, for he had no intention of testing the ability of The Worthy House's ancient pipes to produce drinkable tap water—and quickly drank it down before returning to his beer.

"Yeah, I guess maybe you're right," conceded Phil.

"It wasn't much of a turnout," admitted the third kid.

The three of them continued along in this vein for a while, confronting and lamenting the weak effort Earthpeace had put forth in protesting the airport expansion.

"You know what the problem is?" Phil stated. "Norton is too working-class. It has no pull, none at all."

"Nobody cares about this place," stated Greg, the angry big kid. "Nobody famous is from here, it has a lot of immigrants, too many poor people. Do you think they'd put the expansion down at Avery Airport, where Senator Shea lives?" Greg asked in a mocking, rhetorical tone. "No way!"

Jack, who was silent during all of the conversation between the three of them took notice of what the big kid Greg said. Jack looked around The Worthy House and saw the Earthpeace people might be bug-eyed and paranoid, but there was definitely truth in what they said. He took stock of the gloomy surroundings inside the bar, the dismal atmosphere, the poor lighting, the haggard faces and realized they were right: if it came down to the old mill city of Norton and the tawny town where Senator Shea lived, there was no doubt of the outcome, Blue-Bottled Finches be damned. Nesting habitat be damned, noise pollution be damned, congestion and fairness be damned—Norton would bear the brunt of any inconvenience and pollution. The worn-down buildings, the struggling city budget, the high unemployment— there was no doubt who'd win a tussle between powerless Norton and Senator Shea's hometown. And the worst part was, the expansion wasn't a big issue in the public's consciousness. Elected officials like Senator Shea had no fear of backlash. He'd been an elected official in the state for ages and it would take a lot bigger issue than an airport expansion—which hurt only the city of Norton and could conceivably help everybody else—for officials to feel the backlash, especially when hardly anybody knew what machinations were going on in the backrooms of the state's Department of Transportation.

Not that Jack cared about any of this. It was just a mental observation on his part. He'd met Shea twice casually at public events, and had met much of his extended family at different times as well when he worked in television and had been a roguish, swashbuckling man-about-town, appearing at charity events and in the gossip columns. Go ahead and ruin Norton, Jack felt. He wanted to get the hell out of this town as soon as possible anyway, and so did anybody else with any sense. Now, if he could only take Ava with him on his way out….

"What we need is a hero," lamented Phil pathetically.

"Doesn't everybody?" chimed in Jack suddenly and darkly. He'd been silent for so long, it was almost as if he was no longer there at all and the three of them seemed surprised at his sudden intrusion, and there was a moment of silence as they adjusted mentally to acclimate a fourth person into their conversation.

"I noticed you talking to Ava," said the third kid, whose weak eagerness betrayed the fact he had a crush on the young lass.

"Nice kid, she is," commented Jack noncommittally.

"That's who I feel bad for, people like Ava," said Phil.

"Why's that?" inquired Jack.

"She's super-dedicated," said Phil.

"To what?" asked Jack cynically.

"To the cause—to Earthpeace and stuff, I mean."

"Really?" asked Jack, interested.

"Yup."

Phil looked at the third kid in a teasing manner and said, "She'd do anything for whoever blocked this airport expansion. *Anything.*"

Jack couldn't be bothered to notice how the third kid took the ribbing. He was busy thinking.

"She's that into it?" Jack asked. "The whole environmental thing?"

"Oh, yeah."

"Really…." mused Jack.

"Big time."

Stephen Brown

"How long is Earthpeace going to rent that office on downtown Merrimack Street?" Jack asked. "How long is Earthpeace going to be in Norton?"

"I don't know," said Greg, the big, militant kid. "Two months anyway. Depends on how long this thing goes."

"At least two months, eh?" pondered Jack. That'd be long enough, he was certain.

If Ava was that much into the Earthpeace movement, and Earthpeace needed a hero… perhaps he could combine his interest with theirs. In his old life Jack had long been accustomed to the role of The Hero, maybe he could revisit the role. Win the day… win the girl.

He was conceiving a plan.

"You know guys, maybe I can help. You see, you wouldn't know it to look at me, but I have a background working in the media. I might be able to help out and give you something you need…."

Chapter Four

(Four Years Previous, Early August, 2006)

Jack was walking across the empty parking lot at DeValuvio's, Boston's most celebrated trendy, upscale Italian restaurant catering to the city's movers and shakers. He was wearing the most expensive shoes he'd ever purchased—also Italian, he figured, since they had the name Berluti—and for some reason, he took particular notice of the scraping sound they made as he walked.

Since it was one of the rare moments he was not in among the customary din of activity that typically surrounded him, Jack's sharpened attention turned to the sound breaking the silence. He listened to the scraping noise as he walked and wondered if it were the ground or the shoes that was making the sound. Which one made the noise?

Jack hadn't known what Berluti meant in the fashion world when he'd purchased the shoes, but he *did* know they cost a bundle, and he knew that women responded to such things as stylish, expensive shoes. Plus, the salesmen assured him they were primo footwear and well worth the price. He was a jock at heart, but a jock with a taste for the good life. He didn't know what was good, but he knew he could afford it. Still, in a way, he felt a tinge of melancholy that he'd forever traded in his cleats for fancy dress shoes. Thirty-three wasn't a bad age, it just wasn't a starting point any longer.

He'd bought his Berluti shoes to celebrate his most recent TV contract when he'd signed it. It was a large contract—every year he'd made more money than the year before—and at the time he felt at a bit of a loss over what to do next to celebrate his good fortune. His closet already bulged with tailored finery of every description purchased from the priciest shops on Newbury Street, and he'd realized his footwear needed to go top-notch, too.

Jack was no financial expert, he was a jock who'd made it good, and no matter how much he made, he could always find plenty of ways to spend his money, as he'd ruefully discovered. Despite making a great deal of money as a sportscaster, he still seemed to be always stretching for money, hence his readily agreeing to do the *Daily Number Live!* show. These days, even with that very lucrative gig supplementing his salary, he was looking for more. The more he had, the more he had to chase a little harder for even more….

A smile came to Jack's face as his mind drifted away from his scraping shoes. Life was pretty good, he felt, even considering his peculiar, never-ending need for money. He'd just parted ways with Aleksandra at DeValuvio's door. He'd planned to go to dinner and then back to her place for a romp before heading home, but their passion had proved too strong and the romp had to come first, followed by a late, light meal. Their passion for each other was wild and untamed like that; it was spontaneous, reckless and unrestrained. When he was a running back at a Division Two college, Jack had always burst through the line as soon as an opening appeared, and he was still basically the same now, even in fancy dress shoes instead of cleats. If he wanted a romp before the meal, then so be it. He was a slave to his passions and saw little need to restrain his love of this life.

There were two sorts of trendy Italian restaurants as far as Jack was concerned. The first was the sort of place you went if you had low-key class or if you didn't want to be seen. Usually, out of necessity, that's the sort of place he went with Aleksandra, a place where they could go and have privacy, not be seen and avoid having people coming up and talking to him about the TV station or the local sports scene, or worse yet, have people spot him who could not be trusted to mind their own business.

DeValuvio's was the second sort of place, the sort of place you went when you wanted to see the lights and excitement of the city, it was a place where you'd go to be seen. Visiting pop musicians and performers would go there when in town and would garner a mention in the next morning's newspaper ("Guess who was spotted at DeValuvio's….?"). Jack Webster loved to mix with

Boston's movers and shakers at DeValuvio's, and Boston's movers and shakers loved to mix with Jack Webster, have a good time along with one or two too many trendy martinis at the bar, laugh a little too loud and see where the night went.

However, the public nature of DeValuvio's meant he usually did not go there with Aleksandra. Officially, according to the way Jack introduced her to people at DeValuvio's, she was a production assistant at WKTD and they were there for a working dinner, as the downtown studios weren't far away. This was all untrue, of course, a transparent, paper-thin falsehood, but nobody asked too many questions, especially if Jack and Aleksandra weren't too over the top in flirting with each other while at the place. It was a bit risky to be out at such a high-profile place, but Aleksandra wasn't with him in order to be cloistered away like a monk and live the quiet life. She was twenty-seven, fashionable, gorgeous and feeling her oats. A woman like her needed to be seen, to see the lights and the high life, and Jack respected that.

Jack ponderously got in his Lexus in the restaurant's parking lot and started it up, relishing the tight, almost hungry growl of the engine as he briefly put the pedal down. Years ago, when he'd first started in television, he'd had a sports car, and he'd loved it, showing it off to the local ladies, racing around town in order to appreciate its sleek energy. Now, he was older and a sports car wouldn't quite work the same way it had ten years ago. At thirty-three, he was content to have solid, respectable but fashionable luxury under him; it was part of the transition of age. He still liked to stay out late and live the life—make no mistake, he wasn't old—but a foreign luxury car was the more appropriate way to go now for someone of his station in life.

"Yup, not a kid anymore," Jack said to himself pleasingly, feeling he'd arrived. At least his automobile provided a rare moment of contentment in a restless existence filled with yearning and desire.

With a pleasant martini buzz, he pointed his car home and the engine growled again.

The city was quiet, as it was now fairly late night. The streets were largely empty as he drove through town, and Jack undid his tie slightly so that it hung around his neck with a jaunty looseness. The streetlights flashed across his windshield like a strobe light. He felt like he was featured a stylish car commercial. And he liked it. He felt he must look cool to the imaginary viewer.

"Aleksandra," he thought to himself, "now there's a complicated situation."

Jack was never much one for contemplation. He was about action, pure and unadulterated by endless speculation and contemplation. He might calculate, but contemplation? Not so much. But, in a rare exception, he contemplated now, thinking of Aleksandra. He wasn't sure where it was going with her. He lusted after her and he needed her, that was for certain, but beyond that? There were too many variables. She had a lot going on, a lot of demands. Would she grow tired of waiting for him? Would she drop him if somebody higher up on the food chain came calling, somebody with more money or more status or something?

These were Jack's slightly boozy musings as he drove home. He arrived at his residence in short order. He had a beautiful house in an expensive semi-urban setting just a few miles outside of Boston (he wasn't going to be too far from the lights of the city) called Auburndale. It was an expensive place to live, a desirable town and location. Jack was always thinking about selling it for a hip, pricey townhouse downtown, though. However, everything had gotten so complicated recently that he couldn't pursue that dream very far—not right now anyway. He still hungered for the action and glamour of downtown. He was restless, vaguely seeking a change, and Aleksandra, he knew, fit into it all some way, he just wasn't exactly sure how. Maybe they would spend forever together in a lover's mutual embrace. Theirs was a passionate romance, but there were no guarantees.

Jack pulled his car into the driveway at his house and shut off the headlights with an agitated push.

"Dammit," he cursed, looking at the place. All the lights were on. Jeanine—his wife—was still up.

Jack got out and let himself in. Jeanine, who had seen the lights in the driveway, was standing by the doorway. He knew what that would likely mean.

"Oh, hey, Jean," he said casually.

Jeanine put her arms out, palms up, in exasperation, with an angry, accusing stare.

"What the fuck?" she demanded. "Do I have to call you up to get you home?"

"Oh, sorry 'bout that, it was just that Billy," he explained, meaning his boss Billy Bowman, who was in charge of *Daily Number Live!* as well as the Station Manager at WKTD, "wanted to go out after the show."

"*Billy* did?" Jeanine inquired skeptically.

"Yeah, he had some stuff he wanted to go over with me and Kurt Bevacqua about the upcoming road trip, some features and stuff for the Sunday night show, just a bunch of pre-production stuff," said Jack. Bevacqua was the sports director of the station, and if the station manager and sports director wanted to get together about the direction of the 11:30 half-hour sports show Jack hosted on Sunday nights, there wasn't much to argue about. Or shouldn't be, anyway.

"And you had to go out afterward, to talk about this stuff?"

Jack, who had taken to absently fiddling with the mail on the coffee table by the couch, said, "Yeah, they—we—figured we'd go and eat and talk about it over a couple of drinks."

Jeanine said nothing with exasperation and left the room. Jeanine didn't mind the late nights—she liked late nights at least as much as Jack did—but the obvious problem of him having late nights while she was left behind at home resulted in her being understandably annoyed.

There was a time, back when they were dating and when they were first married, that the two of them cut the impressive couple on the town, hitting all the night spots with their similarly high-flying friends and couples. Jeanine was a year younger than Jack, thirty-two, and those nights now seemed a long time ago. They still went out, but it was impossible not to notice that when together they came home earlier than he did when alone.

Jeanine was a tall, statuesque brunette—one hundred percent Italian blooded, she was proud to say—and once had occupied the same position as Aleksandra did: the beautiful trophy on Jack's arm as he conquered the known world. A two-hours-a-day gym rat and beauty herself (Jack Webster? He wouldn't be caught dead with anything else. The captain of the team, he felt, needed a beautiful woman), Jeanine's fiery temperament was legendary in their circle and stood in stark contrast to Aleksandra's smooth Old World ways.

Jack had loved Jeanine's fire when they first got together. Unabashed and combative, she took a bite out of everything she did and shook it like a wild animal. She was the embodiment of life seized and embraced. A smoking body, a party animal and a demon between the sheets, at the time Jeanine was just what the doctor ordered. A marriage where the wife stayed hot, lounged by the pool and waited for the husband to bring home a big paycheck, that's basically what they *both* had in mind for a future. But things had changed over time. Funny how that arrangement turned out not to be the greatest formula for marital success, Jack mused from time to time.

Where once Jack had seen "fiery" in Jeanine, he now saw argumentative. He used to see strong-willed, now he saw stubborn. Jeanine still liked the party scene out on the town, but her combativeness did not always mix well with alcohol, and moreover, Jack quickly grew weary of his one and only party-partner. Sometimes you like to dance with a new partner, he felt. How Jeanine sized him up as a companion, he cared not to contemplate. They still hit the town together and sometimes even had a really good time (the previous year's New Year's Eve was legendary) but it wasn't quite the same as in the old days.

That was the landscape against which Jack had come across Aleksandra. She'd come on the set to visit her uncle at the studio and the attraction between her and Jack was immediate and mutual despite his wedding ring, and they were soon an item. There had been a whole bunch of other women who had been intermediary steps before Aleksandra, but she seemed to be sticking. She was more serious than the great majority of the others. She was more than a fling.

Jack was reflecting on just this when Jeanine came back into the living room with a suitcase and violently threw it down on the table, startling him from his reverie.

"You didn't forget I was working this weekend, did you?" she asked, at least half in accusation.

"Of course not."

Jeanine started angrily stuffing clothes into the suitcase.

"How's Ronnie doing, anyway?" he asked dutifully. "Business OK?"

Jeanine disgruntledly murmured something Jack could not make out, but he wasn't about to ask her to repeat herself. Best to keep potentially explosive contact points at a minimum, he knew.

Jeanine had a part-time gig. This older guy she worked for, Ronnie, bought various discontinued or off-label merchandise, perfumes mostly, and switched the labels and sold them as the real McCoys. It wasn't actually illegal for reasons Jack never bothered to learn, but it certainly was unethical for reasons he understood perfectly. Jeanine would go to festivals or fairs or trade shows and sell the stuff from tables he'd set up. Human beings named "Ronnie" didn't have great success selling perfumes, which is why he needed an attractive woman for the job. Jeanine got paid for it and got to keep a portion of the proceeds. If Ronnie wasn't paying attention to the inventory, she got to keep a larger portion of the proceeds.

The money Jeanine made with Ronnie wasn't much at all compared to Jack's salary as television personality, but Jeanine was not the type of woman who was going to be beholden to anybody, certainly not a man, not even her husband. Especially not her husband. She wasn't interested in being the happy little homemaker/Stepford wife. She needed to be independent. Jeanine was not the shrinking violet sort, and if she wanted to do or say something, it was going to be done or said. She was not going to be cowed by being indebted to a breadwinner. She'd had a more lucrative part-time gig back in the day, through which Jack had met her, but they didn't discuss that these days.

Jack could see Jeanine seething with fury as she packed and thought he could see rising vapors, indicating a volcano about to explode, and that was something he greatly wished to avoid. He did a lot of avoiding with Jeanine these days. Luckily, he knew just the magic elixir to soothe over her moods.

"Hey," he said, "want to do a line?"

"Sure," she said grudgingly after a moment's pause, still a bit withdrawn and hostile.

Jeanine went over to the hutch and pulled out a small vial from one of the drawers as Jack removed his jacket and his dangling tie and sat down on the couch. Jeanine came over and emptied out some of the white powder on the oval glass table that sat in the middle of the living room in front of the sofa.

"How is Billy, anyway?" Jeanine asked casually, making conversation, showing a small opening in her phalanx of anger.

"Same. You know Billy, he never changes," said Jack mildly as he took out a credit card from his wallet.

"A credit card?" asked Jeanine with annoyance. She always was a perfectionist. "You're going to use a fucking credit card?"

"What?"

"Never mind. Hold on," she said with annoyance as she left the room and came back with a razor.

He reclined as she bent over and started chopping away.

"Jeanine, you know, you look unbelievably great in those jeans."

"Cut the fucking shit, Jack, you know I have a long day tomorrow," she said with hostility, as she crouched over, still chopping away. If he thought he was going to stay out all night with the boys from work and come home to his own personal blow-up doll, she said to herself, he was very much mistaken.

"Going to Springfield," grumbled Jeanine, referring to the far-away town where her weekend gig was taking her. "Who's going to buy anything at a fucking fair in fucking Springfield? Ronnie's a cheap prick, anyway," she complained to Jack.

"You definitely don't seem happy with him lately," noted Jack noncommittally. He felt he needed to say *something.* The chipping sound of razor-on-glass continued to tap through the room.

"He's a cheap fucking prick," Jeanine repeated angrily. She was definitely in a mood. "A bunch of knock-off scarves and perfumes this weekend. I do a lot to help him run his business. He doesn't appreciate what I do for him," she declared. "I don't think anybody does," she added meaningfully, looking at Jack.

For the moment, nothing else was said. It had all been covered before anyway. Five lines of cocaine sat on the glass table. If an observer were looking up from under the glass table, they would have seen the two anticipating faces of Jack and Jeanine hovering above, staring down like eager faces in the clouds watching the earth below.

Jack leaned over and cleaned off one line. When they first began hitting the town together, they'd blow a line half the length of a pencil and just as thick, just to get the night on the town going, to liven things up. Now, they were home on an otherwise uneventful evening and the lines were almost twice as long. Like everything else, things had grown with ever more hunger.

Jeanine quickly polished off two with lusty snorting.

"You always were a vacuum, Jeanine!" chuckled Jack nostalgically recalling the good old days, as he sat back happily, a jolt of energy surging through his head. Jeanine ignored him, absorbing the rush with a quick shake of her head, her eyes briefly crushed together before opening them widely.

"We had some good times, didn't we?" Jeanine said finally, a lightened mood engagingly shining through.

"Yeah, we did."

Then she turned sour again after a moment's flying euphoria. Blow usually changed her mood, but it also fired her up at first before she eventually leveled out.

"Now you're never around," she complained with spirit, but also with lament. "I sit here in this fucking house with nothing to do half the time."

"It's not like you're—we're—in the sticks or something, we're five miles from the city," said Jack defensively. "There's a lot to do. It's not like we're fifty miles from downtown. We have a pretty comfortable life," he pointed out. He knew her charge about his extended absences was true, but he couldn't very well explain Aleksandra to her, so he waved their possessions in front her, illustrating all he'd done for the two of them. There had been other women before Aleksandra, but not one who consumed as much time, and not one who had lasted this long, either. "After you come back from Springfield, we'll get together with a couple people next weekend, how's that?" He sounded as though he was patronizing her, fulfilling a duty. Jeanine picked up on this, and when Jeanine noticed something she didn't like, it was but a short step to expressing it.

"Thanks a lot," she said sarcastically with a glare. "Don't do me any fucking favors."

"I didn't mean it like that," Jack protested. Now it was it was his turn to become annoyed, and as he watched her lean over for the fourth line of blow—that he'd gone through the trouble of picking up, he pointed out to himself—she seemed to pause and contemplate it. "You know this job of mine takes a lot of time and a has lot of strange hours. I'm doing the regular sports broadcast on the news at six, I'm doing the *Sports Finale* show Sundays at 11:30, the hockey games and this *Daily Number Live!*

thing," he said, running quickly over the lottery show, which felt like something he should feel guilty about for some reason, perhaps because of its tenuous connection with Aleksandra. "You know all these duties of mine take a lot of time, I don't just run on the set five minutes before the cameras come on."

Jeanine hunched over and started smoothly and slowly working on the final line.

"You've never complained about the money all these hours bring in. But hey," said Jack provocatively, throwing his hands up in as if to accentuate his victimhood, "if you want to give up all this—the cars, the nights out, the vacations to every island you want to see—we can give it all up along with my job. I can *not* pay for your mother's vacations, your brother's lawyers, your sister's abortions and all that, that's fine with me. We can move to the suburbs and we can work—both of us—nine to five and be the happy little domestic couple and go to PTA meetings and all the rest," he concluded. Jack would have liked to have blamed the line he had just done for his intentionally antagonistic and baiting words, but in truth, he just wasn't the type to sit around and be lectured all night and wanted to take the offensive a bit.

Jeanine, now done with her nose candy, popped her head up and glared at him, clearly pissed, as Jack stood up and with his back to her, walked over by the fireplace and again absently fiddled with the mail, being as casual as possible and ignoring her.

"Fuck you, Jack!" verbalized Jeanine, jumping up and going over to her suitcase on the nearby table. Jack just shrugged at her verbal attack and seemed to pay her no mind, which he knew would get under her skin more than any retort could. "I said, *fuck you*, Jack!"

"Don't worry about it," he said absently and condescendingly.

Jeanine was a city girl from a tough background and when she was spoiling for a fight, his dismissive manner, pretending to be indifferent, only enraged her more, as he well knew.

She grabbed a plate off a little display stand from the hutch. "Asshole!" she shrieked and hurled the thing at him.

Jack only saw her out of the corner of his eye as she'd hopped up and didn't pay her much attention, but he happened to look up at the last second as the plate hurtled toward him. In television and the movies, people always notice a flying plate and duck, leaving it to shatter harmlessly on the wall behind, but this being real, Jack never saw it until it was too late. The plate struck him right above the eye and shattered into a million pieces.

"Oww! Fuck! Christ, Jeanine!" he bellowed, holding his hand to the spot where the plate hit him. He looked down at the largest pieces of the now-decimated plate. "The Patriots plate?!" he cried out. "*The commemorative Patriots plate?*" he wailed in mourning. The New England Patriots plate was a treasure he considered to be a family heirloom, celebrating, as it did, the team's Super Bowl victory three years previous. The thing had been Jack's only foray into the world of Fine Art and it pained him tremendously to see it destroyed. He considered it a great personal and historical loss.

Jeanine grumbled something which Jack was certain was no apology as she violently stuffed articles of clothing into the suitcase she'd placed on the table earlier.

"Jeanine, I have to be on TV, you know," Jack pointed out with aggravation, not quite as miffed as one would have expected.

"Yeah, you told me that a second ago, you fucking asshole!" commented Jeanine vigorously. She was not one to let innuendo and word games linger in the air. If he was going to be passive-aggressive, she wasn't going to play along; if he wanted a fight, he'd get a fight—a real one, not some pointless verbal joust peppered with barbed witticisms. You could always count on Jeanine to escalate a situation.

Jack, still near the fireplace, strategically stood in front of the fireplace poker to conceal it from Jeanine just in case she decided to ratchet up her expression of disapproval. During one tirade not too long ago, she'd rearranged his wide-screen TV with the instrument, and he had no urge to see the scene repeated. Yesterday, the wide-screen TV, today his face, Jack figured. On the occasion of the wide-screen TV's demise, it was suspicions of another woman that had set her passions aflame (ironically, Jack was innocent of the charge that day), and he'd meant to put the instrument of destruction out with the trash, but somehow had forgotten to do so, much to his regret now.

"Jack," Jeanine said pointedly, jabbing a finger towards him, "you told me you're on TV already—"

"I just meant I can't have a bloody face—"

"So then shut the fuck up and don't be an asshole!" she said, implicitly laying the blame for his blood at his own feet. "You know I'm doing my part—that's why I'm working this weekend, so if you want to lord over somebody—do it somewhere else, 'cause I ain't having it!" she declared pointedly. She turned on her heel and stormed off.

Jack calmly went over to the mirror on the wall and examined himself. He dabbed the spot where the plate had struck. "No real blood, just a nick," he declared to himself. "She knows I'm on TV," he mumbled in complaint. "I can't have bloody scars on my face." He shook his head. She had no appreciation of him. Generally, Jack didn't care much about Jeanine's combativeness because she was so damned hot, and she was like that when he first started dating her and he still liked that zest and feistiness of hers in a very real way, but if she messed with his face, she was messing with his paycheck.

Putting it all aside, Jack simply sat down on the couch and reached for the clicker and turned on an out-of-town baseball game as if nothing had happened. "The life of a star sports anchor!" he declared to the empty room. He was not particularly upset about the physical expression of anger Jeanine had leveled against him—Jack was a guy after all—but the endless drama and upheaval were tiring beyond his endurance.

Even though he claimed in his own mind that he was watching the game on his TV to keep up with the national sports scene, in truth, Jack watched the games because that's what he did—he was a sports guy, a jock. That was his world, really; that's where he fit in best and where he thrived. It was the source of his whole identity. And it brought him fame, value and rewards, too.

But Jack quickly got bored with the game. More accurately, he became a bit agitated over Jeanine's outburst and he was still stimulated with the blow he'd snorted and couldn't quite settle down to watch the game. He reached into the drawer of the end table and pulled out some weed. He lit up a joint just to take the edge off the cocaine. He didn't particularly care for the stuff on its own merits, but he was a bit jangled from the blow, and it would mellow him out a bit. By smoking a joint after some blow, he could experience the same sensation as not having done any drugs in the first place. He even considered going to get a beer, but that would possibly entail crossing paths with Jeanine again, and he thought it would be wise to give her a little time to let off some steam and depressurize until she was back to being fit for human society.

Jack absently watched the athletes on TV plying their trade. Now there were some guys who made some real money, he thought to himself.

Money.

Money, money, money. He made tons of it, but it was never enough. It was everywhere and nowhere. No matter how much money he made, he and Jeanine spent it faster than he could make it. He already made a lot of money and he needed more. Always more. Jack mused on his money issues.

He couldn't very well ask the station, WKTD, for more money—he was the highest-paid on-air personality as it was—and he couldn't get any more on-air gigs, as Billy Bowman was becoming concerned about over-saturating the market with Jack's presence as things stood now. He'd just received a big raise last year and, besides, local TV wasn't what it used to be. He dabbled in sports talk radio and had a couple endorsements, like at clothing stores and the like, but that was chump change compared to his ever-expanding monetary requirements.

No, it wasn't his salary that was the problem, it was the lifestyle that was the real issue. Supporting two women—two expensive women—was what was really straining his paycheck. Aleksandra was costing a fortune. He was giving her lots of money and he was taking her on the road with him on the sly as well, and that cost him a bundle, but she loved it, and he had trouble denying her anything she wanted. It was a huge hassle for him to make Aleksandra's arrangements for her hotels and air fare and all the logistical details that went with a trip. The TV station handled those details for him, but if Aleksandra accompanied him on the road, he had to do all that stuff for her independently, discreetly book a room for her after he got his travel plans, and ditto with the airline flights. It was difficult to do, especially keeping it all hidden from Jeanine, and it was expensive as hell. If he went on the road to follow a team, Aleksandra very often went along, as it was a rare opportunity for them to be together without secrecy being the overriding concern. Then there were her regular living expenses, of which he picked up quite a bit, too, and her living expenses were costing him even more than the traveling.

Jeanine cost him a fortune, as well. Her half-witted brother had been busted for drugs again, and his lawyers seemed to do nothing but send bills, which Jeanine had courteously offered to pick up. Jack would just assume see his wayward brother-in-law busting rocks on a chain gang for the rest of his natural life, but "family is family," as Jeanine vaguely and expensively put it, so the bills continued to land on top of Jack's checkbook, nearly crushing the life out of the poor thing. And then there was her mother, whose sole purpose in life seemed to be to act as an object Jeanine could place on a ship headed to exotic locations with the most expensive ticket imaginable. His mother-in-law seemed perpetually on vacation, yet she was also always around, an amazing and maddening sleight of hand on her part that left Jack exasperated as well as broke.

Jack took a deep breath and exhaled the smoke and then put out the joint he'd been holding.

"Ah, Aleksandra!" he thought to himself wistfully. That was the way to go. Aleksandra didn't throw plates at him. Aleksandra didn't have blood-sucking relatives draining the very life from him. She was younger, and after all these years of marriage, she was even more available in the ways that kept a man young. No doubt, Aleksandra was the way to go, Jack mused.

"But if I get divorced…" Jack thought to himself.

If he got divorced, Jeanine would get half of his money, half of everything. Jack had no illusions, Aleksandra might not like him quite so much without his full salary. "Sorry, sweetie," he imagined himself telling her, "no trip to Europe this year, perhaps we can make a weekend to Branson, Missouri instead." No, that would not fly. It wasn't that Aleksandra simply liked him for his money—she'd known plenty of other guys with money that she hadn't taken up with—but at the same time, she'd also known plenty of other guys *without* money that she hadn't taken up with, too. Aleksandra was a woman of high spirit and expensive tastes, and a young woman of Aleksandra's disposition might decide that another suitor suddenly looked a lot more appealing if Jack were going through a horrific divorce that ended up with him broke at its conclusion. A divorce would free him for a future with Aleksandra, but it would mean a huge curtailing of the life to which he'd become accustomed and, ironically, cost him Aleksandra to boot.

A violent man might muse on bumping off Jeanine at this point, but Jack was no murderous criminal. Violence in a bar fight or on the athletic field? Sure, if it was called for, but that's about as far as it went. Besides, it was obvious if anyone was going to be killed in his marriage, it would be him, not Jeanine, he told himself with a sardonic chuckle. No, the answer to his money issues had to be somewhere else.

Then, for reasons he did not understand, Jack's mind suddenly turned back to the senior citizen witness at the lottery drawing from earlier that night, and the vague, crazy daydreams he'd had when the old man spoke to him right before the cameras went on. Jack's crooked smile melted from his face. "*Sure looks like it would be easy to fix,*" the old man had said about the lottery.

"Easy to fix?" Jack muttered. He pictured Bill Hillgrove, the lottery agent in charge of overseeing the drawing, wandering around the studio in the hours before the numbers were selected, not paying any attention to the proceedings.

Easy to fix.

The wheels in Jack's head starting turning....

Chapter Five

(Early August, 2010)

Jack was sitting anxiously in the WKTD building, humbly decked out in a simple plaid work shirt, jeans and New Balance walking shoes, all accented with an itchy beard and slightly unruly, somewhat lengthy hair. He looked like a guy there to change the light bulbs. Jack looked considerably different than the last time he'd been in the WKTD building a few years before. The hundred-dollar ties and even more expensive shoes were now long gone, and he was several pounds lighter, the weight loss a result of decidedly mediocre food the state had served him while he was enjoying their hospitality.

For years Jack was a towering figure at the television station. The most popular, highest-paid personality at the station—even more popular than fellow star news anchor, Gary Gibson—Jack had bestrode the grounds of WKTD like a colossus. Now he sat in a reception area adjacent to the lobby like a common schmuck, waiting for the station manager's receptionist to return.

In the old days, Jack never would have believed there'd come a time when he would be seeking permission for *anything* at WKTD, never mind permission for something as meager as the liberty to freely wander the halls.

Worse still, he was extraordinarily nervous as he waited, his anxiety betrayed by the way he compulsively tapped his forefinger on his chair's armrest. Jack hadn't set foot in his old stomping grounds in almost four years. He hadn't even so much as crossed the border into the city in all that time. There were a lot of memories in this place—and a lot of things he'd planned on avoiding forever.

The place hadn't changed that much, Jack noticed, looking around. Some new chairs, a new carpet and minor changes like that, but the lobby otherwise looked the same. Most of the pictures of the station's on-air personalities were still displayed on the wall. In the place of prominence where his picture once hung there was now only a generic cityscape photograph. Apparently even his visage had become so toxic that nobody was willing to have their photograph occupy his old spot on the wall, as if the location had suffered a contaminating nuclear accident, leaving it poisoned for eons.

But it was business that brought him back to WKTD, not a nostalgic trip down Memory Lane. Jack had called the station manager, Billy Bowman, and Billy had reluctantly agreed to a meeting concerning something Jack would not discuss over the phone.

For several reasons, Billy Bowman was extremely uneasy about meeting Jack. The way Jack departed WKTD left a lot to be desired, to say the very least. Nobody from the station had seen or heard from Jack Webster since the day he went away. It would be a disaster if word got out that the once-great Jack Webster was stalking the halls of WKTD. Such a revelation would be huge news—and a scandalous P.R. nightmare for the station. Every media outlet in the city, and many far beyond the city limits, would be talking about it. To be sure, Jack's memory was a ghost WKTD did not want haunting their studios. As evidenced by the missing picture, the station wanted to bury its association with Jack as deeply as possible.

Jack, even more than station manager Billy Bowman, wanted to keep his visit quiet. Jack had been tremendously anxious to avoid even the possibility being seen by any media members at the pathetic Earthpeace protest in Norton, so walking into the beehive that was a major urban news office wasn't something he was eager to do, but it was a necessary part of his plan—nay, it was the very crux of his scheme. Or rather, it would be.

Luckily, there wasn't much chance of his visit being discovered by the outside world. Jack was unlikely to be recognized since he and Billy Bowman both wanted to keep his visit under the radar and neither had mentioned it to anybody, and thus, nobody was on the lookout for Jack Webster's return. And better still, Jack looked entirely different than he had in his glory days as the biggest local news personality in the city. Before, he'd walk through these buildings at WKTD in the manner of a conquering hero, draped in glory, host to his own spectacular party, friendly with everybody in the building. Everybody had known and liked Jack, admiring him as he toured about the place in splendid, expensive suits, confidently joking and joshing with everybody from the station bosses to the janitorial staff. In his world, he had been royalty.

Now, he hid. From where he was sitting, Jack could almost see Billy Bowman's office door as he craned his neck to look down the hall behind the receptionist's desk. It was a familiar place, yet now a world away.

The young woman who manned the desk for Billy Bowman and kept visitors at bay returned to her desk. She was a beautiful young woman with silky black hair and a captivating, shy smile that admirers remembered forever. Her name, according to the plate on her desk, was Stephanie Dulcinea.

"Billy can see you now," informed Ms. Dulcinea, and Jack stood up.

Before he could ask if it was all right to go back to Billy's office, from the hallway emerged the man himself, Jack's old boss and old buddy, Billy Bowman, coming out to greet him.

Billy, who was a year older than Jack, was a tall, thinnish man, six foot five, with black hair that he kept slicked back. He had a hound dog face with droopy eyes, and in moments when listening to others talk, his mouth was often agape in concentration. Billy Bowman was a creature of the office world, so he always wore a shirt and tie, but usually forgave himself the restraints of a jacket unless some of the station's advertisers were roaming around the offices. His limbs were awkwardly long, and as Billy approached, his hand stretched out weakly from shock, his eyes opened wide in amazement, his jaw almost dropped entirely.

"Jack," he said in almost disbelief, "is it really you?" He spoke softly, almost not ready to believe Jack Webster had really and truly returned from the dead and called for him earlier in the day. He had half expected the meeting to be a practical joke or gag of some sort.

Jack smiled apprehensively.

"Hey, Billy. It's been a long time," Jack said wearily and quietly as he shook Billy's hand, his old cockiness well submerged. Billy, now accepting the reality of the situation, suddenly became exuberant and abuzz with enthusiasm and clasped Jack's arm vigorously as he shook his hand.

"God, Jack, I can't believe it's you! Holy shit, I didn't recognize you at first! I said, 'Who's that homeless guy in the lobby?' then I looked closer and recognized you!" He then struck an apologetic posture, embarrassed for the both them to have made reference to Jack's fallen station. "I mean, what are you doing here?"

"Like I told you on the phone earlier, I wanted to talk with you. It's important."

Billy, who figured Jack was looking to get a job of some sort, said, "Sure, sure, come on in to my office," in a distant and noncommittal tone so as to not betray any misleading zest for the idea of Jack returning to the station, because there was no way in hell that Jack Webster was going to work anywhere near a television studio again, and he didn't want to give his old night-on-the-town partner any false hopes.

Silently they made their way to Billy's office, which had an unobtrusive "William Bowman, Station Manager" nameplate attached modestly to the door.

Billy quickly sat down at his desk and offered Jack a seat across from him.

Settling into the chair, Jack looked around the office as slyly as he could. He used to spend a lot of time in Billy's office, mostly just hanging out, plotting the next triumph or recounting the last. It felt familiar and yet foreign to be there in his old environment again and he did not want to gawk and make an issue out of the fact he hadn't been in the office in a long time. Jack wanted as much of a business-as-usual feeling as possible in order to defuse the discomfort.

Billy looked at him wide-eyed and, reopening the conversation with a friendly posture, threw his arms slightly up and said, "Jesus, Jack, I can't believe it's you! It's really you!"

"Yeah," Jack said with a heavy-hearted and sardonic chuckle. "I guess I'm a little earlier than expected—a few years earlier, I suppose."

"Yeah, you're early…." There was an uncomfortable pause, then Billy slapped his thigh to emphasize his continued amazement. "Jeez, I can't believe I'm looking at you! God—what have you been up to? Where are you now? Are you living back in the city?" Billy asked rapidly and with great animation.

"Well, no," said Jack apologetically.

"No? Where are you these days, then?"

"To tell you the truth, Billy, I'm living in Norton now."

"Norton?" asked Billy, puzzled and wrinkling his brow in confusion. Jack simply did not belong in a backwater old mill city out in the middle of nowhere. He belonged where the action was, downtown in some big city where the lights were bright. It was hard to imagine him in a blue-collar, ratty, old factory town. But then again, it was hard to picture him bearded, twenty pounds lighter and wearing a lumberjack shirt, too, yet there he was.

"Yup, Norton," confirmed Jack. "I was born there, actually."

"Oh, yeah, that's right. I seem to remember you mumbling something about that before. You didn't seem too proud of it."

"Yeah, well, I think these days the town probably isn't too proud to have *me*, either. I was sent there as part of the agreement with the state."

"I see. And what are you doing there? I know they have a local cable TV station out there," said Billy, subtly suggesting Jack would be unwelcome as an employee at his old haunt. It wasn't much of a station that operated in the Norton area, not a tenth of the size of WKTD, but it would at least be a job in the business. "Are you going to try to get in with them?" asked Billy, who figured Jack was preparing to ask him for help in getting him in with Norton's little cable station, covering the University of Massachusetts at Norton's small Division Three football team or some insignificant position like that. Maybe, if Jack started over there in some capacity, Billy figured, he could start rehabbing his name....

"No," said Jack sadly, "I don't think I'll try to get in with that local Norton station. There doesn't seem to be any room for me on television anywhere—in any role—these days. Not after what happened around here four years ago," admitted Jack painfully. "Not yet, that's for sure. It seems even local cable doesn't want me. I'm dead in the business, Billy."

Billy sadly shook his head in confirmation.

"So what *are* you doing?" he asked.

Jack shifted uncomfortably in his chair. He'd fallen a long way since his heady days with Billy and Gary Gibson at WKTD and this meeting was turning out to be as painful as he'd feared.

"I'm delivering carpets, mostly industrial rugs and stuff."

"Seriously?"

"Yeah. It's part of the program. Court-ordered. I don't have much choice right now. I need to have some sort of job and they hooked me up with that."

"I see."

"Yeah, it's tough. But I'm also doing something more interesting on the side. I've been working with Earthpeace. Ever heard of them?"

"Ha ha."

"What's so funny?"

"Earthpeace is an environmental action group, non-profit, the whole nine yards."

"Yeah."

"You're serious?" asked the station manager, astounded. "You're really working with them?" Billy was borderline incredulous. Jack's concern for the environment had always maxed out at recycling shot glasses at trendy uptown bars. And Earthpeace paid next to nothing—and Billy knew Jack always had a high demand for money. What he didn't know, of course, was that Jack's interest in Earthpeace revolved entirely around the girl he'd targeted for his next big romantic adventure, the metal artist Ava Barsi.

"Yeah, yeah, I know, it's a bit of a departure for me," conceded Jack.

Billy noticed how weary Jack had become since the Old Days. Undoubtedly, it was profoundly humbling to confront his spectacular fall from grace. Was Jack really humbled? No, Billy didn't think so, he did not have that in him. More likely, he was just embarrassed.

"I'll say it's a departure for you."

"Yeah, I met a girl there, a young woman who was with Earthpeace and—"

"Ah!"

"Well, anyway," continued Jack, "I met with the Earthpeace people for the first time a couple of weeks ago at a little protest at Norton City Hall."

"Oh, yeah, about the airport expansion," recalled Billy. "I remember them sending a fax or something here to us at KTD, trying to get some free publicity. We passed, of course."

"Yeah, so I noticed that day. You and just about everybody else except the local Norton newspaper passed, and from what I heard even they just gave it a passing mention. Anyway, for the past two weeks I've been volunteering with Earthpeace after working at my carpet delivery job, attending meetings and such, trying to help them out."

Over those two weeks, Jack had taken a role as "media consultant" as a way to become valuable to Earthpeace. He'd volunteered to create the job for himself when the three Earthpeace kids had stumbled upon him at The Worthy House and he'd quickly worked himself into the organization. He hadn't done a single useful thing for them yet, and he didn't intend to if he could help it, but the job got him in the door, and besides, the group was so clueless about what Jack was talking about that they weren't aware he'd just been spinning his wheels.

"Uh-huh," nodded Billy. He knew this was going somewhere. There was no way he believed for a second that Jack Webster was showing up at KTD, facing the humiliation of returning to the Scene of The Crime just to catch up on old times, and he also had a great deal of trouble believing Jack gave a damn about Earthpeace's environmental activism.

And he was entirely correct. Jack did not give a damn about any bird's nesting habitat or the put-upon, leverage-less citizens of Norton having an airport shoved down their throats. Jack Webster had always picked up women by being a hero of some sort—a hero in sports, or by being a big TV personality, now he was trying the only tactic available to him along the hero lines with Ava Basri.

Jack had conceived a vague plan where in addition to winning over Ava by being a hero to the Earthpeace cause, he could maybe begin to rehabilitate his name. He was willing to come out of hiding to win over Ava, and he figured if he played his cards right, something more might come out of it all. Maybe he could use this whole adventure to open a door to a job as a media consultant or maybe a motivational speaker or something. And what better way to convince the world you're no longer a crooked bastard than to work for a non-profit? If he was going to win Ava, he wouldn't be able to deliver carpets forever (not that he wanted to) and at some point he wouldn't be under the state's watchful eye and would have to get another job of some sort. A job on-screen in television was impossible, but he'd have to come clean about his past to Ava at some point, and making a dramatic splash while doing so was just Jack's style. A man with his past would always have fuzzy prospects and he left his exact plans for the future misty for now, but saw this as a first step.

"In any case," said Jack in an apologetic tone, "the carpet job was always going to be temporary anyway, and I think the courts are going to let me switch my employment to Earthpeace. The court really doesn't care if I deliver carpets, they just want me to be doing *something*, you know?"

"Sure," said Billy, as he continued to size up Jack and tried to figure out what he was doing, what the angle was.

"So, anyway, this new-found activism on my part is what brings me here."

"You've been protesting and stuff?" asked Billy, trying to hide his skepticism.

"On occasion, though they don't call it that," explained Jack, subtly and unconsciously distancing himself from Earthpeace by employing the phrase 'they' instead of 'we.' "They call it 'raising public awareness' or some such thing," Jack said dismissively. "And I want to raise public awareness for Earthpeace, you know, for this airport expansion protest."

"You do?"

"Yes. I'm doing what I can," Jack assured Billy convincingly. Jack was a practiced actor and Billy was beginning to keep a more open mind towards his story.

Billy, taking note of the weight loss Jack had experienced since his WKTD days, back when he had a lean, muscular, athletic build of a football running back, asked sardonically, "What, are you on a hunger strike or something?" thinking of something outrageous he could sarcastically ask to break the awkward pause that had taken hold of the conversation.

Jack took Billy's comment to be uttered in jest, and answered in a similar, caustic manner, like he would have done in the old days.

"Yeah," said Jack sardonically, "that's what I'm doing— I'm on a hunger strike." Jack looked away, self-conscious of how much different he looked physically. What he did not notice was Billy's eyes opening wide, mistakenly thinking Jack had been serious about undertaking a hunger strike for the Earthpeace/airport expansion cause. A hunger strike, Billy felt, meant business.

Jack assumed anybody who knew him would never for a second take such a idea seriously—him? On a hunger strike? Risk his health for a protest over a bird habitat??— but he'd undergone so many changes over the past four years and looked so different and had lost so much weight from his days as a TV star, Billy had started to believe anything could be possible. He never believed Jack could be a concerned activist, but (Billy figured) maybe Jack had something else up his sleeve.

Billy Bowman quickly recovered and wiped the shock from his face by the time Jack looked back at him a split-second later. Billy didn't want to embarrass Jack any more than necessary with stunned looks.

Now Jack got around to the crux of his visit, the issue he'd been dancing around since he showed up at Billy's office. He looked suddenly grave and serious.

"Here's the thing, Billy. I'll be honest. I want something I can only get from you."

Now Billy felt the story was more believable. Jack looking for something made things more plausible, more in character.

"What is it you want, Jack?"

"*Publicity.* I want publicity for the Norton airport expansion protest."

Billy looked around sadly, not quite willing to make eye contact and disappoint his old buddy.

"Jack, that Norton airport protest…it's not exactly big news. Senator Shea worked it all out, and Norton's the kind of shithole nobody cares about…."

"I know all that, Billy, that has been abundantly clear ever since Earthpeace showed up in Norton— no media outlet cares, and even if they did, it looks like the expansion is a done deal. That's why Earthpeace needs to rouse public interest. If people knew about the process of approving the airport expansion in Norton, instead of down on the Cape near where Senator Shea lives, there would be public interest."

"I agree, people would probably be interested in the aspect of the powerful, wealthy, connected people like Shea shoving it onto Norton's lap, but…."

"Right. But I'm not asking you give the story publicity out of the goodness of your heart, or because I used to work here with you."

Billy looked at Jack with a furrowed brow.

"You're not? Then what do you mean?"

Jack looked at him intently.

"I'll make it worth your while. I want to propose a trade."

"A trade? What trade?" asked Billy, interested. Jack always delivered something interesting. That's why he'd been Billy's number one star at the station.

"I want to trade an interview—by me, about the lottery scandal—in exchange for an investigative series covering the Norton airport expansion."

Billy was stunned.

"Are you serious?"

"I am."

"Wow," said Billy, thinking on the magnitude of the proposal. When the lottery story came to light four years before, it was just about the biggest story anybody could remember, mostly because Jack had been a household name and everybody, it seemed, played the state lottery. It had become a national story. Needless to say, everybody wanted to interview Jack about it, but not one person anywhere got an interview from him, not even national outlets. It was a huge story, national in scope, and the main participant never spoke a word about it. Even today, an interview with Jack Webster on the subject would be a big deal. A very big deal.

Billy leaned back in his chair and put his fingertips together and intently considered what he'd just heard and paused before answering.

"Jack, I think we can work something out…."

The two of them talked for a bit before Jack left with assurances from Billy that the interview would happen and then the station would follow up the momentum of the interview with a spin-off expose series on the airport expansion. Billy said that he had to do some follow-up with the staff and make sure everything would be OK.

"I think we can work out any issues easily enough," promised Billy.

They agreed to talk again soon to iron out more details, but a deal had been struck in principle: The interview would be about Jack and the lottery scandal, with a "what-are-you-doing-now?" section in Part II of the interview wherein Jack would segue into his activities with Earthpeace. This in turn would lead to the promised two-part exposé on the airport expansion itself. Sure, it would look like a *quid pro quo* deal had been made, but Billy Bowman and WKTD had cover with the claim that Jack gave them the interview above all other news outlets because he still had lots of old friends at the station, and from that the exposé grew organically.

Jack got up to leave.

"Thanks a lot, Billy. This deal is going to help me out a lot. I'm going to be a hero to some of the Earthpeace crowd," Jack said with his trademark crooked smile underneath his beard. He alone knew he was making reference to Ava, the audience of one he was trying to impress.

"Talk to you soon, Jack," said Billy.

"OK."

"Jack," said Billy with a dramatic pause, "nice to see you again."

Jack nodded with a grin and turned to leave.

"Hey, Jack," called out Billy. Jack stopped and turned around. "Do something about that beard, will you? It looks just awful."

Jack smiled warmly at his old friend's barb, nodded and left.

Billy Bowman was lanky and well over six feet tall, so it was difficult for him to recline back in his chair in a thoughtful repose, but he attempted to do so as he considered the magnitude of the story for which he'd just dealt. Then, in a sudden spasm of activity, his limbs flailed as he untangled himself and he picked up his phone to dial and pressed one number, but he got no further before he was interrupted.

By a coincidence, Gary Gibson, the news editor for the evening news and the very person he was going to contact, knocked on his door and poked his head in the office.

Gary, like Jack, had long been a star at WKTD and something of a local fixture himself. Unlike Jack, he hadn't had to leave in disgrace. Gary had been one of the early choices to host *Daily Number Live!* but lost out to Jack, as Jack had been an even more popular and beloved figure. He'd survived the chaos Jack had created at the station, and was in fact largely credited with salvaging the station's place in the local news hierarchy in wake of Jack's scandal.

"Billy, I—"

"There you are, Gary! You're just the person I was looking for. Get in here, quick—and shut the door."

Hearing the urgency in the boss's tone, Gary hurriedly did as instructed.

"Hey, Billy, who was the guy with the beard who just left your office? Was he a homeless guy or something?" Gary joked.

"Just about, he works for a non-profit outfit. Guess who that was?"

"I have no idea," confessed Gary, who had only caught a glimpse of Jack as he retreated down the hallway, unaware that Gary had seen him.

"You know him," teased Bowman.

"I do?"

"Sure do," said Billy cockily.

Gary, Jack and Billy and assorted other part-timer members who made up their after-dark posse had run out on the town together, living the life of local television stars out on the tiles. The three of them had been regular figures at popular bars and clubs around town. Gary was shorter than Jack, had delicately manicured sandy-blond hair and a knack for finding himself in front of a camera. Like Jack, Gary had been known to be mentioned in a gossip column or two, and like Jack, had once in a while been known to leave bars with women who were not his wife. Sometimes Gary would be teased that if he'd been a little better looking or was a little more smooth, he could have been Jack instead of getting his leftovers, comments that Gary would silently file away to resent later, for deep down he knew who was the lead dog in their world, and it wasn't him.

"I don't know, Billy, I give up, who was that bearded guy?" Gary pressed, now that the suspense had been built up.

"Jack…Webster," said Billy in a dramatic tone indicating that this was Big News.

Gary's jaw dropped and his eyes opened wide.

"*That* guy was Jack?" Gary said, pointing a thumb vaguely in the direction of the hallway. "*Jack Webster*?? That guy with the beard, you mean?" he repeated, not quite able to believe it. He'd known Jack at the height of his powers and had trouble reconciling the images.

Billy nodded his head with a smug smile of confirmation.

Gary said, "I thought he was—"

"He was, but he was let out early."

"Are you *sure*?" Gary asked.

"Absolutely. I just spent twenty-five minutes talking to him."

"About what??

"That's the best part. Here's what he came in to talk about," started Billy, who then explained to Gary about Jack's proposed deal—his interview about the lottery in exchange for a two-part story and publicity about the airport.

"Really?" asked Gary, who was shocked that Jack was doing something apparently selfless. He'd been friends and friendly rivals with Jack for years and had never heard of such a thing.

"Yup. So what do you think about the deal?" asked Billy in a serious moment, for he knew this was a big, serious news story despite whatever private thrill they got as a result of their old personal connections with Jack.

"We definitely would want that interview with him about the lottery."

"Yeah, that's a no-brainer."

"Jack Webster talking about the lottery would be big news. *Huge* news."

"I know the airport expansion story is a snooze-fest with the viewers, but I think we can even turn *that* into a winner."

"How?"

"Here's the best part," confided Billy. "I asked Jack, and he said he was on a hunger strike for the Earthpeace cause."

"*What*? Get out of here. Are you *sure*?" Gary asked, not quite willing to believe Jack had abandoned his high-flying lifestyle to go on a hunger strike for an environmental cause. It was all so ridiculous.

"Yup, said so specifically himself. And you saw him, he's already lost weight. Jack Webster's a well-known name—a famous name, especially in this city. We can roll his interview about the lottery into a spiced up story about the airport expansion by playing on his hunger strike and it will sell, and sell big I think, just based on the celebrity of his name. Very dramatic, it'll be. Once the interview is filmed, we'll promote the hell out of it. Gary, you're in charge of content on the news here at Channel Six, what do you think?"

Gary tapped his chin with a pencil, mostly because he instinctively felt it would convey a tone of serious consideration rather than just blurting out the answer they both knew was coming, like he wanted to do.

"Definitely," he said with finality. "I think we can even roll the airport story into a recurring feature on the evening news as long as he stays on that hunger strike and we can tie the two together, playing off his celebrity, like you said. If we tie his name and hunger strike with that stupid airport story, I think it'll be a hit, too. Jack Webster on a hunger strike will be huge, huge news, especially following the lottery interview. Viewers will want more about Jack than just one interview. Keep him on that hunger strike, and anything associated with it will get ratings."

"I'll tell him we have a deal, then?"

"I would."

"Great! That's what I was hoping you'd say. I'll talk to Jack tomorrow and tell him we have a deal."

"Do it ASAP," said Gary. "But there's another angle, Billy," he warned.

"What's that?"

"You know Senator Shea directed that airport expansion to be up in Norton instead of down on the Cape where he lives. He might not like the publicity."

"I know, and don't worry."

Billy picked up his phone again and chuckled before dialing.

"Hunger strike! Jack must be off his onion! I can't imagine what he was thinking!"

"Who you calling, Billy?" Gary asked.

"I'm just covering all the bases," he told her. He spoke into the phone to his personal assistant. "Stephanie, would you get me Rudy Baxter on the phone?"

"Rudy Baxter?" Gary asked.

"Yeah, he's Senator Shea's Chief of Staff," answered Bowman, the phone to his ear as he waited for the call to be made to Rudy Baxter. "Rudy Baxter was our 'anonymous source' on Senator Shea's budget package compromise last month."

"Why are you calling him?"

"Like I said, I'm covering all our bases. If Shea is going to dislike our interview, I'm going to give him plenty of advance notice. I'm going to clue him in every step of the way, that way Baxter will remain a source for the station. Shit, I'll bet he'll give us a good tidbit or two on the story, too. He might even be willing to trade an unrelated scoop or insight for being kept in the loop. It's good to have Senator Shea think of WKTD as a friendly place, you know?"

"Definitely. But isn't that sort of double crossing Jack?"

"Jack's a big boy," Billy reassured Gary, "he knows what the news business is all about. Oh, here he is!" said Billy as Baxter picked up the phone. Billy motioned for Gary to leave.

"I'm going to do some research on this right now," said Gary as he left and shut the door.

"Rudy Baxter! It's Billy Bowman over at WKTD, how are you, sir? Good to hear you, too. Listen, I've got a developing situation here concerning a story close to Senator Shea—literally close to him, if you think of his family's compound on the Cape…. Yeah, that's right, you're very insightful, Rudy. It's a story about the airport expansion issue that went through recently. We've got a story here on my desk and I want to keep you and Senator Shea in the loop of what's going on and how it's developing every step of the way because I value our friendship so much….."

Chapter Six

(August, 2006)

Jack sat reclining in Aleksandra's bed, several pillows behind his back, which was propped up against the headboard. He wasn't smoking a cigarette, but lying next to him, Aleksandra was. It was the only time she smoked. Like many Russians, she had started smoking young, but coming to America years ago, she'd given up the habit, except to celebrate a happy landing.

Jack, with a few well-earned beads of perspiration adorning his brow, had his arms behind his head in stereotyped repose, one of his trademark crooked smiles on his face. He looked longingly at Aleksandra.

"Hope your neighbors aren't nosey. I'd hate to think we bother them."

"They're used to it," she declared through a mischievous grin. He rubbed her back as she sat up.

It had been a whirlwind couple of weeks for Jack since the night of his argument with Jeanine, when she had broken his favorite commemorative plate on his face. In that time, Jack's mind had been constantly racing, alternately proposing, solving and eliminating dangers with his scheme as he ran through his various scenarios. He'd come to a conclusion: it could be done. "It" being fixing the lottery drawing. Right there, in front of cameras, with him standing inches away serving as the host. It was perfect.

Jack had seen Aleksandra a lot recently. He felt close to her. The lottery-fixing scheme had been intimately tied to his future with Aleksandra since he'd first considered it. Now it was time to move ahead. Always a man of action, Jack was not going to endlessly fantasize about his plans; for him, a plan was for executing, not for pondering. It was time to start feeling out his potential conspirators and to get this thing in motion.

"Aleksandra," he started with seriousness, "I've been thinking."

"Oh?" she asked, unimpressed. She thought all the time and wasn't about to give a novice points for beginner's luck.

"Yeah. And I've thought of something I need to talk to you about."

She looked somewhat alarmed.

"What is it?"

"You know how I've been worried about leaving... her," Jack said, tastefully avoiding saying his wife's name. "Well, as you know, I've been worried about her taking me to the cleaners in the divorce." He paused and looked at Aleksandra intently. "I think I've found a way around that."

"You're not thinking of killing her, are you?" Aleksandra asked drably. She'd known lots of guys who announced they were willing to kill their wives for her, but none ever did. She then got up and went towards the closet to put on a bathrobe.

Jack was annoyed to see her blasé reaction to his earth-shattering announcement but quickly put aside his grievances. Aleksandra went over and sat at her kitchen table.

"No, of course I'm not going to kill anybody," Jack continued, giving up on the physical aspect of romance for the moment and joining her in getting dressed. "No, really though, what I meant was, I've got a way for us to be together, finally. Forever."

Aleksandra looked at him skeptically with a one eye cocked.

"What do you mean? What way?"

"Well, I think I've got a way to leave her—but I need help."

"Help?" She sat at her kitchen table. He hurriedly joined her and pulled up a chair. "You want some coke?" she asked in an aside, her slight Russian accent giving her voice a purr, making her sound a bit like a villainess from a 1960s James Bond movie. She pulled out a little vial from somewhere Jack did not notice, seemingly making it appear from thin air like a magician.

"Just a touch," he answered. "Listen, though. What I'm saying is important."

"Then tell me, Jack," she said, preparing the powder. He'd saber-rattled about leaving Jeanine before, so she didn't get too excited about talk anymore. Jack saw himself as a man of action, but she saw him as a shackled husband hesitating over alimony and dividing up assets.

"You know the biggest problem with leaving her is that she'll get half my stuff—the money, the paycheck, the property, everything. Well, what if that didn't matter?"

Aleksandra looked at him with more interest now. "What are you saying?" she asked, then she sniffed a quick, delicate line.

"Here's what we'll do," said Jack. He paused a moment for the unveiling of his grand plan. "We'll fix the lottery," he announced dramatically.

Aleksandra's eyes lit up. If Aleksandra had any moral reservations about the idea of fixing the lottery, she hid them extraordinarily well.

"How?!"

Aleksandra figured if Jack truly wanted to do something, it would happen. He always got what he wanted, he just needed to iron out the details. That's how it worked with him. That's why she figured at some point, when properly motivated, he'd work something out with a divorce.

"There are a couple problems—a lot of problems, actually," he confessed, "but I know we can overcome them," he assured her confidently. He pulled his chair closer. "See, here's one way you come into my plan. I can't win the lottery, I'm an employee of the station and so my winning lottery money is not allowed. I can't claim any winnings. Plus, it would look way too suspicious anyway. That's why you have to be the one to actually *have* the winning tickets."

"OK," agreed Aleksandra enthusiastically. So far the plan was that she'd hold winning tickets worth perhaps a million dollars without doing anything apparently illegal. That was definitely the sort of role she could warm up to.

"Plus, if I have the money, Jeanine just gets half of it, along all with my other assets. However, if *we* have the lottery winnings, where you are the official winner, then she doesn't get any of it, and I don't care about paying a little alimony and losing half the house, right? She'd still get half my assets—but who cares? The lottery winnings would make up for that and it's like I get to leave her for free! I'd replace everything I lose in the divorce!"

Aleksandra nodded eagerly. Jack rubbed his chin.

"There's a lottery agent on the set at all times, he's there to observe the drawing. That's a problem."

"What are you going to do, include him in your plan?"

"No. I couldn't trust him, and besides, I don't want to split the winnings up any more than we have to. Four ways would be too much."

"Split the winnings four ways? It's only you and me, the lottery agent would make three, not four."

"No. We need your uncle, Georgi, to help."

"Uncle Georgi?"

"Yes. He's broke, isn't he?"

"Yes," she acknowledged with animation. Georgi was trying to pay for the relocation of several family members from Russia to the U.S. but was too hopelessly out-classed financially to accomplish the task. "Anyway, he'd do anything for me, even if he wasn't broke," offered Aleksandra.

Stephen Brown

"I'm counting on that," confirmed Jack. "Me, you and Georgi, that's three ways. The lottery agent is a dumpy, balding guy named Bill Hillgrove. Total loser. He doesn't watch what's going on with the lottery drawing at all. He's always gawking at the female interns and raiding the studio crew's commissary food cart to continue his experiment to discover how fat one suburban accountant can get. I can distract him easily enough."

"Are you sure about the lottery agent?" she asked.

"I'm sure. He won't suspect a thing. Nobody would ever have the gall to fix a lottery drawing," Jack said with cocky, roguish pride. "WKTD is a legitimate operation, they'd never allow anything funny to happen even if there weren't a lottery agent present at the studio for the drawing. The Lottery Office has almost total trust in the station. This lottery agent Hillgrove is basically just window dressing. He's tired from working a full day and doesn't have any energy left to stand around the studio downtown for hours just to watch ping-pong balls fly up a vacuum tube. He's not an issue that can't be overcome."

"But if I win the lottery, won't they get suspicious because my uncle works on the show?" Aleksandra asked, bringing up a salient point.

"Not a chance," answered Jack with enthusiasm, glad to have the subject introduced, as it gave him a chance to illustrate that he had done his homework and had total command of the situation. "Not with your background."

Aleksandra was Georgi's niece from his sister's side, which meant she was born with a different last name. Better still, her last name wasn't Russian at all, it was Greek, Maragos.

"The name Aleksandra Maragos won't ring a bell to anybody," said Jack. "There's no documentation of you having any other last name, right?" he asked.

"No," she said. Aleksandra came to this country illegally when she was seventeen (already fluent in English thanks to her education back home) with a Russian last name of Kurtov when she landed on these shores. There was no documentation of her anywhere that would lead back to Georgi. Aleksandra was living under the roof of her Uncle Georgi for a couple of years until she married a local man with the name Maragos. A divorce quickly followed, but by then she was a citizen through marriage and had a new last name, one unconnected with Georgi Sholokhov entirely. There wasn't one piece of paper in America showing them to be related or having lived under the same roof, thanks to her initial illegal status. Because she had an accent and a Mediterranean last name, people who met her often assumed she was Greek herself.

"All you have to do is avoid being seen around the studio, which means no visits to me or Georgi," lectured Jack. Luckily, because he'd been seeing Aleksandra on the side, she was already keeping a low profile, only coming to the set of *Daily Number Live!* after the show was over, intentionally avoiding being seen if at all possible, so no one around the studio connected her with Georgi in any way.

"What is Uncle Georgi's role?" Aleksandra asked.

"Well, the balls are stored in a cage inside a safe in Georgi's office. Georgi—and myself—are the only ones at the station with access to the room where the lottery balls are kept."

Aleksandra nodded. It was becoming more clear now.

"What does Uncle Georgi need to do?" she asked.

"There are still some details to be worked out, but we can cover them later. Besides, I'd rather discuss them with him alone first. Georgi is your blood and worships you, he can be trusted completely."

"Yes. Keeping your mouth shut is a Russian tradition," she said proudly. "Besides, I am dear to him, he can be trusted more than you can trust yourself."

"I agree. So you're on board?" Jack asked.

"Of course!" Aleksandra answered eagerly. Jack had expected a little tougher sell, some perfunctory hand-wringing or something before the inevitable acquiescence, but even such cursory ruminations had not been necessary. Aleksandra, for her part, wondered why he was even bothering to ask such stupid questions. "What do I do?" she demanded spiritedly. She hadn't so much as heard the plan or even known if it was a plausible scheme, but she saw Jack and perhaps millions of dollars within her grasp and was ready to go on that premise alone.

"What I need you to do first is go talk to Georgi—no, not now," said Jack, seeing her starting to get up, "you can go tomorrow, or next week or whenever." Her reaction told him she was going to see Georgi as soon as possible, if not sooner. "Go talk to him and feel him out. Don't just walk up and blurt out something about a plot. He might not want to go along with it. Be coy at first. And here's the most important thing—don't mention my name. Not right away, not until we're certain he's on board. Georgi is your blood, he'd never turn you in no matter what, but with me, you never know. It's a big deal asking him to be involved and he might not want the trouble and for all we know he could blow the whistle. But if it's you bringing it up, we're safe. Once you know he's on board too, then we can introduce my name."

Aleksandra nodded enthusiastically.

"Once you talk to Georgi, we can go from there," Jack said, standing. "After we're done and you get the lottery winnings, I'll start divorce proceedings. And then once that's done, we can start dating out in the open, then we can get hitched up for good and have the money to replace all that I'll lose in the divorce—and then some. It will take a while, but once the whole process is all done, we can be together. Forever." They stood and embraced warmly for a moment, Jack's face nestling against her neck. Then, without breaking the embrace, Jack said, "You know, I think I'll have that line of blow now."

*

Given her enthusiasm, Jack was not surprised that Aleksandra went to speak with her uncle Georgi Sholokhov that very evening. As directed, she had approached him as if there for another reason and subtly brought up the topic of the lottery scheme, but Georgi, who had lived through a variety of repressive regimes and thus was wise and cynical in the ways of man, saw she had another, true purpose to her visit, and soon the topic was broached.

Of course, Georgi agreed to join their conspiracy as soon as the plan came out into the open, and if the spectacular nature of the proposal left him startled or shaken, he did not show it. His agreement to join the conspiracy was as placid as it was immediate.

The day after Aleksandra's visit to her uncle, Jack, coming to the set for *Daily Number Live!*, had gotten word from Aleksandra that Georgi was on board with the plot. Still, Jack did not immediately approach Georgi about his clandestine criminal enterprise. It was such a delicate and dangerous topic, Jack wanted to feel out Georgi himself despite Aleksandra's assurances.

It was afternoon and Jack was on the set for the rehearsal drawing. Before the actual drawing, there was always a rehearsal drawing with the official senior citizen witness. They went through the whole drawing process, except that there were no balls in the lottery machine. After the first week of having a senior citizen witness, it was found that the volunteer inevitably froze once the lights and cameras came on, so WKTD and the state lottery decided to institute a practice drawing in the afternoon, and it was for this dry run that Jack arrived at the set. Most days, like the day Alfred Woodhouse was on the set, Jack would skip the dry run and a stand-in filled his role, but this afternoon there was no way he'd be absent.

Jack showed up earlier than usual, but he did not immediately see Georgi.

"Dammit," said Jack, becoming slightly paranoid at Georgi's absence.

As the set designer and handyman with the title assistant production manager, Georgi had an office, which mostly served as a place to keep his supplies. Jack nervously and guiltily avoided the other WKTD employees and went to Georgi's supply closet/office. He stealthily held a brown paper lunch bag, trying not to flaunt it, but trying not to look like he was concealing it, either.

Jack knocked on the door as he slowly pushed it open and saw Georgi sitting on stool at his slanted, architect's desk, hunched over some hand-drawn design of unknown purpose. Jack took note that, as always, Georgi wore his trademark black apron.

Georgi was not neat and fussy, neither personally nor professionally. His office seemed to have paint spilled on everything, with splatters everywhere from wall to wall. Not a single prop or inch of desktop seemed spared a smattering of paint. There were all sorts of cardboard cutouts, half-done cutouts, plywood palm trees, cardboard storm clouds, cutting and measuring tools, all as if a college theatre supply closet had been shaken like a snow globe. In the back of the cluttered room was a locked safe and inside it was another locked cage, where the precious lottery ping-pong balls sat, ostensibly under WKTD's protection.

"Hey, Georgi," offered Jack with slight trepidation. Aleksandra said Georgi had readily agreed to join in the lottery scheme, but Jack couldn't be sure of his true feelings until he spoke with him about it.

"Hello, Jack," Georgi said with dull, fatalistic undertones, before turning back to his drawing. There was an unnatural moment of silence before Georgi continued. "The WKTD *Morning Show* is doing a feature on preschools and they want me to build an appropriate set," Georgi complained with indulgence. It didn't take much prodding for Georgi to climb up on the cross. He liked it there. He took morose satisfaction from being persecuted.

"'Build a school bus, Georgi!' they tell me!" he said through his gravelly accent, briefly facing Jack again before hunching back over his desk to resume his toils. "So all the wood is outside, waiting for me to turn it into a school bus," he concluded, as though he were faced with a Herculean task. Georgi was skilled at building any background scene out of two-by-fours, thick cardboard, industrial staplers and paint. All the backdrops for the station were his domain. He was considered a magician in some WKTD circles. Other acute observers, like senior citizen witness Alfred Woodhouse, thought the sets thin.

"I'm sure you're up to the task, Georgi, you're the man," joked Jack as casually as possible. It was unmistakable, however, that he wasn't quite his usual glib self.

Georgi grumbled a weary, satisfied complaint that Jack did not pick up.

Jack stiffly wandered next to Georgi's desk and picked up one of the handmade drawings that Georgi had jotted down and discarded. He was preparing to make small talk about it as a preamble to working his way around to broaching the topic of the lottery fix. Georgi, sensing Jack's discomfort and knowing full well the purpose of his visit, brought up the subject first.

"I spoke with Aleksandra last night," he said meaningfully, through the bramble of his Russian accent. "She stopped by my place for a quite some time."

"Oh?" said Jack with unconvincing dispassion. He was a practiced actor after having been on camera for years, but this was different.

"Yes. Now shut the door tightly," said Georgi, still hunched over with a box-cutter razor blade he was using to make a small, thin cardboard mock-up of the bus he was going to build. He turned around in his chair and faced Jack, who had shut the door as requested. "She spoke of this crazy plan. Have you heard of it?" Georgi asked frankly.

"Oh, yeah," Jack answered dismissively with a crooked smile, as if he wasn't taking any plans of hers seriously. "Pretty crazy stuff, eh?"

"Hummm, I suppose."

"Still," said Jack, his smile vanishing as he put his cards on the table, "it could work, though."

"Of course it could."

"She told you the whole thing?"

"Well," said Georgi, through his thick, gnarly Muscovite enunciation, "it was not a whole plan, it was more an idea she presented. She said there were details to be worked out. By you. And by me. But she told me the general idea. It could work."

Jack fixed a hard stare on him.

"Georgi, are you in?"

Georgi nodded sternly. "Of course."

Jack responded in kind.

"Only two people hold the keys to get at the lottery balls, me and the on-site lottery agent, Bill Hillgrove. The lottery agent's keys open the safe, and my keys open the cage *inside* the safe, which actually holds the balls. It takes both of us to get to the lottery balls," Jack said languidly and provocatively, taking the keys out of his pocket and dangling them in his fingertips. "Nobody else has access to the lottery balls."

Georgi slowly—he did everything slowly, deliberately—then opened up his desk drawer and took out a regular, unnumbered ping-pong ball. Because the lottery machine often needed to be tested at night, they kept a few dozen regular balls around to use to test the machine.

"These," he said softly, slowly, "are the same as the actual balls used in the drawing. The actual balls used in the drawing are regular, standard ping-pong balls like you can buy at any sporting goods store, but they have numbers stenciled onto them. What do you propose? Aleksandra said you had an idea how we could fix the drawing and I would have a role."

Jack put away his keys, got up and moved closer to Georgi, fearful and paranoid his voice might carry.

"I have a job for you, a job for me and a job for Aleksandra. I won't bother telling you what I'm going to need her to do just yet," he said. Jack made it sound as though he didn't want to burden the old man and was perhaps was trying to protect Aleksandra just in case the plan went bust, but in truth, he was merely being prudent and protecting himself. If they were ignorant of the plan's details, his co-conspirators wouldn't be able to effectively testify against him if the plot blew up on the launch pad. Later on, yes, they could, but by then, after the drawing, they'd all be in it together and they'd have incentive to keep quiet.

"And what is it you need from me?" asked Georgi. So far, Jack hadn't explained how the actual rigging would take work.

"That's what I need to consult with you about, Georgi. My idea is this: we swap the regular lottery balls with replacement balls. And we'll doctor our replacement balls so that they're all heavier than usual and won't get sucked up the tube to be selected as winners—except for two of them. And then we bet very heavily on those two numbers."

"Why two numbers and not one?" asked the old Russian. "We could cut the options in half and save money on the number of tickets we need to purchase."

Jack shook his head.

"One number might look suspicious."

"I see."

"Here's what we do, and this is where you come in, we make all the balls except two—the fours and the sixes—slightly heavier than our two. Three sets of balls, zero through nine, thirty balls in all. All the balls except the fours and the sixes will be just a bit too heavy to be drawn up into the tube, so the winning lottery number will be a combination of fours and sixes. I'm not sure how to make the balls heavier, but I know you're clever enough to figure it out. I need you to experiment on how to make the balls heavier while making sure they otherwise look exactly the same as they do now. I think you can do it if you buy replacement balls and put a bunch of layers of paint on them."

Georgi nodded in agreement.

"And I have a plan of how we'll actually switch them. Since you actually bring the balls to the vacuum machine and load them for the drawing," Jack continued, "once Bill Hillgrove and I hand the balls over to you, you'll be the only one to see or touch the balls before they go into the machine. Every drawing, Hillgrove and I get the balls from the cage and give them to you to load the machine, and when you bring the balls over to the machine, you'll have the replacement balls hidden on your person. I'll engage Hillgrove in conversation—he's pretty dimwitted as far as I'm concerned and fascinated by my stories—and when you see me distracting him, you do the ol' switch-er-oo and replace the regular balls with our doctored balls. When you load the machine, you just reach into your apron pockets and pull out our replacement balls instead of reaching into the leather bag that holds the real balls. You'll be partially hidden behind the lottery machine, so nobody will notice. Then you just repeat the process in reverse after the drawing."

"Could we not switch the balls the night before?" asked Georgi in his dull, unaffected tone.

"No. I can only open the cage *inside* the safe that holds the balls, the lottery agent is the only one who can open outer safe. Neither Hillgrove or myself can get to the balls alone."

Jack then examined the black cloth woodcutter's apron Georgi was wearing. He wore it all the time when at work. It had four pockets in the front, all deep enough to carry needle-nose pliers and wire-strippers nose down, so that only the ends of the handles peeked out of the top of the pockets.

Jack quickly picked up the brown paper lunch bag he'd come in with off the desktop and started rummaging through it.

"I have thirty ping-pong balls here, Georgi. I bought them last night."

Jack started taking handfuls of the balls, pulled open the deep pockets of Georgi's apron and stuffed the balls in the various pockets. Georgi kept tools and pens and things in the pockets and Jack gruffly pulled those things out as he made room for the balls. Georgi looked on in puzzlement.

"What is this?" Georgi asked.

"You have to look normal when you're switching the balls," answered Jack distractedly. He finished putting the balls in the apron pockets and stepped back to examine Georgi.

"There," Jack said, "just as I thought."

"What?" asked Georgi.

"You look totally normal. Ping pong balls are small, they don't take up much room at all. Even with thirty of them in the deep pockets of that apron, you don't look a bit out of place. You'll be able to walk through the studio with the replacement balls and nobody will suspect a thing, especially after you stick a couple of rolls of tape or something in the apron pockets to hide the balls underneath."

Georgi looked at his apron full of thirty ping pong balls.

"I agree," he said grimly, his Russian accent growling. "I do not look unusual. Nobody will suspect a thing if they see me, the balls will be perfectly hidden in these pockets."

"So…think it can work, Georgi?" Jack asked.

"I do."

"Great, great," said Jack nervously. Georgi had been as easy to turn as Aleksandra. Growing a little paranoid, Jack was eager to tie Aleksandra to the plan, just in case Georgi was just playing along to set him up, maybe collecting evidence. If Aleksandra's fate was tied to his, Georgi could be counted on one hundred percent. "I'm glad Aleksandra talked me into this plan. You know,

Georgi," Jack confided, "a little while after this is done, Aleks and I can go off together forever. I want to make her happy."

"I know. And I wish that. She means everything to me."

"To *both* of us," assured Jack, tying everybody's interests together.

"I will go to the store tonight and buy a lots of ping-pong balls and start experimenting," said Georgi.

"No, no, don't buy a dozen sets of balls at one place," warned Jack. "That could create a trail, it would look funny and stand out. We have to make sure nothing we do stands out in any way. What you do is, drive all over the place, buy two sets of ping-pong balls at each location, buy dozens—as many as you need. We'll only have one chance to get this right. If anything looks funny, we could be sunk, so buy what you need and keep experimenting— but don't draw attention to yourself."

"Good thinking," conceded Georgi, who seem to indicate the plan was in good hands with Jack at the helm. "But how will I be certain the balls will work?"

"Try adding a few milligrams of weight. I have a scale I use to buy…stuff. I brought it today to give you. You work on the lottery vacuum machine all the time, right?"

"Yes, I work on it all the time."

"Well," said Jack, "what you do is, once you've worked on the balls, stay here late—nobody sticks around at night after the show—so nobody will really see what you're doing—and do some dry runs with the doctored balls. If anybody *should* see you running the machine they won't pay a bit of attention to what you're doing because you're always fiddling with the machine, testing it and running the balls through it. Nobody will think anything of it."

Georgi nodded in agreement. Nobody paid any attention at all to the manual things he did around the set. Everybody there, in his estimation, was a blow-dried pretty boy (or girl) and he moved around invisibly. He could craft a bomb and nobody would take notice.

"Once you've got it all worked out as far as which balls will behave the way we want," said Jack, "you will let me know and we'll move from there."

"I will start tonight," declared Georgi stoically.

"Great. Call me once you get started, just keep me updated. I'll consult with Aleksandra." With that that Jack got up to leave to go do his rehearsal drawing with the senior citizen observer.

"Jack," called out Georgi. "Why the numbers four and six?"

Jack stopped and looked back.

"Because," Jack answered with a cocky, crooked grin, "my number in college when I played football was forty-six," and then he strode out, leaving a musky confidence in his wake.

*

The next night, Jack was sitting in a darkened booth in the bar of one of Boston's most prestigious downtown hotels. Aleksandra was with him. Jack knew his time meeting Aleksandra in public—always a dicey situation, even without a lottery plot brewing—was coming to an end, at least for a while, and he wanted to be out with her a few more times and he had business here downtown that precluded him going to her place.

There wasn't much risk of being seen here, at least not where he was sitting. Jack had no fears of their whispered conversation being overheard because of the privacy the booth afforded. Jack was a practiced master at such clandestine activities. He sat in the dark corner, his back to the bar, no booth on the other side, where only the waitress would venture. He had told Aleksandra over the phone where he was sitting so she could just glide in and join him without looking around or drawing attention to herself. She was also practiced at stealth meetings with Jack in public places.

Jack was bringing her up to date about his conversation with her Uncle Georgi from earlier that evening.

"Georgi and I will be taking care of everything with the actual drawing, you don't have to even think about that angle. I need you to work the outside part," he said. Jack spoke in hushed tones, but forcefully. He wanted to be certain nobody would overhear him, but there was an edgy urgency to his voice.

"So what am I to do?" Aleksandra asked, enthralled, excitement racing through her voice. She was very eager to get involved with such a daring and thrilling scheme as a lottery fix. She already had visions of summers down at the Cape, hobnobbing with the idle rich, with little Jack juniors running around and a BMW in the driveway. Maybe two BMWs, a his and hers.

Jack took a long drink and ordered another from the attentive waitress, who was annoying him with her conscientious devotion to her duties, interrupting his disgorging of his conspiracy plans.

"Here's what I need you to do," said Jack to Aleksandra once the waitress had left. "Your role is every bit as critical as ours."

"Yes," Aleksandra assented with enthusiasm and a quick nod.

"Once Uncle Georgi comes up with the right way to weight the ping-pong balls, I'll call you from my new throwaway pre-paid cell. It will be an unfamiliar number, so you have to answer all the calls you get."

"Yes."

"Once the balls are set to be swapped, I'll call you and let you know. The next day, I need you to drive all around Massachusetts, buying tickets."

"That's it?" asked Aleksandra, disappointed and just a bit insulted at her seemingly minor role. "That's easy! Don't you trust me to do more?"

"No—it's not that easy," protested Jack. "You're not just going down to the corner and handing over a twenty dollar bill. It's more involved than that, much more."

She looked a bit mollified at this.

"No," continued Jack, "yours is a very delicate role, and only you can do it—I can't do it, Georgi can't do it…we'll both be in the studio and even if we weren't, we couldn't touch the winning tickets anyway."

"Ah!"

"I need you to go to eight different locations all across the state and play the numbers."

"Why eight?" she asked, perplexed.

"Because there are eight different possible combinations. The two numbers that will be fixed will be four and six. There are three sets of balls, zero through nine, with three of those balls selected as winners. The winning number will be some combination of four and six. That means there are eight possible combinations: 444, 446, 464, 466, 644, 646, 664 and 666. You're going to buy a thousand tickets on each number with the money I'm going to give you. Don't worry about that money, I'll give you eight grand up front to use. You're going to go to one place, buy a thousand tickets for 444, go to the next place somewhere probably half an hour away, buy another thousand on 446, then another place half an hour away and buy a thousand tickets on 464 and so on and so on, until you've completed the semi-circle around the city and played all eight combinations."

"I see."

"You're probably wondering why eight stops where you'll buy all thousand tickets for that one particular number combination and not, say, ten stops where you'll buy a few hundred of each combination—or a hundred stops with ten tickets of each of the eight combinations?"

Aleksandra nodded. She hadn't gotten far down the path enough to ask questions of "Why?" yet, but Jack was anxious to explain his plan and couldn't wait around for her to ask the correct questions, so he had to pose them himself.

"See," he explained, "you could go to one store and buy a bunch of each number at each store, but then when you presented the winning tickets the question would arise as to why you drove all over the place to play that same number at different places. See? Why would you buy the combo of, say, 446, at ten or twelve different stops all over the state? You wouldn't, right?"

"Yes! But," Aleksandra asked, "won't it look funny to have played the same number a thousand times when I *do* come forward with whichever number eventually wins? Why would I buy so many?"

"If anybody asks, you're going to say you had intended to buy them as gifts for everybody at the Russian Club," said Jack, referring to the club where Aleksandra often hung out with other émigrés. "You say you bought them with your boyfriend for all the people at the club, but then you had a fight with him and that's why you never went to the club to hand out the tickets, because you thought he'd be there and so you stayed home instead. That'll help build a cover story for when we officially start dating later on. Of the other seven losing combinations, you will deny ever having any tickets for those numbers what-so-ever, got it?"

"Yes."

"And it's important that you buy a thousand tickets, too."

"Why?"

"Because thousands and thousands of people play the daily number. One winning ticket won't mean squat. We have to make a killing on this, we only get to do it once. There's only one chance so we have to win a bundle."

"OK."

"And here's another thing: Don't buy them all in the same town or anything. I want you to start on the south shore and go all around Boston, stopping at towns circling the city, until you get somewhere near home on the north shore. You live in Somerville, that's just north of the city, you can end there."

"That will take all day," she protested mildly.

"I know, but think of it as an investment. It's not that big a deal considering the payoff."

"But won't they get suspicious if you marry the winner of the lottery a year or so after I win?" Aleksandra asked, the enormity of the thing suddenly landing on her.

"No, not at all," Jack assured her. "There is a photo-op with every big winner. The winner comes to the studio, meets me and a couple other people and gets their picture taken with me since I'm the host of the drawing. When you come down to have your picture taken, that will be our story of how we met. We'll tell everyone that's how we became introduced. You came to the studio and started shamelessly flirting with me since you found me so irresistible," Jack said with his crooked grin, lightening the mood. "Love at first sight. Happens to me all the time."

"Or you could start with me!"

"Well, we can work out that detail later," said Jack slyly. "The important thing is, that will be the story of how we met and started dating. Once you get the money, I will have started divorce proceedings, so by the time of the photo-opportunity, I'll already be separated. It's seamless."

Aleksandra got a worried look.

"Don't worry, Aleksandra," Jack assured her. "The beauty of the thing is that the conspiracy is so small, there's no chance of anyone finding out. It's a safe plan, there are only three of us in this conspiracy, and we're all bound by love of some kind."

"Oh, really, darling? Bound by love? All three of us?" Aleksandra asked with a mischievous Russian roll of the tongue so that her 'darling' sounded like 'dar-link.' "Even you and Uncle Georgi?"

"Well, we do work a lot of long nights together in a darkened studio, you know," said Jack. They shared a laugh and the tension was broken.

"That's more than I need to know!"

"Well, anyway," said Jack, calling the meeting back to order, "here's the thing: once your part is done, you'll need to call us right away."

"O.K."

"It's going to take all day to drive from the south shore to the north shore buying the tickets and there's always a chance something could go wrong, your car could break down or something." Jack paused and rubbed his chin. "Timing is everything. Remember, we can only do this once! So you need to start in the morning and once you get to the last place and buy the last set of numbers, you need to call the studio and let us know it's a go so that Uncle Georgi and I can start our phase of the plan. Once we get the word from you, we can go into action and do our part to switch the balls, OK?"

"Absolutely."

"But here's the thing," said Jack, "you don't call me. I don't want any phone calls coming to me. If they get suspicious and look at anybody, it'll be me, I'm the star of the show. There's always a chance a phone record search could be done of me. What I want you to do is call your Uncle Georgi on your prepaid cell, which is untraceable."

"Yes," said Aleksandra, listening in rapt attention.

"I want you to make sure you call him at his desk phone, and here's the best part: make sure you speak to him in Russian. That way, nobody'll understand what you're saying if they *do* overhear you, OK? Make sure you speak in Russian."

"Good!"

"So I need you to call up an hour before the drawing is supposed to start—that should be the right amount of time in my scenario—and say, in Russian, 'the fix is in.' That's it, nothing else. 'The fix is in,' *in Russian*. Georgi will say 'OK,' and hang up. Nice and quick, that way it'll look like a wrong number in the phone records."

"Jack," Aleksandra said worshipfully, "it is brilliant. I think it can work."

"It's *going* to work, just like that play I called for in the huddle in college that time against Connecticut when I scored on fourth and five with fifty-two seconds left," Jack asserted with a cocksure grin.

Aleksandra had no idea what he was talking about, but nodded happily. She could almost smell the Cape Cod ocean air already.

"OK," continued Jack, "that's the plan." He rubbed his chin again thoughtfully. "Now, I'll call you once Georgi finishes experimenting and works out a system to fix the ping-pong balls and then we can pick out the day you're going to do it. It doesn't matter where you go to play each number, just so long as you play only one number a thousand times at each stop."

"Right."

"And remember, you need to play them all over the state, so start in the south shore and work your way around north in a crescent until you get home in Somerville, north of the city."

"Right."

"And don't forget the part about calling your uncle and telling him *in Russian*, 'the fix is in'."

"Right."

"OK, then. And remember, we can only use my various prepaid cell phones until we're done, right? Good, good." Jack looked at his watch. "Now, Aleksandra, I really should be going. I have a very important appointment I have to get to before going home and Jeanine will kill me if I get home too late again."

"OK, Jack," said Aleksandra, looking at her magnificent benefactor with worshipful eyes. "I'll talk to you tomorrow."

"You should leave first. It won't do us any good to be seen leaving together."

"OK," she said. "Jack?" she said dramatically. "I love you."

"I love you, too, Aleksandra. Everything—all this—is for you. For *us*."

Aleksandra gathered her things, kissed her fingertips and pressed them to Jack's lips and smiled. She strode out and got in a cab and left.

Jack paid the bill, left a generous tip and, instead of leaving the hotel, went into the elevator and went up three floors and got off. He looked around to orientate himself and searched out room 327. He paused outside the door and knocked on the door quietly, lest he attract attention to himself. The door opened, seemingly by itself, the occupant of the room remaining behind the door, and Jack went in.

A beautiful woman came out from behind the door, dressed in a teddy and fishnet stockings.

"Are you Jack?" she asked.

"Yeah, that's me. Gabrielle, it is? It's nice to meet you, Gabrielle. How are you?" Jack asked with a crooked smile as she shut the door.

"Wonderful," she said with a sly smile.

"I'll say you are. Listen, I'm a little tight for time—do you mind if we get started right away?" Jack asked.

"Of course not," she said.

"Great. This is for you," he said, placing an envelope with four hundred dollars on the table as he started taking off his jacket and shirt, unbuckling his pants and sat down on the edge of the bed….

Chapter Seven

(Early August, 2010)

Two nights after he'd spoken with Billy Bowman, the Station Manager at WKTD Channel Six to propose an interview about his notorious past in exchange for publicity for Earthpeace's campaign against the airport expansion in Norton, Jack Webster was at The Worthy House with a group of Earthpeace people. He'd become familiar with them and they with him over the weeks since he'd joined the group… though they were not as familiar with him as they would have supposed. Jack's true efforts with the group were aimed not at stopping the bad environmental decision of expanding the Slocumb Airbase over the objections of the bullied working-class citizens of Norton, but instead were directed at the goals of landing Ava Basri—the beautiful young artist for whom he'd developed a strong desire—and at rehabilitating his sullied name. He planned to use the interview as a jumping-off point to reinvent himself, then perhaps work his way back into the television business or some other career and start a new life that would lead him far away from Earthpeace and places like The Worthy House and the city of Norton forever.

Over the course of his weeks with Earthpeace, Jack had ingratiated and integrated himself with the organization, all in an effort to get closer with Ava. He'd been volunteering for the group and revealed he'd formerly been an employee at WKTD and could be of use as a media liaison, at which point he was appointed a "block captain" and made a full-time Earthpeace employee, and left his carpet-delivery job.

Jack left his former role at WKTD vague. Everyone assumed he had worked in some sort of management capacity, which was an impression he tried very hard to convey. Jack's change in appearance—his beard, his weight loss and the fact he dressed decidedly downscale— usually in a flannel shirt and jeans, in contrast to his sharp-dressed television days—helped disguise his former identity as local television's leading celebrity.

Jack had also gone through great pains to avoid revealing his last name. In fact, Jack had mentioned it just once in passing to Ava. Had he looked the same as in his heyday as the leading local TV personality in town, everyone at Earthpeace would have instantly recognized him, but so far his efforts of disguise and deception had carried the day, and by now Jack had many times congratulated himself on the wisdom of growing his obscuring beard.

Though a block captain was in charge of a geographical group of volunteers, based on his media expertise, Jack became a *de facto* guru to the whole local outfit, a role appreciated by Larry, the aging hippie who was casually in charge of the group.

In fact, Jack was an indifferent guru, being interested solely in getting more chummy with Ava, a goal for which he needed a leadership role. Though he was successful in forming a bond with the beautiful young tree-hugger and consciousness-raiser, in his leadership capacity Jack was proving spectacularly ineffective, though nobody seemed to notice this reality. His ineffectiveness was due not so much to incompetence on his part, but was instead a reflection of his simply not caring. In meetings, Jack mostly just indifferently tossed out a few media-insider buzz-phrases designed to impress the uninitiated. Jack's lackadaisical offerings and random, sometimes contradictory advice added nothing to the cause, but it impressed the locals, and that was more than good enough for his purposes. Often in these meetings, Jack would be not paying the slightest attention when called upon, only to be roused into action, and he would toss out half-remembered consultant-inspired jargonisms and double-speak he recalled from long-gone meetings from his own television business experience, then he'd return to his private daydreams with a wave of impressed novices in his wake.

The Earthpeace campaign against the airport expansion hadn't been going any better since the City Hall protest where Jack had first seen the group. This state of affairs suited Jack perfectly. If the Earthpeace campaign worked too well (he feared) it might end before he had a chance to become a hero to Ava. He was secretly delighted to see the airport expansion plans moving slowly enough to prolong the process while the powers-that-be totally ignored the small band of young, bearded men and young, beardless women trying pathetically to rouse public support to stop it. Jack could only be a hero if he rescued a failing movement; a successful movement served his purposes not one bit.

Jack wanted it underscored that the movement was failing, so he had grown accustomed to lamenting the lack of success Earthpeace was having as he trudged around various locales knocking on doors or hanging fliers with an Earthpeace partner, usually his new great friend, Ava, who seemed to be taken by his re-emerging charisma in this new setting just as beautiful women had been in his old milieu. If he was sent out on his own, Jack would naturally just dump any fliers or handouts into a fortuitous dumpster, stop by The Worthy House for a few drinks and then head home.

But now, at The Worthy House, he had some real interesting material to share with the group.

On this night, Jack had called some of the Earthpeace group together at The Worthy House to drop his big bombshell announcement that he'd struck a deal with some old friends at WKTD—the most popular station in the state—to give the Earthpeace cause some desperately needed airtime and media attention.

Jack sat at the head of the table and lordly glanced over the Earthpeace people sitting there looking up at him. They'd answered his summons to meet him at The

Worthy House instead of at the chilly, sterile office space Earthpeace had rented because he wanted this to be *his* moment, and his alone. There were a dozen members of the organization in attendance, their purpose to act as the audience for him, the star of the production, to be the back-slappers and adulation-givers to the Hero. Ava was present, of course. Greg, the large, angry, militant Jack had met right after the City Hall fiasco, was there, as were assorted other "important" leader-types of the Earthpeace crowd who had descended on the mill city of Norton.

"Guys," started Jack, standing up, "I didn't ask all of you here tonight just to share a couple of drinks, though I'm glad to do that, too," he said to a general laugh. "In fact, I have a big announcement to make."

"You're leaving?" asked Greg with recognizable trace of hostility that he always carried. Jack had noticed with indifference how Greg resented his lack of militancy.

"Not yet," parried Jack with casual confidence. "No, this is big—big for the airport expansion campaign." Everyone became quiet and was listening intently. The Worthy House itself was crowded with neighborhood regulars and neighborhood more-often-than-regulars, otherwise called drunks. A few spare college kids were hanging around, too, having fun slumming, and so Jack did not attract an inordinate amount of attention from on-lookers with his impromptu speech.

"I have a bunch of old friends at WKTD—Channel Six," he added, for the Earthpeace people were not media insiders and called the station by it's number rather than its call letters, as an insider would. "And I approached them the other day…."

The faces in his audience looked at Jack with confused anticipation. Suddenly, even the local barflies not associated with Earthpeace were now paying attention to him.

"What do you mean, 'old friends'?"

"Friends I've known for a long time," said Jack evasively, an annoyed edge creeping into his voice. "Anyway, I approached a few people I know at Channel Six, and guess what? Because I still have some pull over there and I have some people who owe me a couple of favors and, well, the long and short of it is, I've gotten them to do *at least* a two-part exposé on the Slocumb Airport expansion project!"

The table erupted in spontaneous shouts and clapping, so unexpected and spectacular was this astonishing announcement. Jack modestly held up his hands to quiet them.

"I figure *this* ought to get people's attention more than any door-knocking campaign would! You know what? I think we're going to put a stop to this airport project yet!" Jack concluded triumphantly. He wasn't very sincere in that he didn't care about the airport project itself, but he had a role to play, and he was prepared to play it to the hilt. TV news anchors, even the sports guys, were always having to slap on an energetic face on cue, so some phony enthusiasm was a snap for Jack. "They'll film the interview, spend a few weeks publicizing it, then broadcast after they've built up some momentum for it."

Jack left out the details, namely that the interview would at first focus on his past with the lottery before bringing up the airport, for later. It was his moment of triumph and he wanted to enjoy it. Jack knew he'd have to come clean and come out of hiding soon and was planning to clue in Larry, the local Earthpeace director, later that very night.

The faces at the table all looked at Jack in awe, but he scanned for one in particular, and he was pleased to see Ava was beaming at him even more than the others. He felt he was rapidly winning her over. Some of the locals hanging around the bar who had gotten wind of the efforts by Earthpeace to stop the airport and who heartily approved, came over and slapped Jack on the back in thanks and congratulations.

"How'd you do it, Jack?" called out one of the Earthpeace people.

"I'll leave out details of how I negotiated it—for now," answered Jack, who did not feel this was the right time to unmask himself. "But like I said, I still have some pull in the TV business. Once the interview is filmed, Channel Six is going to promote the hell out of it. I'm going to go do an interview at Channel Six about the airport tomorrow morning!"

There was another outbreak of approval and Jack held up his hands to quiet them.

"Everyone at WKTD seems to be under the impression I'm on a hunger strike, and that seems to be pretty newsworthy, so for a while I'm going to have to cut back on meals to give 'em what they want," Jack explained to the group with a grin. He had absolutely no intention of going on a real hunger strike, but he could fake it. That meant only eating in private for a while, he figured.

Jack went on to regale his audience with his behind-the-scenes knowledge of local TV and how he was going to score for Earthpeace's aims. He was dying of thirst and holding a large bottle of water, which he swung like a baton for effect as he told his stories. He was a natural storyteller and raconteur and held the whole table— Earthpeace people and local toughs alike—in the palm of his hand. After his long absence, he was gaining his old swagger back. Granted, it was coming slowly and in modest circumstances, but still, he felt more like his old self than he had in years. Maybe he'd even somehow hit the gym and put some of that lean muscle back on to complete the seduction of Ava.…

After telling a series of entertaining stories, all aimed at impressing Ava, who was staring at him with an almost worshipful gleam in her eye, Jack was satisfied. He'd played his role well and it was getting late. Jack theatrically consulted his watch as he stood there at the head of the table.

"Guys, we're going to have to get either going or find some beds upstairs," he said with a crooked grin, and with that, the table soon started breaking up and everyone headed for the exits, still abuzz over Jack's wizardry at garnering a two-part expose from the leading local TV station in one master stroke that dwarfed all their previous combined efforts.

Ava was among the last to leave, when Jack, still standing at the front of the table spoke up.

"Ava!" he called as she slowly walked away.

"Yes?" she asked with a proud smile upon returning to the table at which only she and Her Hero now stood.

"You know, I'm heading down to the TV station tomorrow."

"Yeah—I'm incredibly excited about it!"

"Right, well, I wanted to know if you'd go down there with me."

"Really?" she asked, with a look of dumb devotion.

"Sure. I'd love to have somebody with me, you know, someone I can bounce ideas off of, remind me of some talking points, someone to break the tension, all that sort of stuff."

"I'd love to do that, Jack," said Ava, her look of worship now complete.

"Great," said Jack confidently. He took a large swig from his bottle of water, for he was unaccountably still thirsty. "There're a couple things I'd like to tell you tomorrow, too," he hinted, referring to his dark, illustrious and hidden background.

"Like what?"

"I'll save that for tomorrow," he said.

"OK."

"I'll call you at ten o'clock."

"OK," she said. "Hey, I have to use the ladies' room. Will you wait for me a minute?"

"Of course."

"Be right back," Ava said happily. She walked off, then looked back towards him for a brief moment and continued.

Jack stood there, smiling, tapping his empty bottle of water in his other hand.

For a split second, Jack was alone at the table for the first time. Just then, a man appeared, coming out of the shadows from the back of the room. The man approached rapidly and with purpose.

"Jack Webster," he announced as more of a threat than a moment of recognition.

The man had been so hidden in the darkness that Jack hadn't seen him sitting there, laying in wait. Jack had noticed the man approaching out of the corner of his eye, but only once the man spoke did Jack become fully aware that the man had timed his approach to wait until he was alone at the table.

Jack noted that the man, once revealed and out of the shadows, stood sharply apart from the regular patrons of The Worthy House. The man was dressed in a full, flawlessly tailored, three-piece suit. His shoes, Jack recognized, were Berluti, the very type he himself used to wear back when he had a lot of money, before he was forced to wear flannel shirts and a beard. Something about the man made Jack uncomfortable.

"My name is Rudy Baxter," announced the stranger, brandishing the name almost as if a weapon.

"How ya' doin'?" asked Jack noncommittally, avoiding making eye contact and looking down, suggesting the man should take the hint and leave. But the man Baxter did not leave.

"I'd like to talk to you a moment, Mr. Webster," he said, emphasizing the name, letting Jack know he was on to him. He was talking like a man who held all the cards.

Baxter wore glasses, but he struck Jack as rather a youngish man (perhaps in his early thirties) to be carrying himself with such an air of importance. There was a vague aspect of menace about him. He had a military-type buzz cut that seemed to reinforce the impression that he was a remorselessly efficient person. The light glistened off his wire-rimmed glasses, hiding his eyes and replacing them with sinisterly illuminated orbs, making it almost seem as though he had glowing, soulless bulbs where his eyes should be.

Jack felt compelled to comply with his request for a moment of his time and sat down, feeling almost like a prisoner. "This is Liberty Hall, Rudy, take a seat," said Jack reluctantly, motioning to a chair.

He wasn't sure how this man Baxter—who plainly was not one of the hard-drinking working-class locals who filled up The Worthy House every night—had tracked him down, for Jack was certain this was no chance encounter.

"It's nice to see you again, Mr. Webster," said Baxter with a poorly concealed air of smugness as he sat.

"See me 'again'?" asked Jack. "I don't remember ever meeting you."

"No, but I've seen *you*. Many times. Not this close up or in person, of course, though you did give a funny talk and video presentation at my college once, accompanied with some funny sports bloopers. It was a big hit among the students. I missed it, unfortunately."

"Chess club meeting or something that day?" quipped Jack.

"No, I was out with the flu at the time," said Baxter bloodlessly. "I meant to say that I'd seen you many times in your previous life on television. You were very big around this state."

"You keep mentioning my name and having seen me on television, is there something you're trying to tell me, Rudy?"

"Just that I know who you are, Mr. Webster. Just a friendly reminder, without having to mention any of the ugliness for which you later became so widely known.

It's a show of tact on my part, which you don't seem to appreciate."

"Thanks a lot, Rudy," said Jack with exasperation, "I really appreciate your efforts."

"You are *the* Jack Webster, of course."

"I've never hidden who I am," countered Jack.

"But of course you have, Mr. Webster, of course you have," said Baxter with confidence. "Nobody around here seems to know who you *really* are. You look quite a bit different now. Significantly different…*entirely* different. You've got that preposterous beard, you're dressed differently and you seem to have lost considerable weight. No, Mr. Webster, you have most definitely tried to hide who you are…. For now."

"What am I supposed to do, carry a sign around my neck?" asked Jack in irritation. "It's not like I'm using a fake name or anything."

"I only meant to say you've kept a decidedly low profile since you returned. You've remained quite hidden and tried to disguise your identity. I've done research, and you haven't tried to get back into the television business or anything like that."

"Yeah, well, the way I left, I don't think there's much room for me in the TV industry anymore."

"You are entirely correct about that, Mr. Webster. Earning a living in television is quite out of the question for you. There is no room for you to earn a living in television. Not as things stand right now, anyway."

"Well," said Jack, standing, "it's great to catch up with an old fan, especially one as devoted as you are, what with you tracking me down four years after I left TV and all, but that young lady who just left will be back in a minute and if you wanted to say 'hello' to me and catch up on old times, you've done it, but I'm afraid I'll be off, unless you have something else?"

"Sit down, Mr. Webster," commanded Baxter without emotion, but sternly, "I do indeed have something more, something you will want to hear about." Jack sat down in a huff. He was agitated at how this man seemed to do everything in a cold-blooded, serpentine way.

"Great, let's hear it—right now. I'm tired of this."

"You see, Jack, I'm the Chief of Staff for Senator Shea," Baxter announced. Jack looked on intently. "It is in that capacity I came to see you—entirely off the record, of course. My official log has me somewhere else tonight. Standard stuff. In my position, you sometimes have to meet with people off the record, you understand."

"Sure," responded Jack sourly.

"Anyway, it was Senator Shea who suggested I come and talk to you. You know, he's a big sports fan, by the way, Mr. Webster, and was a big fan of yours back in the day. He was sorry to see you off the air."

"Uh-huh, well I was sorry to *be* off the air" said Jack, who noticed out of the corner of his eye that Ava had emerged and was detained, engaged in conversation with an older waitress, for which Jack was grateful, as he felt uncomfortable with the nature of this conversation with Baxter.

"Don't worry about the young woman, Mr. Webster," said Baxter without even looking around to follow Jack's glance, giving the unsettling impression he could read Jack's mind, "I'd just discreetly ask her for a moment alone with you if she returned. She'll stay away. I wish for this talk of ours to be kept quiet just like you do.

In any case, what Senator Shea asked me to do tonight was to come down here and talk to you about your little television interview tomorrow with WKTD. Don't look surprised that I know about it, Mr. Webster. Word travels fast, especially when it's word that you're going to do your very first interview on the unfortunate business that so famously entangled you four years ago. That interview is big news indeed."

"Why would an interview by me about my past with the state lottery concern Senator Shea?" asked Jack.

"Oh, it's not the part about the lottery which concerns him. He's more concerned that you are going to trade that interview for publicity about your hunger strike and your work with Earthpeace trying to get the airport expansion at Slocumb Airbase stopped."

There was a mole at WKTD, Jack immediately realized, probably Billy Bowman himself, wanting to keep in the good graces of the powerful Senator.

"Just a citizen airing my views on the subject, Rudy," lied Jack improbably. He didn't care about the airport expansion project any more than the day before he first heard about it.

"Maybe," said Baxter with a sly grin. "But there's another possibility, which I proposed—though Senator Shea would have none of it, he defending your integrity, I promise you. The idea I was kicking around was that you were trying to rehabilitate your image. You know, clean your name and thus get a fresh start in the television business. I did some research on you and your background, Mr. Webster, and there was nothing at all I could see in my thorough investigation that suggested community activism was in your background—or future."

"So?"

"So, clearly it must take a great impetus to get you to come out of hiding like this, something a lot more important than this silly airport issue. This makes me think that perhaps your motives are not what you claim, again suggesting what you really want is to get back in the good graces of the public and get back on television."

"Even if that were the case, what does Senator Shea care?" asked Jack with a defensive note in his voice.

"Senator Shea's family has been prominent in state politics for almost a hundred years. He's very well connected everywhere. He's done a lot of good works—"

"I've seen the Shea family compound on TV, it's a nice payoff for those goods works," pointed out Jack.

Annoyed, Baxter said, "He's made it good in the state, he does good for the state and he wants to make sure other people can make it good in the state. Mr. Webster, I don't want to sit here and play games with you. I know who you really are underneath that beard. You aren't an environmental activist, or an activist of any kind, or even a person concerned about anything at all, except yourself. You've always been totally devoted to your own indulgences."

"And?"

"You know that Senator Shea's home—the Shea family compound—would be severely inconvenienced if Earthpeace were to be successful in thwarting the airport expansion in Norton at Slocumb Airbase. If that project were to be stopped because of public pressure, the expansion would assuredly take place at Avery Airbase, near the Shea family compound."

"Not as near as the current expansion plan will be to Norton," pointed out Jack.

"But still too close for Senator Shea. I know you don't care about the project and are just trying to get back into television, so here is the deal the Senator is suggesting. You drop this bullshit about sticking up for the city of Norton, and the Senator, who as I said, is connected to everybody, will get you back on television. Not with WKTD—he doesn't own *everything* in the state—but on another major affiliate in the city. You pick which one. He can make it happen."

Jack didn't care for Rudy Baxter's attitude, but he never said he was against listening to an offer.

"He could make that happen, couldn't he?" said Jack, suddenly interested and quite certain the Senator could easily put him back on TV.

"Of course he could. It would be child's play for Senator Shea to get you on TV, you know that. This is a man who places billions in government contracts, a television sports anchor job is small potatoes to the Senator, a mere three minute phone call. Maybe two minutes, if he's busy."

"Yeah…."

"Yeah, is right. And you know his word is good, because you could always go back to your interview scheme if he reneged."

"I know he wouldn't do that, Shea cuts deals all the time."

"He certainly does." Baxter paused and looked around The Worthy House. "Look at this place. You don't belong here. I know you, Mr. Webster—"

"—Call me Jack."

"Very well," said Baxter with a smile, "Jack it is. I know you, Jack. You liked the glamour of your old life—"

"I *loved* it," corrected Jack hungrily.

"Better still. You *loved* the glamour of your old life. You don't want to spend the rest of your life in a shithole place like this, surrounded my losers who smell of cheap draft beer and sweat. I know you desire to live high on the hog again."

Jack could not deny the charge. It held great appeal.

Baxter theatrically handed Jack his card.

"The airport expansion project has already been decided on, there's no need to start putting up a stink now. Even just a public airing of your kind would prove embarrassing to Senator Shea, which he'd rather avoid. He's got a legacy to protect. Senator Shea is offering you his friendship just for keeping quiet. And, of course," Baxter intoned, "there is another, less agreeable, side to Senator Shea's connections, as well."

Jack did not need to have this spelled out. He was out of prison upon certain conditions of parole. He could be put back in, and Senator Shea knew people. Senator Shea knew *everybody*.

"You mean I could get in trouble."

"I'm just saying the Senator could address problems with you to the authorities. Or he could make problems go away."

"I see."

"See this: Drop the interview and go back to the high life. Continue with it, and…."

Ava, who had been politely talking to the waitress to give Jack some privacy, had to give up and wandered back over and stood a discrete distance off to the side, but in their orbit enough to communicate that she was waiting.

Baxter saw her approach and he got up, with Jack joining him in standing.

"It's been nice seeing you, Jack," said Baxter pleasantly, smiling now that there were on-lookers to their conversation. He stuck out his hand and they shook. "You have my card, and I'm in the phone book anyway. I'm not difficult to find. Think about it and give me a call before you go on tomorrow and let me know which way you decide."

"Sure," said Jack quietly, looking down at the card absently, "I'll think about it."

"Make sure you do, time's a'wastin'," Baxter said with a sly smile, then he strode off and out the door.

"What was he about?" asked Ava suspiciously, also noticing immediately how Baxter did not fit in with the local atmosphere.

"Oh, he was just asking me what we'd been talking about, the airport issue and all that. Now, come on, let's get out of here," Jack said distractedly, furtively stuffing the card in his pocket just in case he needed it later….

Chapter Eight

(October, 2006)

Georgi Sholokhov approached Jack at the set of *Daily Number Live!* looking just as rumpled and disheveled as always, his appearance an ode to chaos. His head was mostly bald, but the hair on the sides of his head was somewhat lengthy and unkempt, shooting off in every direction from underneath the plain, black scally cap he was wearing. Despite the wild anarchy his locks suggested, Georgi's demeanor was that of unchanging, stoic, fatigued Russian inertia. He was slightly hunched over, and as always, he wore his dusty black work apron around his waist.

"Hello, Jack," said Georgi blandly as he came up next to Jack on the set. Georgi spoke in the same flat, understated monotone he always used, as if nothing out of the ordinary was going on.

"Georgi—where have you been?" asked Jack in a strained, repressed tone. "How's 'it' going?" he asked anxiously. No clarification was needed as to what "it" was. For Jack, "it" now hung heavily in the air everywhere like a clear, odorless smog. Like inflation and misogyny, it was everywhere and nowhere. "It" was, of course, the efforts to complete the fixing of the lottery ping-pong balls in their conspiracy to rig the daily lottery.

"It has been going well," answered Georgi slowly, refusing to further acknowledge the "it" under concern. Georgi, as was typical for him, spoke in a coarse, gravelly voice without looking directly Jack. He was fiddling with a tool of some kind, a tool to which Jack paid no attention, trying to get something unstuck.

Jack paused to let Georgi continue on and tell him about his lottery ping-pong ball experiments, but Georgi—with an implied air of superiority—said nothing. Jack became suddenly irritated at this smugness.

"Well, Georgi," asked Jack loudly and impatiently, in no mood for this game, "how is it going with the lottery ping-pong balls you're fixing? Have you continued your experiments tampering with the balls?" If Georgi was going to act above it all and cop an attitude, Jack would show him he was not above concerns, that he was not in fact running the show.

Georgi looked up with disbelieving reproach, held up his hand and motioned fiercely to keep it down and quietly hissed, "Shhhh!" He stealthily looked around the studio set. Jack was satisfied. *"Not so big now, are you?"* he thought.

"Come into my office," said Georgi with a censorious frown.

"OK," said Jack, "you go first and I'll join you in a moment. No need for us to be seen skulking off together."

A few minutes later, they were together behind the closed door of Georgi's office, with several WKTD stagehands and employees taking unconcerned notice of the fact Jack and Georgi huddled together and then conveniently disappeared moments apart.

"So where do we stand?" Jack asked immediately. "Did you work out something with the balls?"

Georgi took a long, dramatic breath. He looked incredibly fatigued and worn, like an old Russian should.

"It has been a long week," Georgi started wearily, as if recalling a great and trying ordeal, his accented words morbidly stringing along like gloomy boxcars on a railroad track. "Indeed, a very long *few* weeks."

"Yeah?" asked Jack apprehensively.

Once, while in college, Jack had somehow, through a comedy of misunderstandings, ended up taking a literature class on the Great Russians, and to his horror, he discovered the Great Russians wrote very long, dreary books. The unbending professor, who had no respect for Jack's position on the football team, forced him to take the class—to *really* take the class, show up, take the tests, the whole nine yards. After several dozen pages of tortured and laborious reading, Jack had been mortified to see he'd only scratched the surface and sought for other ways to pass the class after realizing the professor would not let him slide through. Had it not been for manipulating a less popular student to do the classwork for him, Jack would never have completed the course in a thousand years. And now Georgi looked as though he was the very living embodiment of one of the particularly dark, bleak Russian tomes Jack had almost been forced to confront back in those college days.

Jack wasn't any more interested in exploring dense Russian stoicism now than he had been back then. He had a conspiracy to run.

"The past week was a very long week indeed," repeated Georgi, his weathered face emoting to the fullest. "It has been a long couple of weeks of endless effort," continued Georgi, squinting his eyes, focusing on Jack, staring at him intently as if to relate how great his efforts had been on their behalf. He seemed to imply Jack was greatly in his debt. "I have been experimenting without stopping, day after day, night after night, never ceasing," he said with strained weariness, using his hands to punctuate the words, painting a vision of endless dark and lonely nights of toil in the cold, deserted studio.

"And how'd things come out?" asked Jack, attempting to nudge Georgi to cut to the chase.

As a response, Georgi wordlessly went over to a shelf and took out a gallon can of paint. He mutedly took out a screwdriver from his apron and started to pry open the empty can. Jack stood, seemingly patient. He knew that this deliberate, melodramatic affectation was just the way Georgi did things, it was very difficult to move him along. The old man finally got the lid off the can and slowly took out two lottery ping-pong balls.

"I knew it would take much, much experimentation before I could get it right, because that's the way I do things—the right way," Georgi said, focusing his intense gaze on Jack, straining his every fiber to illustrate his righteousness in a fallen world.

"Great! So you got it right?"

"I experimented with lots of ping-pong balls. I bought dozens and dozens of sets of ping-pong balls, probably dozens of dozens! I can't even tell you how many," Georgi confided with a rich, Russian roll of the tongue, shaking his head. Jack was relieved that at least he would be spared a merciless, strict accounting of the ping-pong ball tally if nothing else. "I tried many different methods of fixing the ping-pong balls so that I could make them too heavy to be sucked up into the tube, but not too heavy that it would look odd or peculiar, you see?"

"Of course, of course."

"What I did, you see, Jack, I thought to myself, 'How do I make them heavy?' When I looked at the balls, they were white. I thought to myself, 'Ah ha! That is the key!' So I took ordinary latex paint and started putting layer after layer on ball after ball."

"Good," said Jack. "So it worked?"

"No," said Georgi dramatically, slapping the word down like a dead, wet fish, happy that Jack had fed him the line he wanted to hear. "It did not work. Yes, it made the balls heavier, but sometimes too heavy. You see," Georgi went on, "not only did I experiment with dozens and dozens and dozens of ping-pong balls—which I bought all over the place at great expense—but I experimented with almost all of them in The Machine," Georgi said ominously referring to the glass "fish tank" device where the lottery balls were picked as winners for the lottery. "I experimented every night, for hours at a time!" said Georgi, casting himself as a heroically unsung Laborer.

"We owe you a lot," volunteered Jack, who wasn't sincere in this gesture of gratitude, but he wanted to give the old Russian what he so desperately wanted to hear so as to move things along.

Georgi nodded.

"No need to thank me," he said with even less sincerity than Jack had offered. "I do this for all of us," he lectured, parading around his modesty, panhandling for more compliments. "But no matter how long I worked at it, I could not get the layers of paint just right. I would get too much paint or unequal amounts of paint. I discovered, through my long nights of struggle, that even a few millimeters of weight made a great difference!"

"You mean milligrams," corrected Jack.

"Yes, yes, milligrams," said Georgi with irritation, seeing his great narrative passing through the hands of a molesting editor. "I noticed even a tiny bit of weight made a difference, so touchy are the allowances of the machine."

"But you eventually found a way?" prodded Jack.

"Yes!" answered Georgi with drama. He slowly handed Jack two of the ping-pong balls he'd taken out of his paint can. "See those balls? Those are two of the balls I have doctored that we shall use."

Jack examined them intently. "They seem normal."

"As well they should. You see, I could not—by adding paint to the outside of the balls to weight them—precisely regulate the weight of the balls. One would be slightly heavier, the other lighter. They looked peculiar in the chamber when the vacuum was turned on. They did not react normally. Then," declared Georgi grimly and dramatically, holding up his index finger in an act of showmanship to illustrate the momentous unveiling of his genius idea had arrived, "I hit upon an idea. I would inject the paint directly *inside* the balls!"

Jack nodded and looked on with sincere interest.

"By using a needle and syringe filled with paint," Georgi continued, "I could exactly regulate the amount of paint—and therefore the weight—each ball received, even to the tiniest weight and specification."

"Ah, very good, Georgi," congratulated Jack. "You can fix everything around here," he said, stroking the old man's ego.

"And," said Georgi, brushing aside the compliment, "the balls themselves look entirely normal on the outside. The paint re-seals the hole made by the needle. The balls look just exactly as the real balls look, but they will react as we need them," he finished with satisfaction.

"Excellent."

"Yes, excellent. I did another dry run with them just last night, just to make sure it worked flawlessly. And it did. It will work without a glitch."

"So when will you doctor all the other sets of replacement balls?"

"I have already done so," said Georgi softly in dark triumph. "The real lottery balls, of course, remain untouched and will be switched back into place after the drawing. Those doctored ping-pong balls you hold, they will be the ones we use for the fix. I have the others in the paint can. I have done exactly three sets of ping-pong balls—thirty balls, three sets, each numbered zero through nine—all weighted exactly to the milligram as we want them."

"All three sets of numbers are weighted?"

"Yes. Well, except for the fours and sixes. They will be the only balls not doctored. As we discussed, they are untouched and will be the only balls light enough to fly up the tube to be selected as winners. All the others will be just a *bit* too heavy to be drawn all the way up the tube. The winning numbers will be some combination of the three fours and three sixes which are not doctored."

Jack looked at the ping-pong balls.

"Nice. I see you already lettered the replacement balls," he commented as he examined them.

"Yes," said Georgi, also inspecting them, "I did the original lettering on the real ping-pong balls, so it was child's play for me to reproduce the lettering exactly on these replacement balls."

"Boy, Georgi, you do everything around this studio, don't you?"

"I do—I am the only one who will do any manual labor in this place! Everyone else here is so pretty, even the men!" Georgi said, taking a mocking tone as he pretended to fuss with his hair and carry on like the on-air talent, implicitly leaving Jack himself out of his criticism, for he knew Jack was at heart an athlete.

"How did you learn to do such precise lettering work, Georgi?" asked Jack as he continued to examine and admire Georgi's replacement balls.

"I had a sign painting business back in Russia, you know."

"Oh yeah, Aleksandra mentioned that before."

"I was known as The Painter of Signs," Georgi said proudly. "I worked all over the city, lettering signs that I built and hung with my own hands," he said, gently pantomiming hanging a sign for illustrative purposes and dramatic effect.

"OK," said Jack, heading Georgi off at the pass before he could give a history lesson. "So," he said with serious purpose, "are we ready to go?"

"Yes," said Georgi, turning grim.

"I will call Aleksandra and tell her that tomorrow night will be the night, unless you have any objections or reasons why we should put it off?"

"I have none."

"OK, then. Tomorrow will be the night. I will talk to Aleksandra and tell her she must do her part of the plan and go around and purchase all the tickets. You'll be ready to go and do the switch tomorrow night?"

"Yes," said Georgi gloomily. You cannot grow up in a society that produced *Crime and Punishment* and feel that there is ever a good time to look on the sunny side of life.

Jack picked up on Georgi's fatalism and slapped him on the back to buck him up.

"Don't worry, Georgi! This is America! Let's see that can-do spirit!" Georgi looked on glumly. "Hey, a year from now," declared Jack, "I'll be divorced, Aleksandra and I will be together and we'll all have money!"

"Yes, I hope that," answered Georgi.

"Now," said Jack, "let's get back out to the set before anybody notices we're gone."

*

Approximately twenty-four hours later, Jack Webster was standing off to the side on the set where *Daily Number Live!* was broadcast, away from the center of the action. He wanted to give the appearance that it was just another day of business-as-usual. But it was not just another day. This was to be the evening his great conspiracy, two months in the making, was to be launched. This was the evening he and his two co-conspirators were going to bilk the state lottery and the public out of hundreds of thousands of dollars.

Jack fiddled nervously, tugging at the sleeves of his jacket and his tie, trying—and failing—to look casual. He looked at the clock. It was not long before the drawing would take place. Aleksandra would have spent the day driving all around the towns surrounding Boston, buying lottery numbers, one of which they knew would be the winner. Jack had been nervous handing her ten thousand dollars (he'd decided to buy 1,250 on each combination at the last second instead of 1,000, figuring there was no need to skimp on a sure thing). It had been damned difficult to get his hands on ten thousand dollars without his wife Jeanine noticing, but he'd done it.

Jack wasn't entirely confident that Aleksandra might not see ten grand in hand and simply skip town. Not because she didn't love him—he was sure she did—but because, well, that was a lot of money, and Aleksandra was Aleksandra. She could find love again and be up ten grand, right? But those treacherous thoughts were soon banished from his mind. Aleksandra *did* love him—and they stood to win a lot more than ten grand when they won.

In any case, it was too late for doubts now. The die—or lottery ball—had been cast. He was expecting her to call at any moment and tell Georgi over the phone—in

Russian—that the deed was done and the ball-switching could commence.

Jack, giving in to anxiety, ducked into Georgi's office/ store room.

"Georgi," he said with urgency upon seeing the older man, "ready to go?"

Georgi nodded solemnly.

"Good," said Jack. "Heard from Aleksandra yet?"

"No," said Georgi, his Russian accent seemingly a great weight on his words, "but do not worry, she will call. Aleksandra has never let me down, and she will not let me down now."

Just on cue, the phone on Georgi's desk rang.

"Ah!" the old man said, perking up at the thought of talking to his beloved niece, "I bet that is her now." Georgi picked up the phone with a cautious Hello. "Yes, he is here right now." Jack couldn't hear the words on the other end, but he didn't like that she was asking about him. He'd instructed her specifically to just say, "The fix is in" in Russian and hang up. There was already too much talk.

Even if Jack had heard the voice on the other end of the line, he wouldn't have understood, since Aleksandra was in fact speaking Russian. And now so was Georgi.

"<Good. So it's done?>" he asked in the foreign tongue. There was a pause. "<Well done. Well done, my dear. I love you. I will tell him. And don't worry. We will do our part. Goodbye,>" he said, and hung up the phone.

"That took longer than I expected," worriedly commented Jack about the short phone conversation. He wasn't happy about the extra chatter, and he wasn't happy that he happened to be in the room when the phone call came, either. Jack had wanted to be out of the room and far away as possible when the call came, just for deniability's sake. It was his own fault he was there when the phone rang; he had given in to his nervous energy and had come in to consult with Georgi. But what was done was done now, he figured. "What did she say?" he asked anxiously. "Did she finish the job?"

"Yes," said Georgi, dour once again. "She is done."

Jack and Georgi looked at each other. Georgi didn't seem perturbed, but Jack did. Didn't Georgi understand the magnitude of what they were doing? Jack was annoyed that the old immigrant refused to acknowledge the immensity of the moment.

Then Georgi chuckled.

"You know what she did?" asked Georgi with a twinkle in his eye, for his beloved Aleksandra could do no wrong in his view. "To prove she was purchasing the tickets, she held the phone to the machine as the tickets were printed," he said with pride, as if to say, 'Isn't that cute?'

Jack, who had his own ideas of cute, was even more perturbed than before. Playing cutesy with her uncle wasn't necessary. That wasn't part of the plan. Why do something that wasn't in the plan? Perhaps she had felt Jack's slight mistrust when he handed her the ten thousand dollars and was demonstrating her loyalty by proving she'd purchased the tickets? Whatever the case, Jack now regretted his musings on whether Aleksandra could be trusted, and regretted it all the more because she apparently took the risk of holding the phone up to the lottery machine as the clerk printed her tickets because of his mistrust.

"She *was* speaking in Russian, right?" asked Jack, suddenly hit by the fear that if Aleksandra had veered off script in one manner, she might have done so again on another aspect.

"Of course," said Georgi, slightly insulted that Jack could question his little angel. "She was just finishing up the whole process, which I know because she was right near home," he confirmed proudly.

"OK, we can go forward now," Jack said to Georgi, who nodded without enthusiasm. "Let's get out there," Jack continued, referring to the studio set. "I've got to go get ready for the drawing with the senior citizen witness."

They started out the door.

"You said Aleksandra was near home?" asked Jack. "Where was she?"

"She was at a place near her home," Georgi said casually.

Jack stopped.

"She bought them at a regular haunt?" he asked, not liking the sound of this.

"Yes," answered Georgi. "We felt it would be only natural to buy one set of numbers at a place she where she was a regular."

Jack was going to pursue this angle further, but then the show's director, Linda, poked her head in the door.

"There you are, Jack!" she said. "The senior citizen witness is getting fidgety out there. She wants to meet the most popular TV personality in town!"

"Oh, sure!" said Jack, suddenly turning on the charm like a spotlight. "Here I come!" he said. Even to his friend Georgi, it was amazing how Jack could turn on the charisma like flipping a switch. Seeing Jack change personalities like changing hats, Georgi felt suddenly suspicious, a feeling he'd never had about Jack before. They went out onto the set, Georgi a step behind.

Jack, as per the plan, immediately spied Bill Hillgrove, the lottery agent assigned to be the auditor of the drawing. Hillgrove's job as auditor was basically to oversee the whole drawing process. The job was largely perfunctory, as it was widely assumed nobody would ever be so audacious to actually try to rig a lottery drawing. This assumption gave the set an air of complacency about the drawing as far as security went. Only Hillgrove and local legend Jack Webster even had access to the balls, and both, plainly, were trustworthy and beyond reproach.

Jack had regularly made small talk with Bill Hillgrove over his time as auditor. They were hardly buddies, but Jack always found time at some point before the show to talk with him for a moment. Jack was like that, he made friends with most everybody, but especially with people in some position of authority, or who might someday be in a position of authority. There wasn't a cop in Boston with whom Jack hadn't shared a moment. That sort of thing came in handy if, say, a drug bust produced your name in the address book of a dealer's phone. A higher up in law enforcement might make suspicions go away if you were a beloved figure in the sports world. And needless to say, DUIs were out of the question. Celebrity had its benefits.

Bill Hillgrove loved it when Jack chatted with him. Hillgrove was in his forties, overweight, with a little bit of comb-over and had always been a something of a nerd. Older, middle-aged accountants did not have much in common with a local hero like Jack, and Hillgrove always enjoyed a little reflected sunshine from Jack's star quality.

Bill Hillgrove led as suffocating and mild a domestic existence as an observer might imagine, and the window into the young, sexy, thrill-filled world Jack described delighted and titillated Bill to no end. He tried to act casual when confronted with such stories, as if to suggest, *Yeah, we've all been there*, but the way his eyes lit up while being held in rapt attention suggested something else entirely. It was not unfair to say that he hung on Jack's every word. It was actually not unlike the relationships Jack had with dozens, or even hundreds, of Bill Hillgroves throughout his life. They were the audience in Jack's triumphant victory parade through life.

"Hey, Bill," said Jack as he approached Hillgrove.

"Hey, Jack!" said Hillgrove, attempting to be nonchalant. He didn't notice that Jack was not quite his usual confident, cocky self.

"What's going on, Bill?" asked Jack, as his eyes darted back and forth, not taking much time to look at Hillgrove.

"Nothing, Jack!"

"Great, great."

"Almost show-time," hinted Bill happily, eyebrows arched.

"Oh, yeah, you're right. You ready?" asked Jack.

"Yup," said Bill merrily.

Without a word, the two of them repeated the process they executed every day, and they went walking across the set and down the hallway towards Georgi's office, where the lottery balls were kept.

Jack realized an awkward silence had taken hold and an image appeared in his mind of Bill Hillgrove on the stand giving testimony that "on the night in question Jack was acting strangely, he seemed tense and did not talk like he usually did." Jack wanted to make sure everything was as normal as always, so he spoke up.

"How's Cindy's soccer team doing?" he asked, referring to Hillgrove's daughter.

"Oh, great! They're going to make the state tourney if they can win the next two games! And thanks again, Jack, for going to her school that day."

"Don't mention it," said Jack with a casual wave.

"It was a big deal to the kids, they're still talking about it! It's not everyday a TV star shows up in class and talks to the kids for two hours!"

"Glad to help, Bill."

They arrived at the safe in the office, where the balls were locked.

Jack had got Bill talking to distract him, and while Bill was continuing to yammer away, Jack took out his own set of keys which opened the inner cage and positioned himself close to the safe.

Hillgrove then took out his keys—the only set of keys that opened the outer safe—and unlocked the door.

Hillgrove continued to talk as Jack casually unlocked the inner cage and took out the leather bag that held the lottery ping-pong balls. "I've got it," he said as he shut the safe door. "The state tournament, eh? Your daughter must be excited?"

"Oh, she is!" Hillgrove went on for a bit, vigorously outlining various scenarios concerning his daughter's soccer team's fortunes, but Jack only feigned paying attention as they started walking out to the set. It had been a non-issue when, as usual, he took the small, leather bag which held the lottery balls out of the inner cage; nothing seemed out of place.

The satchel looked like a bowling ball bag and Jack held it by the handles as they walked and talked. Jack and Hillgrove approached Georgi on the floor of the *Daily Number Live!* set, Hillgrove still prattling on about his various domestic dramas.

Jack felt nervous. The transfer of the balls was one of the most dangerous parts of the plan, dangerous because Georgi had the doctored balls on his person, in the deep pockets of his black apron.

Georgi looked normal, even with thirty replacement ping-pong balls hidden in his apron, but Jack had made sure Hillgrove didn't get close enough to accidentally spy the balls in Georgi's apron. If Hillgrove noticed Georgi holding a spare set of identical ping-pong balls on his person, even a dim-witted, dumpy civil-servant like him would follow up on it with some elementary inquires.

Jack, making sure to keep himself between Hillgrove and Georgi, stood next to the little Russian and stuck the bag out towards him, keeping eye contact with the jabbering Hillgrove, who never even glanced at either the bag or Georgi. Georgi took the bag and walked away. Hillgrove never stopped looking at Jack, who was smiling at him, nodding at the salient points, keeping the pudgy accountant engaged and focused on him.

Seeing Georgi move away safely, Jack felt a wave of relief. It went perfectly. Hillgrove never suspected a thing.

Jack noticed he and Hillgrove were still in the same spot—a bit too close to Georgi for Jack's liking

"Hey Bill, buy you a coffee?" asked Jack.

"You got it, buddy," answered Hillgrove merrily, happy to be on the team.

They walked the other side of the studio set where a coffee machine sat to dispense free drinks to the crew.

Standing there, Jack was paying a heavy price to distract Hillgrove, as the contented suburbanite continued to ramble on about his relentlessly tedious life.

"….And so when they brought the big screen TV into the house, the workmen couldn't fit it up the stairs!"

"Oh, no," said Jack with disguised sarcasm.

"Yeah, the banister was in the way."

"Gosh, what did you do?"

Jack sighed internally. This man was boring him nearly to death. He was really earning his cut of the lottery money.

Jack returned his mind to the task at hand: distracting this oaf so that Georgi could switch ping-pong balls without anybody observing him.

Luckily for him, Bill Hillgrove was so still so star-struck that any critical thoughts about Jack never entered into his mind. Jack, as his eyes continued to dart distractedly around the set, taking note of where everybody in the room was, noticed Georgi milling about, unable to get to the lottery machine to load the balls—and do the switch—because two cameramen happened to be lingering nearby. That meant Georgi was holding two sets of the balls on his person, a very dangerous situation that made Jack very nervous.

"Jack," started Hillgrove anxiously, wanting to show he was One Of The Guys, "who is that new intern I saw be-bopping around here?" There was a pathetic eagerness with which Bill Hillgrove pursued the topic, trying to suggest that if he only weren't married, the tight young co-ed might end up seduced by his paunchy charm. He'd seen his hero Jack flirting with every variety of young women on the set—and stories of Jack with the interns were legendary, much to Hillgrove's delight—and it was important to Bill that he communicate to his hero that he, too, had an eye for the ladies.

"Huh?" asked Jack, not paying attention. "Oh, yeah, that young college girl? I don't remember her name. Paige? Sophie? I can't remember." Then Jack noticed that Hillgrove was disappointed his little sensation wasn't considered newsworthy in Jack's eyes. Jack did not want this, he wanted Bill Hillgrove's attention focused right on him as Georgi was preparing to switch ping-pong balls.

"Say, Bill," started Jack, suddenly turning on the charm and giving Hillgrove all his attention, "did you see Hazel Whitney at the game last night?" Hazel Whitney was a sideline reporter for the city's cable sports station and quite a looker, as is apparently listed in large, bold type as part of the job description for female sideline reporters who work for sports stations.

"Yeah, yeah," said Hillgrove with enthusiasm. "She's the best," he commented weakly. "Say, Jack," he suggestively offered, his eyes alight, "why don't you take a run at her?"

"Oh, jeez!" said Jack, throwing up his hands in mock protest. "That girl's nothing but trouble—from what I hear anyway!" He had an ingratiating smile and made Bill Hillgrove feel like the most important person in the world. This was a real talent Jack had: he could make anybody feel like the most important person in the whole world. Jack could make people feel important, because he himself was always important.

"Come on! Jack Webster's never been afraid of a little trouble!" kidded Bill worshipfully, as though he were in on the joke.

Jack never ceased being amazed at the number of overweight, middle-class domesticated 'men' who fluttered around him worshipfully, living vicariously through him, viewing him as some sort of sexual cartoon character, only needing to snap his fingers to be surrounded by beautiful young women. Certainly, Jack—ever popular and usually semi-famous wherever he'd been—never had trouble with women, but just how much time did these guys think he had? He was married, for Christ's sake, dating was a big chore for him. And there were only so many one-or-two night flings to be had out there. Couldn't these tubby, hen-pecked suburbanites worship elsewhere? They were always underfoot when he didn't need them, thought Jack to himself with a snarl.

Pushing these contemptuous thoughts aside, Jack continued to pour on the charm to his captive audience of one, Bill Hillgrove, the large bureaucrat with the small life.

Jack managed to steal a few peeks at Georgi, who was lingering calmly, puttering with busy work, waiting for the two cameramen to vacate the area around the lottery machine so he could do his handiwork of switching the lottery balls.

"What have you heard about Hazel Whitney?" asked Hillgrove breathlessly.

"Oh, jeez, where to start?" asked Jack rhetorically. He'd heard nothing particularly salacious about Ms. Whitney, but he wasn't about to admit that to Hillgrove and have him wander over and shake down Georgi, so instead it was slander for Hazel. "You know that pitcher the Sox got rid of last year?"

"Yeah, yeah," prompted Bill Hillgrove eagerly.

"Because of Whitney. That's why they let him go. Don't have the details right now," admitted Jack, who hadn't thought of any on the spot yet, "but I hope to hear something soon."

"Wow. I'd leave town over her, too!"

"Right, right," said Jack distractedly, for he noticed the two cameramen had moved along. Georgi casually waited a moment and then moved to the lottery machine, where he could load the balls, standing behind the table, partially concealed behind the device and hidden from the waist down, just as Jack had planned. Georgi's hands were shooting back and forth, grabbing a ball then quickly loading it into the tubes of The Machine.

Jack then noticed Hillgrove's eye following his own towards Georgi. "She likes to party, you know, that girl Whitney does," said Jack in order to recapture Hillgrove's attention. It worked like a charm. Hillgrove dropped all interest in the old Russian Georgi puttering around and was again fixated on Jack, hoping to hear some salacious sex stories about the young woman who, in fact, lived as clean a life as her dad might have drawn up for her.

"No!"

"Oh, yeah. I heard she was seeing a married guy on the team, snorting coke, following him on the road, the whole deal," confided Jack, creating a biography for the young woman that sounded suspiciously like Aleksandra's. That's all he could come up with on the fly. He wasn't a great inventor of stories, like, say, one of the Great Russians.

"Really?" asked Bill Hillgrove.

"That's what I heard."

"Wow," commented Bill, awestruck.

Jack snuck a glance and saw Georgi finishing his assignment and walking away from the lottery machine. Georgi had switched the lottery balls. The fake balls had been loaded into the lottery machine and the real balls were now hidden in his pockets.

Ever invisible and left to his own devices, nobody had noticed Georgi stealthily reaching into the pockets of his apron to pull out the fake ping-pong balls—instead of the leather bag that held the real balls—as he went about loading the machine. Even if someone had been watching, they wouldn't have seen Georgi's hand slip into his apron instead of the leather bag that held the real balls, as he was standing behind the table, half hidden.

"So who's the player Hazel's screwing now?" asked Bill with an eagerness Jack found pathetic and off-putting.

"Hey, I'm going to have to finish this story later," said Jack abruptly, as he saw Georgi disappear with the incriminating lottery balls, presumably to his office. Jack didn't want to take a moment more than necessary chatting with this fat load, Bill Hillgrove.

"Oh, OK," said Bill, disappointed.

"Catch up with you later," Jack said as he slapped him on the arm, a sudden rise in his spirits now that the lottery ball switching had been accomplished without a hitch, and he virtually sprang from the spot and headed off in the direction of Georgi's office.

*

Jack grabbed the handle to the door of Georgi's office. Even though he was initially frustrated to find it locked, he quickly mentally congratulated Georgi for his good sense to lock the door.

Jack quietly, yet frantically, knocked on the door.

"Georgi!" he said in a hushed, yet frantic, voice. "It's me, Jack!"

Georgi cracked opened the door.

"Everything go OK?" Jack asked in a husky whisper.

"Yes, yes," answered Georgi impatiently, waving his hand. "Now go back out to the set! It's time for the drawing! Somebody is going to come looking for you!"

Jack, without a word, nodded in agreement and started hurriedly scampering back down the hallway towards the set, where the live drawing would soon be occurring. Sure enough, as Georgi had feared, Linda, the director, approached him, wearing a headset and holding a clipboard.

"Jack! There you are," she said in relief. "We didn't know where you went off to."

"Just had to use the facilities," explained Jack as they both headed back to the set.

"The sponsor tonight is Okee-Dokey Supermarkets," Linda said to him. "Don't forget to mention their name right before the drawing," she lectured. Jack hardly noticed what she said, however. He had bigger things on his mind.

Before he knew it, Jack was standing in his familiar spot, next to the lottery machine with the senior citizen witness, Violet Lowry. Linda Showalter, the director, pointed. It was on.

The nightly disembodied voice sang out, "It's time for the live, daily drawing of the Massachusetts lottery! The daily drawing is for today, October 9th, 2006. Now, let's play the Daily Number... with your host... Jack Webster!"

The lights came on, giving Jack his cue to start.

Every other night when the lights came on, so did Jack, smiling, being outgoing and gregarious, loving the camera and the camera loving him. This night, however, it wasn't the same. He was flat. He seemed distracted, almost nervous.

"Hi, everyone," said Jack, without his usual welcoming, confident tone. "Welcome to *Daily Number Live!*" he said without spirit. "Today is October 9th, the lottery drawings are audited by Maynard-Holtzman, CPA, an independent accounting firm, and the official overseeing the drawing from Lottery Security is Bill Hillgrove," Jack announced with a rapid mumble. "Tonight's senior citizen witness is Violet Lowry. A reminder, the guaranteed annuity of the Daily Three Pick drawing tonight is *at least* one million dollars. And don't forget, the lottery benefits every one of the three hundred fifty-one cities and towns in the Commonwealth of Massachusetts."

The enormity of the fix, and the consequences of things going wrong, were affecting him. Jack then realized he was coming off differently, lifeless, so he made an effort to spice it up with some energy.

"Where you from, Violet?" he asked, putting his arm around the old black woman, who, in her role as senior citizen witness, was something of a surrogate for the television audience at home.

"Hyde Park," she said.

"I used to live there!" Jack said buoyantly, suddenly feeling like himself again. He was a master of putting on the charm—it came naturally to him—and he soon found himself totally at ease again. He could have been a great con man, he said to himself in a congratulatory tone without a trace of irony.

There was a bit more happy chatter and Jack found himself laughing heartily at something inane the woman said.

"There are three sets of balls, numbered zero through nine," Jack explained to the television audience, again, rapidly, for there were virtually no new viewers to *Daily Number Live!* but it was a formality that needed to be done. "The drawing begins when the balls are released and then mixed into the machine," said Jack. "Now Violet," he counseled, "we're going to release the ping-pong balls. Are you ready?"

She nodded. Jack pressed the button on the side and the three tubes angling down released three sets of balls numbered zero through nine into the main chamber, with Jack well knowing that the fours and sixes tumbling down the tubes were his way out of his marriage and into the arms of Aleksandra, along with lots and lots of money.

"Now, Violet, if you would, go ahead and press the button to start the machine." Jack's heart raced, his destiny a push of the button away. Violet pressed the button and the air started filling the fish tank chamber.

Jack could barely contain his fascination as he watched his long-planned scheme go into effect. Each four and six ball was a piece of a puzzle he'd been trying to solve, a puzzle that created a picture of wealth and freedom for himself. He tried focusing on the magic four and sixes, but he quickly lost track of them in the jumble.

Jack, though you could not tell it to look at him, was fixated on the balls with an intensity he had never before known as the vacuum device kicked on. The time elapsed seemed an eternity to him. Was the air always so slow to begin flowing? Of course not, it was just his imagination, he knew. It had taken a split second as always.

Soon, the familiar sound of the air currents wafted about his ears as he watched the balls start to dance, as if by magic.

Jack was immediately gripped by panic. The replacement balls were not moving in the fish tank like the real balls did. Usually the balls bounced and danced, now they were just bumping up and down. Georgi's tampered-with balls didn't look normal, thought Jack in a panic. Only the fours and sixes were reacting normally—because they were un-tampered with, of course. It was madness not to have watched any of Georgi's experiments! How could he have trusted such an important thing— namely, the way the tampered balls look in the chamber—to that old fool without seeing it for himself?! It was stupid, insane of him not to have personally supervised this most important aspect of the plan! All because he was afraid of raising suspicions of people who might—*might*—see him hanging around the machine late at night as Georgi played with it! *Madness*!! "*What was I thinking*!?" he screamed in his head.

"No," Jack assured himself in a commanding inner voice. "It's only my imagination."

He looked at the senior citizen witness—he'd already forgotten her name—and the other WKTD employees on the set and they were reacting as if everything was perfectly ordinary.

He noticed the balls acting differently only because he was fixated on them. To all the people observing, they looked perfectly fine.

And so, too, did Jack look perfectly normal. For all the tempest of emotions in his heart, he never betrayed any unusual emotion. He kept a straight face as the balls jostled around.

"Now, Violet," he said after peeking at the older lady's handwritten name tag, "I'll press the button and select the winning balls." Jack pressed a button on the first receiving tube. The button opened the tube, causing a ball to fly up the tube where it was caught in a box at the top, making it a winning number.

"Six!" said Jack with faked surprise as the first winning number was selected. "The first winning number is six!" he said with his usual enthusiasm, though of course he wasn't not surprised at the number, knowing the winning numbers would all be either fours or sixes.

Jack moved a half-step to the second receiving tube and pressed the button. The second winning ball immediately shot right up the tube to the waiting catch-box.

"Another six!" said Jack with excitement, his millions and his freedom getting closer. "The second winning number is six," he said with even more animation. He always showed a lot of enthusiasm as the winning number came closer to being revealed, as if he was right there with the winners. Jack expanded with pride for his great scheme as it finally unfolded, right there in front of the whole world. He figured he had more guts than anybody in the whole world.

Jack moved another half-step and pressed the third and final button on the third and final receiving tube. The last ball shot immediately up the tube.

"And the last winning number is..." said Jack with rising excitement, "six," he said in a slightly dulled voice. "The last number is six." Jack seemed momentarily shaken. "The winning number is 6-6-6," he said in a monotone voice, as if it were a harbinger of ill fortune. He almost felt cold wind blow through him. "The Daily 'Pick Three' Number for today is 6-6-6." He collected himself. "Well, goodnight, everybody!" he said, regaining his composure. "Hope you won a lot of money tonight! See you tomorrow!" he said as sign-off, with a jaunty wave. The studio lights went down.

Then the magnitude of it hit him: He'd done it. A wave of relief swept over him. It was over. He'd made himself a million dollars. Maybe more.

He'd done it.

*

The cameras went off. The show was over. Cameramen and assistants started wrapping things up, collecting wires, walking over to the set.

Unexpectedly, Bill Hillgrove wandered inconveniently over to where the drawing was held. Usually he couldn't be bothered to do even that, and Jack couldn't remember the last time he'd done so. Typically he wandered around backstage someplace, amusing himself slovenly, unconcerned with the drawing. It was only by sour chance that he had come along hazardously this night.

Removing the tainted balls from the lottery machine was now very dangerous with Hillgrove underfoot.

Georgi stood off to the side, betraying no anxiety and not moving an inch from his spot. Georgi was expected to grab them right away as usual, but he didn't want to be in possession of the balls until he saw that Bill Hillgrove, the lottery office auditor, was engaged and distracted.

Noticing Georgi's reluctance and correctly reading the situation, Jack sprang into action in the midst of the crisis and instantly hurried over to Hillgrove.

"How'd you like the drawing tonight, Bill?" asked Jack, once again full of charismatic charm now that the deed had been done and done well.

"Pretty odd, that winning number was tonight!" Hillgrove mentioned in a jolly manner.

Georgi saw what Jack was doing and immediately made his way to the lottery machine the moment Jack had created an opening.

"Hope you're not superstitious!" joked Jack, slapping the paunchy man on the back, looking directly at him. Jack could give anybody a direct look and his full attention and charm them, make them feel important.

"That winning number's a little weird if you ask me," said Hillgrove.

"Weird? What do you mean, 'weird'?" asked Jack defensively, fearing the worst.

"6-6-6! You know the Mark of the Beast!'"

"Oh, yeah. I know, all the religious people will probably get all bent out of shape over it, that's all," said Jack in annoyance, keeping one eye stealthily on Georgi, who was by now fiddling around the machine, collecting the lottery balls and cleaning the machine or some other wizardry he performed in the way of regular maintenance.

"That's a bad omen for somebody," said Hillgrove ruefully.

"Bad omen?" asked Jack, agitated. He would tolerate no bad omens on this night. "Why would you say it's a bad omen? Do you think people with winning tickets think it's a bad number? This isn't a magic world we live in. Shit, somebody just won—rather, a whole bunch of people just won—a whole lot of money off that 'bad omen' number, how bad a number can it be?" demanded Jack. The idea that his scheme would be met with a bad omen rankled him. He had beat the odds, he'd won out—who was this fat ass desk-jockey loser from the lottery department to rain on his parade? What was he doing, trying to ruin a good time?

"I don't know..." answered Hillgrove, oblivious to Jack's change in mood and blissfully ignorant that the always-personable Jack had become annoyed and almost argumentative.

"Well, I'll bet lots of winners out there disagree with you," said Jack with a surly twist, ending the thread as if slamming a door shut in the face of an unwanted visitor.

Annoyed with this narc from the state lottery office, Jack was happy to see Georgi in his peripheral vision, moving away from the lottery machine, coming towards him. Jack looked at Georgi's apron. Anybody who didn't already know the replacement balls were hidden in the apron pockets would not have had any idea they were there, as Georgi had repeated the switch of the balls in reverse.

Georgi silently held out the leather bag that now held the real lottery balls. Jack took it.

"Come on, Bill, We've got to go lock the balls away," Jack said abruptly, trying to shove Hillgrove from his consciousness.

Bill and Jack walked silently to Georgi's office, Jack resentful at Hillgrove's warning of bad omens, Bill Hillgrove blunderingly heedless to his mood.

"You know," started Bill with roly-poly joviality, "I heard some guy in Sacramento won with 6-6-6 and ended up dying the very next week!"

"You don't say," said Jack, piqued, as they went into Georgi's office.

"Yup," said Bill. "Hit by a bus."

"Bad luck for him," said Jack.

"Yup," continued Hillgrove as he used his key to open the outer safe, "and a guy in Pittsburgh won with 6-6-6 and was dead within a month. Ate some peanuts and had an allergic reaction. From what I heard, he was just praying for death at the end," he concluded jauntily.

"Well," said Jack, tossing the leather bag into the inner cage with annoyance, "I don't believe in omens," he declared with irritation, and he slammed the safe door, sending an echo through the room not unlike a cell door slamming shut.

Soon, the entire staff and crew, along with Bill Hillgrove, had all gone home. Jack, who courteously offered to lock up the studio for Linda, the director, was left alone with Georgi on the set. They both did a quick reconnaissance of the studio to make sure that it was indeed empty and took a quick peek down the hall.

Georgi then came out of his office holding the paint can by the handle, a can of lighter fluid under his jacket and a newspaper tucked under his arm to hide any suspicious bulge from the can of fluid. He stood by as Jack locked all the doors.

"OK," said Jack, holding a bottle of water, "let's go."

The two of them passed the security guard at the front desk with Jack nearest him to shield Georgi, and then they briskly went down to an alley between the WKTD studios that provided a great deal of privacy. Jack, in fact, had often done a couple of lines in this private alleyway with guests of his Sunday night late sports show *Sports Finale* after filming. Jack watched Georgi squirt lighter fluid into the can and stuff some of the newspapers in there as well.

"Very good," mumbled Georgi. He threw a match in the can and covered it with the lid. The can burned for a few moments. Ping-pong balls are made of celluloid, a colorless flammable thermoplastic material, the same ingredients used to make photographic film. Learning this, Jack came up with the idea of burning them rather than merely tossing them out in the trash someplace.

"Let me see," said Jack. He knocked the lid off and they looked in. The balls were a smoldering ruin, totally unidentifiable. Jack poured some of his water into the can to douse any embers. "OK, Georgi, you know what to do now?"

Georgi nodded grimly. "I am going to drive out to the wharf on the way home, put rocks in the can and throw the whole thing into the ocean when nobody is looking."

"Right," affirmed Jack with serious purpose.

The two of them wordlessly shook hands quickly and with a nod, parted company.

Jack hurriedly walked out to his car. Once inside, he took out his pre-paid, impossible-to-trace cell phone. It was dark and the parking lot was empty, Jack's car being the only one in the employee lot. The light from his cell phone was the only light in the car and as he dialed the number, Jack's face was illuminated with an eerie green, as if he were holding a lime flashlight under his chin. The phone rang and he held it up to his ear.

"Sweetie? Aleksandra? It's me, Jack."

"Thank God you called!" she gushed. "I can't tell you how I've been waiting! I was watching and waiting on pins and needles!"

"What'd you think?"

"You looked great! Perfectly normal. But I've been so scared!" she cooed.

"Don't worry, Aleksandra," Jack assured her. "Everything went off without a hitch," Jack said. He paused, "Without a hitch," he repeated, almost as if to convince himself.

"Are you sure?"

"I'm certain," he said. They talked a moment longer and Jack hung up his phone and sat there, looking off absently. He felt a gnaw. He thought of the balls not quite looking normal when the lottery machine had been turned on. Surely he noticed a difference in them only because he was in on the secret. Surely it was just his imagination noticing something that wasn't really there.

Softly, Jack spoke out loud to himself, "There's nothing to worry about." He wished he did a better job of convincing himself....

Chapter Nine

(August, 2010)

Jack stood in the Executive Washroom in WKTD's downtown offices the day after Rudy Baxter approached him with an offer by Senator Shea to get him back on television in exchange for his dropping his interview concerning the Slocumb Airport expansion.

Jack had decided to forego the offer and pursue Ava by going through with the interview, an interview for which he was currently preparing. He was half bent over the sink as the water ran unchecked. Placing the razor blade he'd been using on the sink's edge, he turned off the faucet. He stood up straight and looked in the mirror. Jack smiled his cocky, crooked grin and rubbed his bare chin happily. He had just finished totally shaving off his beard, and he liked what he saw in the mirror.

He looked like himself again.

Not only did he look like himself again for the first time in a several years, he felt like himself, too. He continued to rub his face as if to physically enjoy the beardless feel once again and welcome back the old Jack Webster to the land of the living.

Jack had been growing back into his old self over the last month, since he'd met Ava. He'd worked hard to bring himself into her good graces, and with this program proceeding swimmingly, he felt good enough to unveil the old Jack Webster that everyone in the city and the entire state had known.

Billy Bowman had suggested to Jack that his interview about the lottery scandal would require the viewer to see the old Jack Webster they'd known for all his years on television, and Jack readily agreed. He had grown the beard to stay hidden, and now with the hugely publicized interview at hand, he was going to publicly out himself anyway, so he might as well look good while he did it.

Jack left the washroom and went out to the studio area. It was his old stomping ground, and it was with a wave of nostalgia and melancholy that he looked around. The studio where he was going to be interviewed about the lottery was next to the set where the evening news was broadcast, and it was on the evening news broadcasts that he became a household name in the city. Jack was never really one for reflection, but it was impossible not to ruminate a bit as he looked around. In a sense he was returning to be reborn in the place of his past life.

His musings were interrupted, however, as he saw Ava come virtually rushing over to him.

Jack had left her name at the door as his guest—his only guest for the interview appearance—and she'd shown up just as she had promised. Jack smiled broadly.

"Hey there, Ava," he said buoyantly.

She looked at him, astonished.

"You shaved!"

"Yup," he said, "thought I'd take the ol' mug out of hiding."

She eyed him with wonder.

"It *is* you! It *really* is!"

"Yup."

"You are *the* Jack Webster from the lottery!"

Jack shook his head ruefully.

"Yeah…."

"This morning the guys down at the Earthpeace office said it was you! They said you talked with Larry last night to tell them about your interview and you told them you were Jack Webster, the same guy who used to do sports and the lottery show on Channel Six!"

"That's me. Everyone was kind of wondering where this interview came from," Jack explained, "so I filled them in."

"Wow," she observed with awe. Ava eyed him closely, from every angle, her mouth half-open in awe. "I can't believe it! I had no idea. I didn't recognize you from your TV days with that beard! No wonder you were able get Channel Six to do an interview and an exposé on the airport! You said you were going to be interviewed by Channel Six, but nobody at Earthpeace knew it was going to have anything to do with the lottery."

"Yeah, first lottery talk, then airport talk. I didn't want to tell everybody at Earthpeace about the lottery part, not right away, anyway. I didn't want to show up and say, 'look at me!' And I thought you guys either knew my background or didn't care."

"Oh, I don't care," she said happily, "You're a celebrity! I barely remember you mentioning your last name to me."

"What's a name, right?"

"Your name is a little different than most, everybody knows you. And you're in Norton with the rest of us, fighting for a good cause and you're famous and everything. I really admire that," Ava said worshipfully.

"Oh, you know how it is, in life you grow sometimes," Jack admitted with practiced and false humility. He was delighted. His celebrity, even the notorious aspects, worked like a charm on young Ava. People her age cared so much about celebrity that there was really no bad kind.

"I really admire you for what you're doing, going on the air and talking about the lottery scandal to get us some exposure. It must be difficult for you. You're making a huge sacrifice."

Jack nodded modestly.

"The least I can do," he muttered humbly.

She looked at him so rapturously that he considered grabbing her and kissing her for an hour or so until he'd gotten his fill, but that would look bad while in the studio. He could wait until he got outside afterward.

"I remember once back when you were on TV and doing sports radio and stuff, you came to my high school to do some sort of talk. It was a funny routine, you brought a sports blooper highlight reel or something. I had to sit way in the back because it was so crowded, I could barely see you."

"Oh, yeah, I used to do that for years, all the time, all over New England," Jack recounted with sincere wistfulness. It was a more pleasant recollection than it had been when Rudy Baxter mentioned the same thing.

"All the girls thought you were really good looking," Ava confessed coyly. "Seeing you without the beard, I can remember it all now."

Ava looked at Jack with such worship, he was practically ready to ask her what she liked for breakfast, so much did he now look at her as a sure thing. She was on the hook and all he had to do was complete the ridiculously simple task of reeling her into the boat.

"Well," said Jack, "there's a lot of time left in the future. But for right now, I've got an interview to do—and an airport expansion to stop," he declared dramatically, striking what he felt was a sensational note.

"You're the best, Jack," Ava gushed.

"Yeah, I'm pretty hot stuff, all right," he said as a modest joke, to which they both laughed. Jack felt they were bonding more than ever and he was about to win Ava over for good.

"And to think," he continued, "you were so late arriving here today I was getting worried you were going to stand me up and weren't going to show up."

"Oh, I'm sorry about showing up late. I was so excited about all the stuff going on with you that I had to call up my boyfriend and tell him all about it, you know, who you were really were and stuff."

Jack's face went blank.

"Boyfriend?"

"Yeah. George. I think I told you about him, didn't I? He's out in California for a few months until he comes back permanently around the holidays. You'd like him. He's working for his father's company right now. It's a lumber company—but don't worry, they're environmentally responsible! I thought I mentioned George. He's my fiancé," she added casually, looking all around the studio in wonder at the behind-the-scenes stuff hanging all around.

Jack stared at her, stunned, as Ava's gaze wandered guilelessly all over the studio. He hadn't heard anything about a fiancé or anything of the sort.

"I've never been in a television studio before," commented Ava, totally oblivious to Jack's reaction. "What does that thing do?" she asked innocently, pointing to a piece of equipment.

"It's called a Balbox," Jack said flatly, without emotion, anger slightly suffocated beneath the words. "It's an analogue audio to digital audio converter. It allows serial digital video to be sent over a Cat5 cable." He was staring bitterly ahead. All his time, work and emotional investment disappeared into the single word "fiancé." Just like that, it was done. He stewed and boiled for a moment. "I'll be right back," he said coldly to Ava, who did not notice anything odd about Jack's suddenly stiff manner and tone.

Jack angrily went off and filled up his liter bottle from the water cooler and took a big, long drink from it. His mind racing bitterly, he turned on his heel and rejoined Ava.

"Ava, I'm sorry, but something's come up. I'm not doing the interview."

"What?!"

"Yeah, sorry," he said flatly, taking caustic enjoyment at denying Ava and Earthpeace their triumph.

"But—"

"Sorry, can't be helped."

"Can it be rescheduled for—"

"I don't know what to say. Why don't you go wait outside, and I'll see you in a minute, OK?" Jack commanded. "I've got some people to talk to and I need privacy."

Ava looked at him, stunned. Jack's expression was hard and stern, his glare piercing.

"OK," she acquiesced submissively. Whatever it was, Ava figured, it looked serious. "Well," she said, "I'm sorry."

"I'm sorry, too," said Jack sincerely, thinking not of interviews.

Ava left and Jack immediately went over to his old friend who was slated to conduct the interview, Gary Gibson, the lead anchorman of the evening news.

"Gary," Jack declared, "I need to use your phone."

"Sure, Jack, you know where my office is" Gary said, not knowing his big interview was about to cancel and pull the rug out from under him.

Jack quickly went into the office, shut the door and out of his pocket pulled the card that he'd been holding onto since the night before. He looked at it and then dialed the number off a card.

"Hello? Rudy Baxter? This is Jack Webster. Listen, the situation on the ground here as changed entirely. Is that deal you offered me still on the table? Good. I've changed my mind. You've got a deal, I'll drop the interview and take you up on your offer to get back on television. I'm getting out of the interview right now. Yeah, I guess I didn't know a good thing when you first mentioned it."

*

Later that evening at a lonely table at The Worthy House sat Jack Webster. Now clean shaven, but still thin, even more so than just a month ago due to his recent 'hunger strike,' staged to heighten WKTD's interest in his now-aborted interview, Jack finished off a large mug of cheap, stale draft beer and put down the glass with authority. He was thirsty, but he passed on having water. He'd been drinking for quite some time and he wasn't going to slow down his momentum with any water. It was dark outside and he'd come into the place when it was still light. He was very much drunk. He had a slow, soaking intoxication that had taken over him, one that hadn't blitzed his brain, but rather one that had slowly and thoroughly permeated every cell in his body.

It was dark and dank inside the bar, which fit his mood. Jack looked around The Worthy House. It was filled with the usual losers, he observed. Men with worn jeans, women with worn faces. All their eyes glassy from yet another night of drinking after yet another day of working at jobs that were loud, dirty and left them covered in grime and paid not enough. Young men waiting to take the seats of the old men, as it had been for years and years. Jack shook his head.

The old waitress came over.

"Another one, Jack?" she asked sympathetically.

"Yup," he said plainly and without interest in her.

"OK," she said disapprovingly. Since he'd been coming in there regularly, Jack had become a welcomed face around The Worthy House, as it always was wherever Jack went. Then once it became advertised by Earthpeace that he was going to go on television and stop the hated airport expansion, he became a hero, and when it was revealed that he was *the* Jack Webster, the famous sports guy from Channel Six, well… he immediately stopped being a hero and became something of a god to the locals. That's why the waitress looked on in such distress, seeing Jack drowning his sorrows for hours, now sitting there, drunk, his eyes glazed and half shut, brooding and scowling in obvious distress, anger and resentment.

She returned to the table with his beer.

"This is from Lenny," she said, pointing out the guy at the bar. "He says 'thanks'."

Jack paused for a second to try and figure out what she meant.

"Thanks for what?" Jack asked blurrily.

"Didn't say," she said. "Probably just for everything you're doing for everybody." Then she left.

Jack waved limply and disinterestedly and went back to drinking. Clearly they didn't know he had backed out of the interview.

Jack was musing darkly on Ava. He'd invested weeks and weeks on her, he contemplated bitterly. "That was time I could have spent running down some other piece of ass," he told himself.

Sadly, he realized his words were mere bravado. It wasn't an investment of time he'd lost, it was hope. It wasn't just that he'd missed out on the chance to bed a hot young woman. He had come to truly enjoy and admire Ava. He'd tried to learn something about her artwork, something he never could have imagined doing before.

Granted, he hadn't learned much—he never did—but that wasn't the point.

As the weeks had gone by and he became more enamored of Ava, the more clearly he could imagine a future together with her. The thoughts were at first misty and clouded, but they had continued to take a more and more distinct shape.... He saw himself returning to television somehow, maybe as a consultant after time had worked its magic and healed the wounds associated with his name, or maybe just as lowly cameraman or something...Ava pursuing whatever it was people with master's degrees in art did with a master's degree in art. Jack had smiled at the prospect, and it had been a long, long time since he had smiled when thinking of the future. It had been years since the future held any promise.

Once upon a time, before The Lottery, the future had been a magical place, a place of unending triumphs and ceaseless delights, a place with no limits. Then, after the lottery scandal, the color of the world was drained and replaced with a drab gray, a prison gray. Hell, who was he kidding? The magic of the future had been banished long before the lottery scandal. Maybe it hadn't ever really been there at all.

Jack heaved a sigh.

"I'm better off this way," he mumbled into his beer.

He was better off this way, he reassured himself. Better off without the shaky and uncertain roll of the dice that throwing his lot with Earthpeace against the powerful Senator Shea would have entailed. Getting back on TV—that was the way to go, he told himself. You could get more babes being on TV than you ever could any other way, he well knew. Ava was just one chick, but being on TV...the sky was the limit. Plus, he could earn a living on television. A real living. He could get back to making some serious coin, he told himself. Whatever future he imagined with Ava, it would not have involved making the type of money he would make being back on television, and Senator Shea was going to make that happen with one phone call. Hell, Ava was young and it probably wouldn't have lasted anyway. Or he'd grow bored with her like he'd done with Jeanine after they'd gotten married. Then were would he be? Nope, he told himself, he was happy to be right where he was, with Baxter's deal in his pocket.

Just then, the door of The Worth House opened, letting in light from the street lamp stationed right outside the door. Jack grimaced. He saw four of the Earthpeace kids coming in and behind them Jack noticed there was a steady, relentless drizzle outside. The Earthpeacers shook off the rain, looked around and spotted Jack. Much to his disgust, they made right for him.

Greg, the big, aggressive kid Jack had come to dislike, was leading the charge. Phil, the very first Earthpeace kid Jack had spoken to, was there, too. However, there was no Ava.

The four of them stood at Jack's small table. Jack ignored them.

"We thought we'd find you here. What happened?" demanded Greg.

"Whatever do you mean?" asked Jack with drunken sarcasm.

"Ava said you weren't going to do the interview," yammered Phil, "and when we called to find out why

Channel Six postponed it, they said *you* canceled it—and that you weren't going to do it at all!"

"That's right," grumbled Jack argumentatively, looking down into his glass.

"Why?" asked Phil, pleadingly.

"I guess I just got tired of my hunger strike and got the munchies," said Jack sardonically.

"The airport protest is going to die on the vine if something doesn't happen soon, and you're the only hope to provide a spark," pleaded Phil. "We can raise a big stink and nobody's going to care. The city of Norton can't go up against Senator Shea if nobody sees what's going on at the airport— but you can bring attention to it"

"Dammit, you promised you'd to this, you phony!" protested Greg, the big, angry kid who hadn't show much interest in the plan before. "You can't just sit here and get tanked all night."

"Sure I can," replied Jack.

"Ava's supposed to stop by, will you talk to her about the interview?"

Jack looked up at them with disdain.

"Hey, guys, I just don't care about it, OK? I'm just not interested in the airport expansion issue, all right? I couldn't care less. I'm not some silly college kid tilting at windmills before mommy and daddy send me off to law school—I have real-life concerns. Now get lost, I'm meeting somebody here about a new job," he said. He meant, of course, he was meeting Rudy Baxter, Senator Shea's chief of staff about the deal to which he'd agreed.

The Earthpeace people mumbled amongst themselves as they retreated off to a little table around the corner to lick their wounds and wait for Ava to arrive while they tried to figure out what had happened to all their grand plans.

It was just a moment later when the door to The Worthy House opened again. Jack saw a man immaculately dressed, with an umbrella and a military-type buzz cut and eyeglasses that reflected the light so as to make him look like a devil with lights instead of eyeballs. The man looked around the place, as if searching for someone as he folded his umbrella and leaned it against the wall near the door. Jack waved to him lethargically, and the man, Rudy Baxter, spotted him and confidently strode over.

Just as he reached Jack's table, an old woman grabbed Jack affectionately around the shoulders from behind and hugged him.

"Give 'em hell at the interview, Jack!" she urged.

Jack recognized her. She was an off-duty waitress with whom he'd spoken a few times. She beamed at him. She didn't know his role in stopping the airport expansion had come to an abrupt end, either. Jack smiled back at her weakly, then she left, giving him an encouraging thumbs up as she walked away.

Rudy Baxter sat down, smiling a cocky, crooked smile.

"Friend of yours?"

"I guess so," said Jack slowly and drunkenly, a little embarrassed, "she sure acts that way." Jack wasn't exactly sure what he was embarrassed about, but he knew it wasn't his association with the woman that left him feeling sheepish.

"Friends in low places," said Baxter with a grin.

"Right…."

Baxter made himself impressively at home, like a regent visiting his peasants rather than a customer.

"I brought the television contract from WLOX Channel Nine," he announced with great arrogance.

"Great," said Jack drunkenly, with seeming disinterest.

"I'm bringing it with the full knowledge of the station's management, you understand," Baxter said. "It's their contract, I'm just acting as a courier. You see, Senator Shea simply wants to wrap up this situation as soon as possible and wanted me to expedite the conclusion of this situation." Baxter pulled out a twenty-page document out of a manila folder. "Standard stuff," he said, tapping the stack of papers sitting in front of him. "The Senator is a busy man with a lot of work to do on behalf of the state and he wanted your name on the dotted line right away so he could put this unfortunate airport-Earthpeace issue out of his mind and put it to rest once and for all."

"Good," said Jack without enthusiasm, not making eye contact. There was a brief, odd, moment of silence.

"You were smart to take this offer," teased Baxter.

"Oh?"

"Oh, yes. I mean, Senator Shea is a powerful man, but it's not like he could snap his fingers and get you back on television anywhere, you see. He couldn't get you back on WKTD, for example. But he's got friends. Lots of friends," bragged Baxter. "Senator Shea is very friendly with the people at WLOX Channel Nine, to cite but one example." He paused to let Jack jump in and gush about Shea's importance and how thankful he was to the Great Man, but Jack said nothing. Baxter was disappointed. He'd expected a bigger reaction, but Jack barely blinked and didn't seem at all enraptured with his tales of power. "In any case, it's better if you sign this and keep everything about this deal to yourself. Of course, for the record the Senator had *nothing* to do with getting you this job—got it?"

"Right," said Jack, feeling discontented. He felt a growing revulsion toward Baxter.

"You'll be much happier, Mr. Webster," Baxter reiterated condescendingly. "The night spots downtown are where you belong, not with these... people, I guess you'd call them," said Baxter scornfully with a wide, sardonic, crooked smile as he twisted around in his chair to survey the Norton locals at The Worthy House. "What filth they have here," he commented absently.

"Yeah," said Jack in a low, guttural mutter, not quite willing to look directly at anybody as the waitress came over with his drink.

"Thanks for going on TV for us, Jack," she said. "I used to love you when you did sports on TV," she gushed.

Baxter chuckled as she left.

"She's going to be disappointed! Good thing you'll never see her again. Oh well, the upside is that she'll get to love you on TV once again, Jack," he said with a quiet cackle. "There's a foul smell in this place," observed Baxter accurately. "That's why Senator Shea had no qualms about pushing state officials to put the airport expansion in Norton instead of near his home on the Cape."

"Why's that?" slurred Jack drunkenly.

"Because this place is already horrible," explained Baxter with surprise, startled that there even an explanation required. "The lives of these people are already ruined, a little airplane noise won't matter. For that matter, a *lot* of noise won't matter, either," chuckled Baxter. "They've got nothing going for them, anyway."

"And the wildlife habitat?" inquired Jack with a sardonic lilt in his voice, making eye contact with his benefactor for the first time.

Baxter waved it off.

"The senator's record on the environment is strong enough. Don't you worry, Mr. Webster, his seat in the Senate is very safe," explained Baxter, taking a sip of the beer the waitress had brought. "Boy, even the beer is terrible here," commented Baxter.

"Yeah, I've had better."

"And you will again, now that you've made this wise choice! Well, in any case," started Baxter, spinning the contract on the table so it faced Jack, "here you go, Jack, we just need your John Hancock on the dotted line to make things official. Once you sign, it'll all be yours again, Mr. Webster. The fame. The money. The broads… the blow," offered Baxter temptingly, but contemptuously, too. The high-achieving Baxter had a Puritan's fascination with Jack's underground reputation as he gazed longingly at the forbidden fruits in which Jack had been known to indulge. Baxter seemed to enjoy buying off Jack with nothing more than a few crumbs of Senator Shea's influence. It cost Shea nothing to get his way; it was almost an afterthought to buy back Jack's future.

Ava suddenly opened the door and came into the bar, a look of distress on her face. Ava went over and talked briefly with the group of Earthpeacers. She looked around and spotted Jack at his table. As Baxter prattled on about some of Senator Shea's past triumphs and string-pullings, Jack noticed some of the Earthpeace kids talking to some of The Worthy House employees with hurt in their eyes, all of them then looking toward Jack. The Earthpeace guys, looking deserted and defeated, left *en masse*, letting The Worthy House door slowly shut behind them and a few of the locals turned their backs and sadly went back to what they were doing. For some reason Jack didn't want to look at Ava and the rest of the people by the bar and turned his attention back to Baxter, who hadn't stopped his bragging chatter about Senator Shea's worldly influence.

Ava came over to Jack and interrupted Baxter.

"Jack—what happened? I thought you were just putting things off, but they said you didn't just postpone the interview, they said you won't reschedule the TV interview at all, that you dropped it altogether. Is it true?" she asked pleadingly. "Are you really going to leave us, Jack?" Ava asked, a look of hurt and betrayal all over her face.

Jack guiltily—he couldn't ever remember feeling guilty before—avoided Ava's face and as he did, his eyes swept across the barroom. The faces he saw were of grim despair, almost hopelessness. For a moment, he unwillingly drank it all in. He glanced back at Ava, who was still looking at him for an answer, and he felt a great burden.

Baxter, immediately reading what was going on, took control of the situation by shoving the contract in front of Jack and handed him a pen.

"Well, Mr. Webster, it's time. It's time for your last chance. It's now or never. Your old life is anxiously waiting for you, Jack. Do we have a deal?"

Everything he'd longed for, everything he'd missed and hungered for over the past three years were finally back within his grasp—all his for the taking just by signing his name. For three long years of deprivation behind bars, Jack had ceaselessly yearned to somehow return to his old life of endless pleasures, and here it was for the taking. Inside the pen was his signature, for now concealed and jumbled in the ink. He needed only to put pen to paper and let it out.

Jack felt the weight of the locals looking at him, and then he looked at Ava.

Jack took the pen and looked at it for a split second and thought of his high life of fame, money and women, all just a pen stroke away.

He put the cap back on and laid down the pen.

"No, Mr. Baxter, we don't have a deal. You can keep the contract. I think I'm going to do the interview after all."

Chapter Ten

(October, 2006)

Jack sat behind his desk in his office at the WKTD studio, leaning back in his chair, fully at ease, brash, full of swagger and exuding a jock's confidence. Chair life did not suit him in general, as he was a man of action and sitting behind a desk was an unnatural restraint on his hungry, competitive, racing temperament. But for the moment, he was quite happy to kick back, take a seat and enjoy his good fortune.

Gone were any feelings of anxiety he'd had during and immediately following the rigged lottery drawing. As he carried on around the studio, Jack was once again his vaguely cocky, yet gregarious and approachable self, smiling a crooked, rakish smile, striding confidently and quick with a teasing, endearing comment.

Right at the present moment, however, he was simply reclining in his chair, relaxed, talking on his untraceable pre-paid cell phone. Jack had started using pre-paid cell phones a while back, right after he got married and found dating to be more difficult to give up than he had imagined, and he had come to find them indispensable.

A saucy smile on his face and feeling on top of the world, Jack was talking with Aleksandra. They had kept their distance leading up to the lottery fix and talking with her had been a rare treat the past few weeks, so he was very much enjoying her company over the phone now.

Jack's joy was especially acute since Aleksandra had recently been officially declared a winner in the lottery drawing Jack had labored so exhaustively to fix. She had come forward with her winning tickets forty-eight hours after the drawing, which was a bit unusual. Winners typically come forward immediately, for obvious reasons, but Aleksandra—for reasons Jack did not understand—felt she would look more "unconcerned," as she put it, if she came forward two days later, presenting herself as a casual, or even indifferent, winner.

This policy she'd independently enacted had upset Jack (who considered it lunacy), but when no one cried foul at the lottery office, he lost interest in arguing about her tardiness in claiming the prize. Better still, there was no way Jack could possibly argue with the overall results of his bold and audacious scheme: Aleksandra—and her two silent co-conspirators, her Uncle Georgi and, of course, Jack himself—were big winners. Through sheer good fortune, Jack had virtually struck gold. The drawing that night was actually the largest ever for the Daily Number.

Aleksandra's tickets accounted for almost a third the total $6.4 million payout that night. They were going to split up $2.1 million dollars. Even a jock-at-heart like Jack could do the math on such a bounty: $700,000 each.

Jack and Aleksandra were, of course, planning a life together, so their combined take would be $1.4 million. Jack figured that Georgi, who was family too, after all, would take his $700,000 and head for a much more comfortable retirement fairly soon. It all came to a quite robust and satisfying conclusion, felt Jack.

The marketing people from the lottery office had sent a breathless, excited memo to their partners at the TV station explaining the circumstances behind the large play the lottery received that night, but Jack just glanced at it and threw it out. Reading memos were for the nerds, management types and accountants. He had bigger and better things with which to concern himself.

"What luck," Jack had thought to himself, "to pull it off on the biggest night of action in the Daily Number's history!" For quite a while he sought in vain for a way in which he could give himself credit for clairvoyance in picking the correct night on which to enact his plan, but credit eluded him, even by his own biased calculations. He vaguely asserted that he must have done *something* right to come up with the right night on which such a large jackpot was available. "There are no such thing as coincidences," Jack haughtily proclaimed to himself in his victorious musings.

Even if he couldn't exactly peg what he'd done right, he assumed his unwavering instincts must have unconsciously led him to the correct course of action. It was not unlike in sports, he figured; an instinctive reaction was really just genius done immediately, in an unconscious way. The same natural instincts that served him so well in the athletic world and made him a natural leader everywhere else must surely have shined through with the lottery fix as well, right? "Whatever," he told himself, closing the book on this line of thought, "I'm freaking rich!"

In his mental victory lap, Jack also congratulated himself on the wisdom of choosing the conspirators he did. The setup was perfect: He and Aleksandra were lovers, this cemented their bond and made their part of the conspiracy leak-proof. Nothing could come between them. Georgi was, of course, family to Aleksandra. Georgi loved Aleksandra like a daughter and admired Jack; he would never in any way betray such a bond with a virtual son-in-law. And, Jack conceded—less charitably—they all shared the same fate. The two family members could never harm him without taking down the other relative. It was a fool-proof setup, a perfectly tied Gordian Knot. The conspiracy's seal seemed perfect.

Despite his previous brief, low suspicions, Jack felt closer than ever to Aleksandra. Theirs was a bond deepened even further by the lottery fix. And now they had much to discuss.

It was late afternoon, two weeks after the drawing and Jack was chatting up a storm with Aleksandra in his office. They were discussing her adventures in going down to the lottery office and claiming her prize.

"Did they say when you'll start receiving the checks, babe?" he inquired happily.

"They told me, but I was so excited, I forgot what they said! They told me the date, but I can't remember. Not too long, though! I'll have to call back and ask again."

"So they weren't suspicious with you at all?"

"No!" she recounted merrily. She still had a vague accent, but it was not nearly as thick and intrusive as her Uncle Georgi's, but enough of one to give her an exotic, sexy flair. "They did ask why I had one thousand, two hundred tickets of the same number, but it was just asked in conversation."

"And what did you tell them?" asked Jack, seeing his vision coming into fruition. He had, of course, expected this to come up.

"I told them—just like you instructed me—that I had planned for the tickets to be a gift, but that I broke up with my boyfriend right before I gave them away. I said I dumped *him*, of course," she said with womanly pride. "They believed the whole thing entirely!"

"Good, good," said Jack. The part about buying the large amount of tickets as a gift with a boyfriend who was now history was a bit part in his plan. It was a nice cover story for when they went public as a romantic item as to why she just happened to be available right around the time she became rich.

"I miss you, Jack," she said gruffly.

"Not half as much as I miss you," Jack said sincerely. "It's murder to me."

"Me too!"

"It'll all be worth it, though," Jack promised her. "Now remember, we can't be seen together, or have anybody realize that we even *know* each other."

"I know," she said sadly.

"I hate to hear you sad, babe. But it'll all be worth it in a year, when we can be together forever, out in the open, with no more of this crazy hiding."

"I can't wait for that," she said hungrily.

"Once they send the first check, I'll know we're in for good and I'll go to Jeanine and start divorce proceedings. Once I file for divorce, it'll go quick. I won't put a big fight and I'll give her whatever she wants just to move things along as fast as possible. Once she and I are separated, you and I can come out of the closet, if you know what I mean."

"Don't give her too much!" urged Aleksandra, always keeping an eye on the bottom line.

"No, no, I won't. I just won't fight a long court battle. I don't want to spend any more time in the court system than I have to. I can afford to end things with her quickly now that we've got this money from the lottery," he said openly and without fear. "I never could have afforded to leave her without it," Jack said, leaving the implication unsaid that Aleksandra desired a life only his full salary could afford.

"If only—"

"Now, Aleksandra," said Jack, interrupting, "just a reminder of our cover story. After a big winner comes forward, a few weeks later, the winner always comes down to the studio to pose with me for a publicity photo."

"Right, they mentioned that to me down at the lottery office."

"Good. When you come down, we have to not know each other, right?"

"Right."

"And you *definitely* don't know Uncle Georgi, of course."

"Right."

"So when you come down, we're going to make sure Uncle Georgi calls in sick that day, just in case somebody slips up and says something or something like that. And like we discussed, when you show up for your publicity photo, you and I will flirt—just a bit."

"OK."

"We'll make sure to do it in front of everybody."

"That's going to be fun—like we get to meet again for the first time!" she cooed.

"Right. Anyway, we'll make sure everybody sees us. That's going to be the cover story of how we met."

"I can't wait!"

"Then, once it's established that's how we met, in a few weeks, I'll be starting divorce proceedings and be separated. Then we can date openly. Then," he said, wrapping up the happy tale, "we'll live happily ever after."

"Oh, Jack, I cannot wait for that," she said with yearning.

"God, me too," he said. "This past month has been crazy."

"The process with the lottery seems to be going so slow," Aleksandra observed with a tremor of fright peeking through her voice.

"It *is* going slow," agreed Jack dourly. "I don't know what the issue is. I'm not an expert on what happens with paying out to the lottery winners, but they seem to be taking their time with you. It seems usually everything is finalized after this amount of time."

Silently, they both wondered if the lottery officials were secretly questioning her story about having twelve hundred tickets of one number. They were both thinking it and they both knew they were each thinking it; it didn't need to be said, but neither had the courage to verbalize their thoughts any more explicitly.

"Don't worry, though," said Jack, "as long as we don't admit anything, there is *no way* they can do anything more than have suspicions. They'll never have a lick of proof. I'm not worried a bit."

Just then, there was a knock on his office door.

"Somebody's here. Gotta go!" Jack said in a urgent, hushed voice, and then he hung up. Aleksandra didn't take such a quick sign-off as a slight. It happened all the time, and, given they'd been a secret couple for a long while, she knew it was necessary sometimes.

Jack quickly hid his secret cell phone.

"Come in," he called out to the hidden knocker.

The door opened and the gloomy personage of Georgi poked halfway in, he still rumpled in dress with a long Russian face.

"Jack, there is a man to see you here," he said, pursuing his official duties as production assistant on this visit.

Jack saw the silhouette of a man looming patiently behind Georgi in the hall right outside the doorway. He looked official in countenance. Jack did not like the look of him.

"Sure, who—"

"This is Detective Dietrich," said Georgi meaningfully though his thick Russian accent. His words, accent aside, hung heavily between the two of them. Although Georgi did not change his expression one bit, their eyes locked meaningfully for a brief moment.

Jack had a split-second of panic race through him before quickly composing himself.

"Oh?" he said, realizing the detective could easily overhear them. "Send him in, by all means, send him in," Jack said warmly and ingratiatingly.

Georgi moved and let the man in.

Detective Dietrich, all business, came in an offered his hand.

Dietrich was clipped, in a black suit, semi-buzz cut dark hair, total Joe Friday getup. He was a middle-aged man, not the grizzled veteran a step away from retirement like the stereotype in the movies or on TV shows.

Jack shook his hand, and although he did not betray it in the least, he felt suddenly cold. The detective wore a straight poker face and Jack could get no read on the man, and this concerned him.

"Sorry to bother you, Mr. Webster," the cop started. The man spoke softly with no bluster in his voice.

"No bother at all," assured Jack. "Sit down," he said, offering a chair with an outstretched hand.

"Thanks, I think I will," said Detective Dietrich with a friendliness that Jack did not trust.

Jack knew everybody who mattered in the city, including the cops, as they liked him and such relationships came in handy for him. Important public officials liked hobnobbing with the city's local celebrities, and the local celebs such as Jack liked having strings available for the pulling.

"Hey, how's Lieutenant Cruz doing?" Jack asked immediately, wanting to establish that he was untouchable, that he was One of The Boys. Whenever he got pulled over for DWI, Jack was always quick to name-drop. Worked every time, especially when you were well-known and admired, like he was.

"Couldn't say," said Dietrich quietly and with a half smile in a face that was still somehow stony. Unspoken in Dietrich's response to Jack's attempt to give himself immunity was that this sort of name-dropping would not work with him. It must be a serious matter, Jack decided. He wondered if somebody had murdered his wife Jeanine? That would make things even easier, he chuckled to himself sardonically.

"Anyway," said Jack, "tell me what's on your mind." He spoke confidently, ingratiatingly, and they both sat.

"You know, Mr. Webster—"

"Call me Jack, everyone down at Area B does," Jack interrupted, casually dropping the name of the nearby Boston police station downtown.

"Sure, Jack it is, then. In any case," started the detective quietly and slowly, "you know, Jack, I'm quite glad to meet you."

"Oh? Sports fan, are you?"

"Sure. And I've been watching you on TV and listening to you call the hockey games for years."

"It hasn't been *that* many years!" protested Jack with mock indignity. "It's been almost ten years on Channel Six, but I'm not quite thirty-four yet, you know."

"Yeah, I know," said the cop with a soft chuckle. "Hell, I'm forty-two myself. You've got a lot of life left, that's for sure. In any case, I remember watching that night you were interviewing your buddy from the Bruins on your *Sports Finale* show that Sunday night a couple of years ago."

"That was a very celebrated and well-remembered night!" conceded Jack with a jocular, matey laugh.

"You both had had a couple pops, I'll wager, and you guys started going back and forth, kidding around, then he took offense at something and he socked you right there on live TV! That was incredible, it was all anybody was talking about the next day."

"Jeez, that was a lot of fun," said Jack, recalling the night for the millionth time with well-practiced intonations. "That was a good time."

"It *looked* like a good time," conceded Detective Dietrich with a smile.

"Well, except for getting punched, anyway," said Jack with a grin. "But that goes with the territory, right?"

Jack was nervous, although he didn't let on. The cop was trying very hard to be casual and ingratiating. Jack did not like it.

"You know, detective, I know all the cops in town— or so I thought," said Jack, "but I've never seen you before. Are you investigating a murder here at WKTD? Or do you need me to talk to the news division about revealing a source?" joked Jack. "I'm just a sports guy, after all."

"Oh, no, nothing like murder," said Detective Dietrich with a gracious chuckle.

"Good. I mean, as a taxpayer, I like to see you guys downtown earning your weekly envelope, after all, but murder's a bit much. Tickets?" offered Jack. "That I can do for you. You know, there's a big Patriots game coming up next week. How'd you like some primo luxury box seats?"

"Oh, God, I can't do that, I can't take favors in this job. But I am anxious to see a couple of those games this year. I actually got tickets a while ago. How do you think the team is going to do?"

"Excellent. A couple of big off-season pickups should put them over the top. My sources inside the locker room are keeping me well-informed with the behind-the-scenes stuff, too. I'd be happy to spill the dirt with you sometime."

"Great. Maybe some other time, though. Anyway," started Detective Dietrich, more casual than ever, "business is what brings me here—my line of business, unfortunately."

"Ah," said Jack noncommittally.

Dietrich was absently fiddling with a souvenir baseball on Jack's desk.

"Anyway, like I was saying, I'm here on business. I'm sure you've heard rumors about the lottery."

"The lottery?" asked Jack innocently, raising his eyebrows. He shifted in his seat uncomfortably.

"Yeah, a few weird rumors about the daily lottery drawing you host every night," started Dietrich laconically. "What's it called, the Triple Play drawing? Anyway, you know the one. Turns out some street level book makers are refusing to pay out on one of the drawings because they say it was irregular. See, street bookies run parallel games on the daily number, because the daily number is a game everybody knows is on the up-and-up, and people are willing to bet on it with bookies because with a street bookie you can bet over the phone, bet on credit, avoid income taxes and so on. It's pretty big business, these parallel street games. And like I said, some of these street bookies aren't paying out on one of the drawings. That's probably where some of these rumors get started, rumors you might have heard."

Jack had heard a few squawks on the street around town, but he'd assured Aleksandra that was just because of the weird 6-6-6 winning number and otherwise considered them too inconsequential to even think about.

"Oh, I heard something in a bar one night, I overheard two idiots say something, but I hadn't heard any details," offered Jack improbably.

"Oh, OK. Maybe I can fill in some of the blanks for you. It was... let's see," said Detective Dietrich, theatrically pulling out and consulting a small notebook, "October 5th. No, wait, October *9th*. Yeah, October 9th." He looked Jack directly in the eyes. "Does that night's drawing mean anything to you, Mr. Webster? Or should I say, Jack?"

Jack shifted uncomfortably again. He realized the conversation had suddenly gotten very serious. October 9th was, of course, the night they'd rigged the lottery drawing. Jack knew this Detective Dietrich was trying to get him to say something—anything—on record, not necessarily to confess or implicate anybody, but to just get him to make a statement, anything that could be contradicted later in another interview. That's how it worked, once you said something in a statement, later on you'd say something else that didn't mesh with what you said at first and then they'd start whittling away until you had to come clean. Even though he realized fully what was going on, Jack felt he had to say something. He had the right to refuse to talk to a cop — indeed, any defense lawyer would have urged him to do so — but he felt doing that would place a bull's eye squarely on him. He felt he *had* to say something.

"Hmmmm. No, not off the top of my head. I don't remember anything in particular. Not about that night, or any other night, really."

"You don't? OK. Let me refresh your memory, it was only a few weeks ago, after all. The winning number was 6-6-6. Sound familiar now?"

"Oh, yeah, I remember that night. I can't keep track of all the nights and numbers. They're all alike if you do that show every day, like I do," explained Jack with a bit of an edge creeping into his voice. "I didn't know what date that was, but I remember that number. That number 6-6-6 will come up once in a great while, just like any other number. In reality there's nothing special or magical about it."

"Yeah…so, anyway, you *do* remember that number coming up? So you know there were whispers of the number being fixed?"

"I vaguely heard something about a fix, but of course I didn't think anything of it. Like I said, I know that's what those idiots I overheard in the bar were talking about. I wasn't even sure what night they were talking about. That sort of thing happens whenever that number comes up. Makes the religious people go crazy," suggested Jack dismissively. "Puts them in an uproar, you know? Triple numbers always bring out weirdoes, but that number in particular does. The station gets all these crazy letters every time."

"Right."

"Say, detective, I'm not in some sort of trouble or under suspicion of something, am I?" asked Jack aggressively. He had no urge to sit there and endure an inquisition from this cop all day.

"Oh, no, no," said Dietrich softly and with a wave. "Just standard stuff. There are some people whispering on the street and we're just doing a routine follow-up, you know?"

"Sure."

"I mean, nobody thinks *you've* done anything wrong, of course."

"Good, good. In this business I don't need my name dragged into something like this. I mean, it won't go anywhere—the investigation, I mean, because the drawing happens in this studio where all the station's people are here and a lottery agent is always present," said Jack, taking the offensive, "but you know how rumors can hurt a person like myself who is in the public eye, you know?"

"Of course. It's a very serious matter, which is why, even though I agree with you that there's likely nothing to the rumors, it's in everybody's interest to keep our interview low-key."

"I appreciate that, Detective Dietrich," said Jack sympathetically.

"Yeah, anyway," said Dietrich, still in a slow, gentle voice, "I doubt anything will come of it, but I want to talk to all the principals involved, you know?"

"Right."

"Even though we know *you're* not involved, there's a chance that something you say—or somebody else here at the station might say—could mean nothing to you, but might be important to me when I put it against somebody else's statement."

"Right."

"For instance, you could very well say something that makes me think somebody else is lying to me. You tell me one thing a guy did the night in question and he tells me he did something else, and now I know he's lying to me, right? Makes him look suspicious, like somebody I should look into a little bit more, you understand?"

"Sure, sure," said Jack, who was afraid he knew exactly what the detective meant. He was warning that if Jack lied to him, somebody else would point it out, perhaps innocently. Jack ran through everything he did the night of the fix and tried to recall who might have observed him, even though it was impossible to recall everything under this sort of pressure. He was reacting just the way Dietrich wanted him to react, but was powerless to stop and get off the treadmill.

"I just feel I have to follow every lead—just to make sure," said Detective Dietrich. "You understand, right?"

"Of course I do. I appreciate your thoroughness," said Jack, vainly hoping to ingratiate himself with the suddenly menacing investigator. He felt the conversation had somehow turned into a very serious interrogation, and he'd gotten into it without a lawyer. He desperately wanted it to end, but he dared not say he was unwilling to talk for fear of throwing more suspicion on himself. What if the interview really *was* completely innocent and Jack overreacted and blew it by calling for a lawyer? What if he did so and called attention to himself over nothing? Jack felt completely trapped.

The room seemed to Jack to be maddeningly silent. Time seemed to pass painfully slowly. It felt like Dietrich had been in the room for hours. Now totally humorless and in command of the situation, Dietrich continued his grim march.

"Did you notice any suspicious activities on October 9th or any of the days and weeks leading up to the 9th?"

"Oh, uh, no, not at all. Nothing I can remember."

"No need to be nervous, Mr. Webster," counseled Dietrich, "this is just a routine interview and you're not under suspicion. You don't even have to talk to me if you don't want to."

Jack felt he had no choice but to continue, even though he knew the cop was lying. He knew damned well he was under suspicion. Worse still, he knew he was guilty.

"I'm fine," Jack said, trying—and failing—to sound nonchalant.

"Did any of the employees of the station or anybody connected with the lottery office act oddly?" asked Dietrich dully and remorselessly, pen in hand, pausing over his notebook, ready to jot down answers. The man's drab and dogged pursuit was unnerving. Jack felt blocked in and hunted.

"Not any more oddly than usual," joked Jack, trying to use his charm to defuse the situation. He felt he could bluff his way out it by acting confidently. Would a guilty man joke, after all?

"Please don't joke around, Mr. Webster," said Detective Dietrich seriously, fixing a stern eye on Jack.

"Sorry," said Jack, chastened. "Uh, no, I didn't notice any odd behavior by anybody."

"Did any employees of WKTD or the lottery office meet with strangers or people you didn't recognize around the studio set?" asked Dietrich after scribbling down Jack's denials, his voice now less soft, now with a hard edge underneath, and with even less emotion than before.

"No," said Jack flatly, his life flashing before his eyes, his head swimming. He thought he might be sweating, but he wasn't sure and didn't want to mop his brow to check, lest he betray any more nervousness.

"Good. Now, did you have any reason what-so-ever to think that the lottery drawing on October 9th , the night of the 6-6-6 winning number we've discussed, was tampered with in *any* way, or that anything unusual surrounded that night's drawing?"

Jack thought for a moment, trying to buy himself some breathing room.

"No, not off the top of my head."

"What do you mean 'off the top of your head'?" asked Dietrich pointedly and quietly, in an accusing manner.

"Well, like I said, that seemed like just another night to me, and besides," added Jack defensively, "it's not like I can remember every detail of every night. I'm a busy guy, you know."

"I understand, but it's not a difficult question, Mr. Webster: Do you remember anything unusual in that time period or do you not remember anything unusual?"

"Nothing unusual," said Jack flatly with a tone of defeat.

Dietrich wrote down what seemed to Jack to be a lot more than necessary.

"No phone calls that stuck out in your mind?"

Jack became rattled internally, feeling besieged on every front. Why was Dietrich asking about phone calls? Jack's mind raced to try and remember if he or Georgi or Aleksandra had messed up with any phone calls. Everything seemed difficult to recall and it seemed impossible to have faith in anything they'd done. Demon doubts gnawed at every corner of his mind. Anything seemed possible.

"Not that I can recall."

"Good," said Detective Dietrich as he wrote. "So nothing at all unusual in any way?"

"No."

Unexpectedly, just when Dietrich seemed to have Jack completely on the ropes, the cop snapped his notebook shut. Jack felt that maybe the worst had passed and he was home free.

"Excellent,' said Dietrich. "You know, Jack," he consoled, "there's nothing for you to worry about."

"Oh, I'm not worried—not about myself, anyway," declared Jack. "I'm just a little worried that the station could be hurt by rumors, you know?"

"Certainly."

"There's no way to defend against that sort of thing, you know? Rumors, I mean. Rumors are impossible to stop and can be very damaging. This sort of talk could be devastating to a news organization."

"Well, don't worry, Mr. Webster," said Detective Dietrich sympathetically, rising from his chair, which Jack did as well. "These sorts of interviews go on all the time, very routine."

"Good. Hopefully it'll go away. WKTD doesn't need this sort of thing growing into a cloud." Jack felt he was making progress charming the detective and throwing him off the scent by professing concern over the station's reputation instead of for his own well-being.

Dietrich extended his hand.

"Well, Jack, thanks for your time," he said softly with a smile as he stood. "Like I said, it was a pleasure meeting you after all these years. You're quite an institution around this city."

"Thanks. You know, I'm not a sports anchor imported from another state like some other guys who do sports in town. I grew up around here and I can't tell you how much I love the city and what I do. Say, detective," said Jack, brightening, "if you're at the game and you see me down on the field doing a live shot before the game, come down front and say hello. I can take you on the fifty yard line and maybe show you around a bit."

"Thanks, that'd be great. I might just take you up on your very kind offer. My boy would get a huge thrill out of that."

"Anytime," said Jack with fraternity. He smiled broadly, but on the inside his smile was even far more expansive. Not only had he defused the situation, he'd won over the investigator. Detective Dietrich, he figured, was no longer a force to be reckoned with or feared. He was on Team Webster, just like everybody else.

"Guess I'll be off now. I'll see myself out," said Detective Dietrich quietly with a comforting half-smile.

"OK, great," said Jack who went to sit back down.

As Detective Dietrich opened the door to leave, he paused. Jack, as he was pulling out his chair, noticed Dietrich out of the corner of his eye and stopped in mid-motion. Then Dietrich turned around, as if remembering an insignificant detail.

"You know, Jack, I can trust you, so I don't mind telling you because you're probably wondering why we're even bothering to look into this. I mean, what are barroom rumors after all, right?"

"Uh-huh…," offered Jack cautiously.

"Well, we got a tip from an establishment about the lottery drawing."

"Oh?" Jack asked skeptically. He didn't trust any supposed anonymous tips. Invented "anonymous tips" were a trick often used by authorities to rattle someone into talking.

"Yeah. Turns out somebody working at this place overheard a customer who was buying a whole bunch of tickets talking on the phone about fixing that night's drawing." The lawman paused. "Well, see you later!" Dietrich concluded happy with a lilt in his voice. He then shut the door and was gone.

Jack was shocked. That seemed far, far too close to home to be a fake story designed to shake a suspect into talking. The detective hadn't been thrown off by his denials at all. Those stories Dietrich had about 'rumors on the street' were probably not made up, but were just a ruse, an excuse to get Jack talking and looking in another direction, and it all worked like a charm. Jack had thought the law's suspicions had been based on rumors on the street, but it was really about overheard phone calls, a fact he didn't let on until he was done.

Dietrich knew a lot more than he was letting on, Jack realized. And he was letting Jack know that he knew. He was trying to rattle him. And that worked, too. Jack wanted to ask Dietrich if he'd talked to anybody else about these rumors to see what the man knew, but of course he couldn't; police interviews only went one way. Worse still, Dietrich said he was going to talk to everybody—that meant Georgi and probably Aleksandra as well. Could they be trusted to issue stout denials? Jack couldn't be certain. He had held up well enough under the assault with denials, but what about them? They could screw up or break under pressure.

Jack fell in a heap into his chair and stared off into space....

Chapter Eleven

(October, 2010)

It was the morning after Jack's rededication to his WKTD interview, and Earthpeace's rented office space on Main Street in downtown Norton was abuzz over the news.

The Spartan accommodations that were serving as Earthpeace's temporary local headquarters until the Slocumb Airport expansion issue was settled wasn't truly an office in any meaningful sense of the word. There were no cushioned chairs, no receptionist's area, no furniture of any significance at all. There were rows of cheap, folding chairs and flimsy, collapsible tables, the scene humbly crowned by an unobtrusive wipe board at the front of the room. Mostly just a place to keep signs and meet with protection from the elements, the room looked more like a Red Cross blood donation station than an office.

Everything there was a stark reflection of the shoestring budget that comes with community activism.

As the Earthpeace meeting was preparing to get underway, some of the clattering, tinny, dark brown folding metal chairs were occupied, but most Earthpeace members milled around in small groups, everybody talking and consulting with each other about the drama concerning Jack's announcement of the previous evening. The Worthy House was only half a mile from the office Earthpeace was renting, but even if it had been much farther, the news would have reached this room long ago. The emotional roller-coaster of Jack's off-and-on relationship with his interview had riveted the Earthpeace people in Norton, being as it was their last hope.

Everyone in the group had been informed that Jack had dropped the interview and they'd been dramatically updated that it was back on, all for reasons that were mysterious, and everyone seemed to provide grist for the rumor mill by advancing their own pet theories.

Ava stood in urgent conference with a couple of the leaders of the Earthpeace chapter.

"Are you sure?" asked the older man, Larry, the titular head of the local organization, his skepticism evident and plain on his face.

"Yes!" Ava assured them with urgency, "I was standing right there! Jack said he was doing the interview again! It is back on."

"I don't trust him," announced Greg with hostility. Greg was the big kid Jack had labeled a hothead on the first day he'd seen Earthpeace protesting. Greg hadn't taken much of a shine to Jack the day he first saw him and nothing about his stance had softened since. "Who's to say he's not some sort of double agent? He was talking to that guy in the suit at The Worthy House when I last saw him, and the guy in the suit was offering Webster a job."

"No way," protested Ava, "you left and didn't see it. The guy in the suit—Baxter, I guess his name was—handed Jack a contract and Jack rejected it and told him flat out that he was doing the interview after all."

"Could be a ploy," countered Greg tenaciously.

"Don't be ridiculous," scolded Ava. "That guy Baxter was *royally* pissed. He told Jack that he had 'made a very big mistake' and that Senator Shea was a important man and that Senator Shea knew people and that Jack had made a very powerful enemy and he'd regret it someday soon, real soon. Then this Baxter guy—who Jack says works for Senator Shea as his chief of staff—grabbed the contract angrily and stormed out."

"What did Jack do after that?" asked the old hippie Earthpeacer.

"Nothing, really. He just finished his drink and left without saying another word."

Greg looked on skeptically. "Let's forget about him and get going," he said. Then, with a scowl on his face, he stalked over and stood at the front of the room, next to the wipe board, with Larry, the director, following sheepishly in his wake.

"OK, everybody, could we all sit down? We've got a lot to work to do here," Larry, the baldish director announced apologetically from the front of the room. Everybody was sitting down in the rows of cheap folding chairs facing him.

Just then, the door opened and, unexpectedly, Jack stood momentarily in the doorway. All the chatter in the room immediately died down as everybody looked at him, not sure what to make of his reappearance. The room fell almost entirely silent.

Jack, feeling the full weight of the room on him, was acutely aware everyone was looking to him.

"Am I late?" he asked.

"A little," said Greg from the front of the room. "A little late to all of this, actually."

"I thought you were out, Jack?" asked the old hippie director, Larry.

"No. Not anymore. There's been a change of plans. I'm doing the interview after all," Jack said calmly, without drama, his eyes moving quietly around the room. He held simply a liter bottle of water, which had lately become his constant companion.

"There's some trail mix on the table over there, if you're hungry, Jack," offered the old hippie gently.

"No, thanks. Channel Six has been giving us publicity about my hunger strike so now that's back on, too. I haven't eaten anything in twenty-four hours, so I guess I'll have to pass."

"Well, take a seat, Jack," said Larry.

Jack went and sat at the back of the room, being as unobtrusive as he could be, but all the attention of the room was clearly and silently on him and he felt a bit embarrassed about it.

Previously, whenever he'd been at an Earthpeace gathering, Jack had scowled and maintained a hip cynicism concerning the proceedings, keeping himself aloof and above the group's proceedings despite the fact they looked at him as a sort of guru. In spite of that guru status, he'd mostly given almost totally useless advice, dealing out platitudes laden with buzzwords and the like. Nobody knew that when left to his own devices, Jack was tossing all the fliers he was supposed to be handing out into the dumpster or ducking into The Worthy House tavern when he was scheduled to be knocking on doors. Only he knew the extent of his interest in the entire project had originally been to ingratiate himself with Ava and boost his career plans.

After she'd announced her engagement, there no longer seemed to be any reason for him to be there, but here he was now, defying Senator Shea's offer to return him to his former glamorous life on television.

Before, Jack had always worn a crooked smile, or depending on Ava's involvement in a particular topic, a furrowed look of concerned intensity. Now it was unmistakable to Ava, as she looked at him, that Jack had a calm about him that hadn't been there previously. He looked focused and oddly untroubled. Jack had a serene countenance and the only time he seemed to move at all was when he took long, deep drinks of water from the bottle he was carrying.

Larry, the director, talked at the front of the room about various campaigns involving Earthpeace as Ava slipped into the chair next to Jack and whispered to him.

"That Baxter guy looked really ticked off at you last night."

"Yeah, he was mad, all right," Jack whispered back. "I can't blame him, I backed out of our deal."

"He said Senator Shea would get revenge, what did he mean?"

"I'm not sure exactly. Senator Shea knows a lot of people. I'm sure he meant what he said, though. A guy like me can find himself in a lot of trouble."

Greg, who had been standing agitatedly next to the Larry, finally got the floor. He was still carrying a look of anger.

"OK, look," he said, addressing the group, "I'm sick as shit of all this passing-out-pamphlets crap we've been doing for months here. It's a goddamned waste of time. It's a waste of my time and it's a waste of your time, am I right?" he asked, the stress and agitation playing plainly on his face. "What we need to do," he declared, rapping the table, "is start with some more confrontational tactics—let them know we're not going to just be a bunch of ineffectual paper-passer-outers!" he concluded awkwardly.

This got the attention of the younger set especially, most of whom nodded.

"We need a big confrontation, like you see at the G8 meetings! I was at the G8 protests in Mexico, and we got tons of media coverage! A lot more attention than you'd get from a local TV station, that's for sure," he sneered, looking over at Jack, who was listening, unruffled. "The World Trade Organization and G8 protests are huge events, but the protesters dictate the discussion! That's because of the confrontations. Once the tear gas starts flying and a police cruiser is overturned, nobody ignores you! That's the only thing the powers-that-be will listen to. That's what we need to organize!"

The room seemed taken by this line of thought.

"Now obviously, we aren't going to have a couple thousand protesters like at a World Trade Organization meeting," Greg conceded, "because this isn't as big as global economic exploitation, but I know plenty of G8 protesters—we all do. Most of the younger people in the room belong to a variety of newsgroups and organizations. We need to organize a call to arms. I figure we can have a hundred protesters in the city of Norton in a week—easily. Once we plant a hundred anarchists here, we can have our confrontation—then we'll be dictating the discussion of the issues, not handing out fliers and having doors slammed in our faces," he concluded with satisfaction.

The younger people of Earthpeace looked on, mostly excited, nodding and talking quietly to themselves with approval as a general murmur took over the room.

Jack, seemingly the lone dissenter (along with the old hippie director, who looked on with dismay, but said nothing) shook his head. In a soft, yet commanding voice from the back of the room, he spoke up as he stood up.

"No, no, no," he said, putting his hands out gently. "This airport expansion is strictly a local issue. Tear gas, police with batons, signs touting anarchy, those things don't belong here. This is a local issue that requires local action, not riots."

Jack was standing in the back, and he walked gently to the front of the room. It was only right then that everybody else noticed the change that had overcome him. Before, Jack had been content to be in the background, seemingly bored with the proceedings, almost scornful, his participation in media discussions a façade, though nobody had realized it at the time. In fact, he had been entirely indifferent to everything Earthpeace was doing and only hanging around long enough to score with Ava. Now, however, he was involved, the look of indifference on his face was replaced with a focused, commanding, yet serene look.

"Because the airport is a local issue, you're going to need local participation, not outsiders showing up and causing trouble, all that will do is alienate the locals, who then won't want anything to do with you. The only ones who care about the G8 and WTO clashes are college bloggers and the French. You guys are going about this all wrong. You've got the wrong media contacts," Jack explained. He had spent his whole working life around news institutions and station managers like Billy Bowman and he knew how they worked. "A letter the editor? Who cares? The Internet? That's preaching to the choir. You can't self-direct like that. You guys never worked in a business requiring public relations or public outreach. I'm going to do this interview, they'll come for the scandal and they'll hear about the airport. We'll have a much more clear view of how to reach out to traditional and non-traditional media after that, and more importantly, an idea of who is listening to us."

Jack had suddenly, subtly, taken total control of the room, in command and full of sincere charisma. Everyone watched him as he spoke and he was forceful and engaged, but comfortable and not domineering.

"I'll do this interview next week, then we'll come back here that night and come up with a more complete plan of how to spread our story about what's going on with the Slocumb expansion project. I believe next month Senator Shea is scheduled to visit the Slocumb Airbase. I say we should plan to have a big—peaceful—protest there. By then, the interview will have attracted some public interest and we'll keep that public interest alive with my hunger strike, which WKTD thinks is really big news and something they want to *make* big news, so I'll keep it going. I'll help come up with more useful media contacts to spread and reinforce our narrative about the airport project. I have a lot of ideas already."

Greg, seemingly shrunken, fumed off to the side, his idea of a giant clash with authorities having wordlessly been shot down by the Earthpeacers, a reality even he could see.

"It'll never work," Greg mumbled, shaking his head at Jack's plans.

"OK, then, we agree," said Jack, "I'll go to Channel Six tomorrow and we'll meet back here to decide what we'll be implementing for the big protest when Senator Shea shows up at the Slocumb Airbase next month."

Soon enough, after some other business was conducted, everyone was getting up and the sound of folding metal chairs scratching across the floor filled the room as people stood and the Earthpeace group broke up, some leaving right away, others congregating in small groups to talk.

Ava approached Jack as he stood alone.

"Jack, you never got to finish telling me, what are you doing here?"

"What do you mean?"

"I mean, when that Baxter guy gave you that TV contract, I thought you were leaving and you were going to make a million dollars and drive a sports car and everything and we'd never see you again. He was going to give you your old job back and you turned in down. What happened?"

"Well, I guess I had a change of heart. I'm this far into my hunger strike and I realized just how much money I was saving on food, right?" Jack joked with a sardonic chuckle.

"Ha, yeah…. You know, Jack, you've lost a lot of weight," Ava commented, suddenly taking note of his appearance after his mention of the now-famous hunger strike.

"I know it. Back when I was on TV, I had all these gym memberships and more muscle on me. I'm practically wasting away."

"No," she said, becoming concerned, "I didn't mean since your TV days, I mean you've lost weight just since you first showed up around here. That hunger strike has really kicked in."

"Yeah, I guess so," said Jack, tugging at his clothes to illustrate how loose they had become. "When I went to WKTD and first proposed the interview, the station manager thought I was staging a hunger strike, so I had to kind of go along with it. Now I'm really on a strict hunger strike, not eating anything and just drinking diet shakes because the hunger strike is a big part of the story the TV station wants. Lots of box office appeal in the dramatic gesture, I guess. If we want to keep the airport story in the news, I'll have to keep it up and not eat. I guess the hunger strike is working—in more ways than one, because not only am I dropping weight, the TV station keeps asking me about it constantly also. It's funny, I've been having nothing but liquids, but I'm thirsty as hell," he said, taking another long drink of water from the bottle he'd put down on the table.

"Well, be careful," said Ava. Jack smiled at her. It was no longer a crooked smile, but an even, reassuring smile. "Feel like going out for a drink?" Ava asked him sprightly.

"No, I'd better not," said Jack. He was no longer hitting on her or putting on a show for her. For Jack, it wasn't about Ava anymore. "I think I should go home and *not* eat," he joked. "I've got to prepare for the big day at WKTD. They're going to do a ton of promoting for this thing and a lot of people will be watching, and this interview is going to be broadcast live and rebroadcast again later and I want to make sure I'm rested and sharp."

*

Sitting in his chair in front of the cameras at the WKTD Evening News studio the next day before the much anticipated and much-delayed interview was to begin, Jack patiently took a drink of water from his bottle just before the station's makeup artist came over and put on the finishing touches by patting his face with some powder to avoid glare from the studio lights.

"All set," she said perkily.

"Thanks, Holly," said Jack with a friendly smile

"It's nice to see you again, Jack," she blurted out, breaking into a personal tone with him. She'd vowed to keep a professional distance when Jack came back to the studio for his interview, but at the last second, she just couldn't.

"Nice to see you again too, Holly. How's Annie doing?" he asked, inquiring about her beloved dog.

"Great!"

"That's good."

Holly had worked with Jack years before when he was the star of the station. She hadn't wanted to talk to him too much upon his return, partially because she'd felt let down by him and partially for fear of embarrassing him about the nature of his departure after the lottery scandal.

"You look good, Jack," she said. Then, observing him closer, she added, "but you've lost weight, try to eat something!"

"Eat something? Haven't you been paying attention, Holly? I'm on a big diet these days, you know," said Jack with a broad, even smile. "Hunger strikes are big news around here. Though to tell you the truth, I do find myself tired a lot these days."

"Well, rest up. And knock 'em dead, Jack!" she said, and in spite of herself, gave him a quick good-luck hug before scurrying off.

Gary Gibson, WKTD's star news anchor and Jack's friend from the old days came rushing over seemingly at the last moment and sat next to Jack, across from the cameras.

"Ready to go, Jack?" he asked energetically as stage assistants fluttered about him, affixing his microphone and touching him up with makeup.

"I'm ready, Gary."

"God, Jack, you look awful," Gary said, taking close notice of Jack for the first time.

"Awful?" asked Jack, taking a drink from his water bottle.

"Yes, awful. You've lost a lot of weight."

"Yeah, they didn't feed me so great when I was away. Bread and water, you know."

"But I think you've even lost weight from when you first came back to see Billy Bowman about doing this interview last month."

"So I've heard. Everyone keeps saying that to me lately. Even Holly just mentioned it before you came over. I'm just tired is all. Anyway, I'm supposed to lose some weight. Don't forget, Gary, I'm on a hunger strike."

"How could I forget! You must have seen the advertising promoting this interview, right? It's been everywhere. They've really been promoting the shit out of it since you rescheduled the interview. *'Local television star talks about The Lottery Scandal—and what is driving him to risk his life now?'*" he said, running his hands across the air, as if framing the words on a giant, invisible marquee. "Great stuff," commented Gary to himself with satisfaction. The theme music started and the director signaled that they were to begin filming in a moment. "Put that water bottle down out of camera shot, will you, Jack?" muttered Gary out of the side his mouth.

"Three...two... one... go!" said the director. The red light above the camera came lit up, signifying there were on.

"I'm Gary Gibson and I'm here with an old friend everybody in Boston knows well—Jack Webster, who is making his first public appearance since 2006, when he was involved with the infamous lottery fixing scandal known coast-to-coast as 'The Triple Six Fix.' Welcome back home, Jack," said Gary, turning to Jack as the last words left his mouth.

"Nice to be back, Gary," answered Jack, looking utterly relaxed, but not cocky like he'd always been before on TV.

"Jack, you're recently back on the outside and this is the first time you've spoken publicly to anybody anywhere about the scandal that led you to be banished, is that right?"

"It is. I've never spoken about the lottery scandal before, anywhere. Nobody's ever really heard how things happened back then."

"So why don't you take us back four years, to the beginning, and tell us about the infamous Triple Six Fix scandal and tell us—in your own words—exactly what happened and why."

"Very well, Gary, I will," began Jack. "It started one night while doing the show, *Daily Lottery Live!* right in the studio next to where we are right now, as a matter of fact. At the time, the state's lottery office didn't have facilities to televise the drawing, so this station, WKTD, broadcast the drawing right here on-premises. Anyway, on this particular night, the senior citizen witness made a casual, off-hand comment to me about how it would be easy to fix the drawing. His words stuck in my head as soon as I heard them. You see, Gary, I was in a great deal of turmoil at the time. In fact, it's fair to say I was struggling with personal demons, if you'll allow me to use a cliché. At that time, I was leading what you might call a complicated life. Now, the fault was entirely mine—please understand that I don't want to convey anything else. But this is how it was…" started Jack.

For the better part of the hour, Jack laid things out, just as they'd happened. He talked about his infidelity and drug use and how, despite having co-conspirators, he in fact was the driving force and hub of the conspiracy. He was blunt and honest, never pointing fingers at anyone else and did not dodge any questions and or evade responsibility for what he had done. He laid his motivations for the scandal at the feet of his own naked desire and greed. It was compelling viewing, even being called "riveting" in the next morning's newspapers.

Even Gary, his old friend, was spellbound at the story Jack told, filled as it was with stimulating, raw elements, all laid out dramatically by Jack's natural skills as a raconteur. Gary interrupted only occasionally, jumping in to ask a question or ask for a clarification.

"And then, eventually, after getting out, I found myself starting out on a new life, walking out of a barbershop in the old mill city of Norton," concluded Jack, "and that's how I ended up back here at WKTD—for one evening, at least—back at my old stomping grounds and among my old friends."

"It's an amazing story, one nobody around this city will ever forget," commented Gary. "And what are you doing now, Jack?"

"Well, television work seems out of the question, of course, but I'm doing something very rewarding right now. I'm working with Earthpeace, the environmental activist group. They're well known around the country for their work on a variety of issues from air pollution to baby seals."

"Yes, certainly."

"I got involved because when I came to the city of Norton, I discovered something about what was happening there, and I've felt compelled to help."

"And what's going on in Norton? You mean the Slocumb Airport expansion project?" asked Gary leadingly.

"That's right, Gary, the Slocumb Airport expansion," said Jack. "I'll tell you why I felt it was necessary to be involved."

With that, Jack launched into a passionate and eloquent monologue about the expansion project, the environmental impact it would have and how the working-class people of Norton were powerless to stop unnamed "powerful interests" from shoving the project down their throats instead of placing it where it made more sense, namely on The Cape. Everyone from Earthpeace, watching their televisions, was stunned to see how persuasive and articulate Jack was on the issues. Of course, having been a TV pro for years, Jack was a natural in front of the camera and could deliver a perfectly professional delivery, but what struck everyone was how emotive and passionate he was. It was a performance that was moving and engaging. Nobody knew he had it in him. And until recently, he hadn't.

Gary (and WKTD management) was more interested in the celebrity-driven lottery scandal, and though he knew Jack's discussion of the airport expansion was good copy, he was preparing to turn towards the final leg of the interview.

"Good stuff, Jack."

"And," interrupted Jack, "as you've been reporting on this station, that is why I've launched this hunger strike."

Gary's eyes lit up.

"You mentioned that before we went on air, I'm sure viewers have noticed you've lost weight since your days doing sports here on WKTD."

"That's right. This issue is so important, I've decided to pursue this hunger strike further, until we can get an open-air hearing at the State House about the Slocumb expansion issue." Gary opened his mouth to say something, but Jack jumped in front of him, "And to that end, in approximately three weeks, on the 9th of this month, Earthpeace is going to have a major protest at the Slocumb Airport, which, coincidentally, is the day Senator Shea is scheduled to visit the base for a small ceremony as his plane lands from Washington, according to his official itinerary posted on-line. I'm going to read a statement there at the main entrance of Slocumb, updating the progress on our efforts to get a hearing at the State House and also giving an update on my hunger strike, and Gary, I'm personally inviting you and WKTD to cover the event because I'm sure the Senator will not want to change his plans and miss it."

This was not something they'd talked about beforehand and it put Gary Gibson in quite an awkward spot. He didn't break his smiling countenance, but inside, he was boiling mad.

"Sure, Jack, that sounds great, we can do that."

"Excellent, thank you, Gary, see you there."

The cameras soon went off and the stage crew started walking back and forth, coming over to de-microphone the host and guest, telling them both what a great interview they'd just done.

"Jesus fucking Christ, Jack—what were you doing with that?!" demanded Gary, throwing down his notes on the floor, leaving them scattered.

"What do you mean, Gary?" responded Jack innocently. "Look around here, everybody thought that was a killer interview. I'll bet you get nominated for a local Emmy for it."

"That's not what I meant and you know it! I meant that bullshit about inviting me *on air* to cover that stupid protest speech of yours. You already had a deal in place for a two-part story on the airport expansion just for doing this interview—then you go and put me on the spot like that!"

"It'll be big news, Gary. Hey, now you've got another big event to cover." Jack handed his microphone clip to the stage assistant. "Gary, you'll thank me when the time comes." Then he left the studio.

*

The next afternoon, the Earthpeace people were back in their strategy room, deciding what would be their next course of action. The airport project was becoming closer to reality with every passing day, and there was rising anxiety that they'd not done enough to change public consciousness about the expansion. There was a palpable feeling that it was now or never.

Greg, brooding over Jack's newfound status as the emotional driving force behind the local Earthpeacers, listened to the others congratulate Jack on his interview, which was, as predicted, a huge television event all across the state. Greg was a hothead and found all the endless talking to be totally useless.

"I can't believe how many people on the street have talked to me about it today," gushed Ava, joining the chorus of accolades.

"Yeah, nice interview," injected Greg, "but we need more action. No—we need *some* action. Anything. We need to revisit my plan of a call to arms and provoke a G8-style confrontation."

"Jeez, Greg, we already talked about this," said Jack wearily, for he was exhausted, brushing aside the young hotspur's attempts to bring about a general agitation. "Mayhem is not the answer—not for an airport expansion, anyway, that's for certain. This is a civil society we live in and sunlight is the best disinfectant. Eventually public pressure will come about and win out, either that or it wasn't meant to be. We need to win public opinion and we do that by showing them what's going on, not by trying to blackmail them with demonstrations of anger. It's a little slower and not as immediately satisfying, but it's the only path that really makes sense. Am I right, Larry?" Jack asked, turning to the aging hippie director of the local Earthpeace chapter.

"Yeah, that's right," the older man said quickly, seemingly wishing to be invisible.

"Good," said Jack, brushing aside Greg and seizing the narrative, "now my source at WKTD says that people really responded to the hunger strike and the interview in general. WKTD will show up for our protest if there's a reason."

"Like a G8 riot," offered Greg sardonically.

"No, not like that. Here's what I have in mind. On the 9th, Senator Shea—the man who directed his state allies to put Slocumb airbase on the expansion list—will be arriving at Slocumb from Washington. As a government official, his plane always lands there. He can't back out and change his plans now because we've already called him out in public. I think we should go ahead full bore with the protest, call in everybody we can. We'll make a big deal—backdoor—through the media that we're going to unveil the charges against Senator Shea of using his influence to direct the project to Slocumb. And to make sure we get coverage, I'll be the spokesman and we'll tell the TV station and papers I'll be giving a speech."

"Why you?" asked Greg with a tone of accusation.

"Because the media loves the hunger strike angle. That'll guarantee they'll show up. Plus, the public knows my name. I can put my lottery scandal notoriety for good use for once."

"Are you sure about the hunger strike, Jack?" asked Ava. "You don't look so great these days."

"I'm fine, just tired and worn down" said Jack, who wasn't really feeling so great, but refused to own up to it. Jack then took a drink from the bottle of water that had lately become such a constant presence that it almost seemed an extension of his hand.

"Are we going to be allowed on the airport, Jack?"

"No. That's the good part. They police will force us to leave—we won't fight them over it, of course, Greg—but having the police remove us in front of the media will send the message we want, it will show how powerful interests are controlling the entire process."

"How do you know that's what'll happen?"

"Because it happened before. Remember when you guys were kicked out in front of the Shea compound down on the Cape a while back? We'll get the same thing, but this time it'll be in front of the cameras for everybody to see."

"Who cares?" snapped Greg. "That won't make the state government change their plans for the airport. That won't do a thing."

"Maybe not," said Jack. "There's no guarantee any action—or non-action—we take will work the way we want. We'll do our thing and see what happens. Once you throw a baseball and it leaves your hand, you stop trying to control it. Same thing here."

Greg sulked, seeing the room was not on his side.

"So," asked Jack, "is that the plan? OK, then, we'll break out into smaller groups like we talked about earlier to work out the details about what we're going to be doing over the next few weeks."

Everyone got up and went on their separate ways, until finally only Ava and Jack were alone in the room, and Ava approached Jack and spoke to him in a low, conspiratorial voice.

"Jack?"

"Yes?"

"I need to talk to you."

"Oh? What about?"

"It's personal."

"Is there a problem?" he asked.

"A little bit of a problem, well not really a *problem*…. Anyway, see, I've been watching you lately, and I've gotten to know you since you arrived."

"Me too. That is to say, same here."

"And the thing is, I think I'd like to get to know you more. Know what I mean? I'd like to move things along—personally, I mean."

Jack was startled.

"What? But I thought you were engaged to some guy you went to college with? George, the prince of the lumber world, wasn't it?"

"Yeah, I know," said Ava with a pained, embarrassed look on her face. "It's pretty confusing to me, too. I mean, I know it's lousy—but I just feel like I have to know. I don't want to spend the rest of my life wondering if I made a mistake, you know?"

Jack smiled sardonically and rubbed his chin.

"A couple weeks ago, I would have loved to have heard you say that."

"Well, what's changed?" she asked, her face contorted in confusion, thinking it was something she'd said or done.

"I'm not sure," said Jack absently, slightly shaking his head. "But I know it has nothing to do with you. It's hard to explain. Not long ago, I used to look at the past and it seemed so fixed and permanent, and the future stretched on to infinity, and the present was just an insignificant blip in between. Now it feels just the opposite, *right now* is the thing that goes on forever."

"I—"

"No, no, it's true. What I mean is… I don't know. Things are different now. You're fantastic, and any man would be thrilled to have you in his life. You're just getting out of college with that crazy degree of yours. You have your whole future ahead of you. And I have what they call 'a past,' and it'll probably catch up to me before I'm done. And my future… I don't know. It wouldn't do you any good. It probably wouldn't do me any good, either," he said with a chuckle. "Hell, you work on all these art projects and stuff that I don't understand at all. I'm just an old, dumb ex-jock and you're probably going to go places and talk to people I'd understand even less than your artwork." Jack wasn't even sure what he was talking about himself. "I just know you have a good thing going, and there's no way for me to fit in there. Your life's going to be great, I can see that. I had my time, now it's your time." Ava looked at him, not knowing quite what to say.

"OK, if that's the way you feel…."

"Now," said Jack with happily, but with fatigue, "we have to get back to this business of the Shea's visit on the 9th. There are a couple of things I need you to do…."

Chapter Twelve

(October, 2006)

Later on the night of Detective Dietrich's disturbing visit to his office, Jack sat sullenly on his couch at home, a look of gloomy concentration having taken over his face. The television was on, but the sound was down low. The lights were off, and in the near-total darkness, only the screen's glow illuminated Jack as he sat. A potent Jack Daniels and Coke sat in his hand, mostly untouched. The drink was going slowly because it was his fourth one since dinner and a dark mood had come over him as he sat and brooded.

Jack had recorded the infamous "Triple Six" drawing from October 9th for all posterity. Intended as a keepsake of his great triumph and the beginning of his new life, after Detective Dietrich's visit, the recording had an entirely different, ominous implication now.

Jack had served as his own Recording Angel, keeping a perfect chronicle of his sins and was now grimly examining the record. He was sitting there, alone in the dark with his drink, watching the drawing over and over again, meticulously studying and examining the ping-pong balls in the lottery machine's glass chamber. The balls weren't acting normally, he could clearly see. It hadn't been his imagination after all. The balls they'd tampered with were sluggish. Nobody except him noticed at the time because he was the only one paying close attention to the way the balls moved. Now, law enforcement, state lottery officials and WKTD's station manager Billy Bowman—everybody was going to be closely examining the same video. And they'd notice the listless balls as surely as he did.

Jack's wife, Jeanine, entered the room and he switched off the DVR recording of the lottery and put a baseball game on the TV. He didn't want her asking any awkward and inconvenient questions about why he was watching a recording of a weeks-old lottery drawing. In an optimistic and supportive mood, Jeanine slid up next to him. This was the side of her everybody had trouble reconciling with the angry and impulsive Jeanine. When things were going well, she could be quite supportive and accommodating, coy and friendly.

"What's wrong with you tonight?" she asked softly, placing her head on his shoulder, her hand rubbing his chest.

"Me? Nothing," Jack answered distantly. He was desperate to be left alone, but of course could not say so. His acute insight into human behavior told him she would not be receptive to commiserating about his anxiety over having fixed a televised public lottery with the help of his mistress.

"Can't you tell me what's on your mind?" she asked.

"I'm just wondering why this guy doesn't make a pitching change," Jack answered absently, referring to the game on the TV.

Jeanine's countenance changed entirely and she glared at him for a long moment.

"You can be real fucking asshole, you know that?" Jeanine declared, abruptly rising. She was not one who took negative feedback well, and less so from the man from whom she'd lately felt a growing estrangement. That Aleksandra had secretly entered the picture and was at least partially the cause of (or perhaps the beneficiary of) the estrangement Jeanine couldn't have known, but it would not have completely surprised her.

Jeanine angrily left the room. Jack glanced at her as she left, but said nothing. He sat in silence, uninterested in her ire and immersed in thoughts of Detective Dietrich's visit, contemplating where things might go from here.

The detective had let Jack know that he was under suspicion, that he hadn't bought Jack's denials. He let Jack know all this in order to increase the pressure. He wanted Jack to think somebody screwed up and for the conspirators to crack, to break ranks and to get them to turn on each other.

And Jack was about to take the bait.

Jack looked at the clock on the wall. It was 9:45. He desperately needed to talk to Aleksandra. He'd been calling her all night, ever since his talk with Dietrich, but he dared not leave a message on her phone.

Jeanine came by with her coat on and keys in her hand.

"I'm going out," she declared as a challenge. Jack said nothing but a mumbled "OK" and nodded. A woman who declares in a huff that she is leaving is not looking to be met with indifference. "Is that *it*, Jack?"

"Yes."

"Weren't you going to ask me where I'm going?" she asked with irritation.

"Sure. I was just waiting. I figured you were going to tell me if I didn't interrupt you, that's all." It was a feasible lie. Normally he would have tried to sooth her bruised feelings before she expressed herself with a verbal barrage, but he had so much on his plate with this lottery situation, he couldn't possibly juggle all of his concerns at once. Plotting his divorce after a successful lottery scam was problematic enough, but throwing a potential police investigation on top of everything else, that was too much.

"I'm going to my mother's."

"Oh. OK."

She glared at him.

"What?" he asked with irritation. "OK, OK, when are you coming back?"

"You'll know when I get back—later."

"OK."

She left in an understandable huff. There was, of course, the predictable slamming of the door.

"I don't have time for this crap," grumbled Jack to himself, adding another piece of string to his giant mental yarn ball of resentment while taking a long drink from his warming Jack-and-Coke, ignoring the pungent taste.

Seeing the headlights of her car leaving the driveway, he heard the chirp and squeal of the tires as Jeanine sped off.

Getting up quickly, Jack went out to his own car in the garage. He kept his secret prepaid cell phone hidden there. He took it out of his hiding spot inside the car and dialed Aleksandra's number. He stayed in the garage to talk to her rather than go back inside. Somehow, even with Jeanine gone, using the phone in the house seemed suicidal. It felt safer in the garage for reasons he could not have fully articulated, even if he'd wanted to.

It seemed the phone rang forever.

Aleksandra finally picked up.

"Hello?"

"Aleksandra," he said, "it's me, Jack."

"Hello, my sweet thing," she purred, "I've missed you, it's so nice to hear your voice."

"Same here," he said hurriedly, "but there's no time for that right now. Listen, we've got problems."

"Oh?"

"Oh, yes. Listen, I got a visitor today."

"From who? Do I need to be jealous?" she asked in a flirty tone. She still didn't realize how serious he was.

"Now's not the time," he urged. "Listen to me, it's very important. I got a visit at the TV station today, from a man named Detective Dietrich."

This got her attention.

"Detective?" she asked in an appropriately concerned tone.

"Yes, *detective*. And you can imagine what he was asking about. Here's what happened," Jack started. He went on to relate his conversation with Dietrich in detail, including his interpretation of the meaning behind every phrase the cop had used. In an act of deceit against his fellow conspirator, he left out the comment made by Dietrich as he'd left the room about a tip from an establishment concerning someone overhearing a ticket-purchaser talk about a fix. This overheard talk was the key to the whole investigation, so Jack himself wasn't sure why he left out any mention of it. Perhaps, like Dietrich, he wanted to hold back a bit of knowledge to make sure he had a superior hand. Jack did not care to examine his motives, but it felt like he was trying to extract information from Aleksandra, not share concerns.

"Oh my God, Jack," Aleksandra whispered in a hushed tone.

"Yes, that's right," said Jack, glad she appreciated the seriousness of the situation.

"What are we to do?"

"It's very simple, don't say anything. Not a word. He hasn't tried to contact you, has he? Nobody from law enforcement has tried to contact you, left a message or anything?" asked Jack, suddenly paranoid that perhaps her phone was bugged and being recorded after she'd decided to co-operate with police behind his back. The world seemed suddenly filled with pitfalls, traps and double-dealings, with danger lurking everywhere. No, he assured himself, Aleksandra would never do that. She would never turn on him. Plus, they'd only just started looking into the lottery drawing, they couldn't have flipped her already.

"No, nobody's talked to me at all," she answered.

"OK, good. Now here's the thing—Dietrich *will* contact you, I guarantee it."

"You're so certain?" Aleksandra asked.

"Yes." Somehow, Jack felt better expressing confidence in something about the investigation. It made him feel more in control of the situation, whereas things had felt totally out of control since Dietrich's visit. "He'll contact you for sure. You won a lot of money, you're an obvious starting point. So when he does, you have to make damned sure you stick to the plan. Remember the contingency plan we had? The one where if someone asks why you'd buy a thousand tickets on one number—"

"It was one thousand, two hundred and fifty," she corrected.

"Whatever," he said. "Do you remember the plan?"

"I'm to say that I bought them as a gift, but changed my mind and kept them."

"Exactly. And this is hugely important, do *not* mention that you played any other numbers! Remember, you only bought the *one number*, the winning combination. If you said you bought ten thousand dollars worth of tickets, the whole thing will be easy to figure out and it'll be as good as a confession, got it?"

"Of course."

"So the only tickets you bought were these twelve hundred and fifty tickets on what happened to be the winning number, got it?"

"Of course," Aleksandra said in rapt attention. She fully understood the seriousness of the situation.

"Good, good," said Jack, sounding and feeling a bit relieved. "Remember, as long as we stick to our stories, there's nothing they can do or prove. As long as we hold together, there's nothing they can prove. I talked to Uncle Georgi in private before we left the studio today, he's up to speed and I know for sure he can play his part," Jack said with confidence. Georgi was reared in the Soviet system, where keeping silent and avoiding suspicion from the authorities was a way of life.

"Oh God, Jack, this is awful!"

"Don't worry, babe," he consoled her. "We just need to keep quiet for a few days and this'll blow right over. God, I wish I could be with you now with all this going on, so you wouldn't have to face this without me," he said.

"Me too," she said with legitimate affection.

"This is just one of those hurdles we talked about that we'd have to get over in order for us to be together."

"I know," she said sadly. "But what I don't understand is how this Detective Dietrich came to become suspicious in the first place," she asked.

"Who knows? Dietrich did try bluffing me, though."

"Bluffing you? How?" she asked.

"He told me he had a tip that the lottery was fixed," said Jack, deciding to come clean upon feeling a degree confidence in his handle on the crisis.

"What sort of tip?"

"He said," recalled Jack, "that they got an anonymous tip from a person who overheard somebody on the phone mentioning a fix while buying lottery tickets. But the more I've thought about it the less sense it makes. At first I bought it hook-line-and-sinker, but now that we're talking, I'm skeptical."

"Oh, good."

Deep down, Jack still believed Detective Dietrich was on to something, but his ego would not allow a show of weakness or fear, so he was content to lie, even to himself.

He coyly sought a way to test Dietrich's story without exposing himself as a man not in control of the situation. He wanted to keep up the façade to himself was well as to Aleksandra.

"But let's not leave any stone unturned," counseled Jack. "Let's run through everything you did on the day of the drawing from the time you got up until the time you bought all the tickets." Jack sought to somehow convinced himself Dietrich was bluffing. "What did you do when you first woke up?" Jack asked, playing the role of detective himself.

"Well," Aleksandra started, "I showered and had breakfast." She then recounted her entire day in excruciating detail, recounting that she'd started to drive around the parameter of the city to purchase the tickets. She started by driving down on the South Shore, going from small city to small city, making her way up and around Route 128, the highway that made a 180 degree arc around the city. She recounted, in piteous detail, all the little convenience stores she'd visited to purchase the tickets. She bought $1,250 worth of tickets at each stop. One thousand, two-hundred fifty tickets of 444 at the first stop, one thousand, two-hundred fifty tickets of 446 at the next stop, one thousand two-hundred fifty tickets of 464 at the next location, and so on, all the while driving north in a semi-circle around the outskirts of the city.

Aleksandra mentioned details about each stop, all that she could remember, in recounting the trip to Jack— who was gluttonously hungry for every detail—with Jack asking pointed questions such as, "Did you say anything to anybody while you were there?" Each time, Aleksandra did not report anything out of the ordinary.

Finally, arriving near home at the end of her travels, Aleksandra described her last stop triumphantly.

"So I went in to buy the very last combination," she said, "which, of course, was the winning number."

"666?"

"Right, the triple six."

"And where was this?"

"Well, like you said to do, I figured I would finish close to home, and I knew that the place that sells the winning ticket gets five percent of the winning jackpot." Jack became vaguely concerned. "So I went to the Russian-American Club here in Somerville to play the last lottery number," said Aleksandra nonchalantly.

"The Russian-American Club?" asked Jack, almost in bewilderment. He knew the place. Georgi and Aleksandra were regulars there. They were friends with the owner. Kasatonov was the owner's name, as Jack remembered, Victor Kasatonov. Kasatonov ran a small-time book-making operation for the locals. Jack recalled Georgi describing it.

The 'club' was basically a dump, an old, plain, run-down building where local Russian émigrés gathered, mostly old, plain, run-down émigrés. It looked like an aged American Legion hall. It was not exactly a trendy spot. The club was drab on the outside and worse on the inside, dimly lit, generally occupied by mostly working class locals getting plastered on cheap booze served in small, dingy glasses or large plastic cups. Jack recalled seeing the locals buying lottery tickets at the counter by the bar. The club got quite crowded sometimes, depending on the occasion or the entertainment. That's when a younger crowd came out. Aleksandra had dragged Jack there on a couple of occasions, wanting to have him to herself on her home turf, saying that the locals didn't care who he was, and it would be safe for them to be seen together there and it was a chance for her to introduce him to some of her Russian neighborhood friends.

"Yes, I figured Victor," Aleksandra said, referring to the owner, "could use the five percent cut. Why not help him out, too? That's what I figured."

"You didn't tell him what you were doing, did you?" asked Jack, becoming alarmed.

"Of course not!" retorted Aleksandra, laughing at the suggestion.

"Thank God," said Jack. "Still, it was dangerous to do this there," he lectured.

"Why?"

"Because people know you there, they know Georgi is your uncle, for one thing. Somebody could figure it out and talk."

"Oh, don't worry. The Russian community is like family anyway. It's always like that with a community of immigrants."

Jack was disturbed she'd decided to go to the Russian Club to buy the fateful tickets without consulting him, and for her part, Aleksandra was growing more than a little tired of his constant lecturing about his conspiracy plans.

"Well, at least it'll be easy to explain why you bought the tickets there, anyway. Since you go there a lot, it wouldn't be unusual for you to stop in there."

"Yes, see? I'm not stupid."

"I mean, it makes sense you'd buy them there, close to home, where you are a regular and everything."

"Exactly," she said with satisfaction. "It was very crowded that evening, anyway, with the after-work crowd. I'm sure I blended in when I bought the tickets. I got them right from Victor himself, he sold them to me."

Jack suddenly had an epiphany. A terribly disturbing realization descended on him.

"Wait a second," he said with rising alarm, almost panic. "You bought the tickets in the club, right?"

"Yes, that's what I just said."

"Hold on, hold on—you didn't call Georgi from inside the Russian-American Club, too, did you?" Jack asked pointedly.

"Yes, that's what you said to do. You said to call Uncle Georgi right when I bought the last of the tickets. I took out my phone and called as I was purchasing the last tickets, I held the phone up to the machine so Uncle Georgi could hear."

"And did you do what I said—did you tell him just what I told you to say, did you say, 'the fix is in,' *in Russian*?!"

"Of course," said Aleksandra, defensively, as if there was nothing else she could have been expected to do.

"What?! You said, 'The fix is in' *in* Russian—*in* the Russian club?!?"

"Well, yes," said Aleksandra, now very defensive. "That's what you told me to do," she retorted in accusation.

"Not *inside* the fucking Russian-American Club!"

"But...but...." stammered Aleksandra. Jack had gone on and on and on about the need to follow his plans and instructions to the letter and now he was ranting about her doing just that.

"*What the fuck were you thinking*??" Jack bellowed.

"I just did what you said to do!" she protested.

"I never told you to speak *Russian* in a club full of fucking Russians!"

"You told me to say it in Russian—you never said why!"

"Don't you understand?" Jack pleaded. "Don't you understand what's happened?!" he screamed in a rising, nearly-shrill voice. "Detective Dietrich said he got a tip from an establishment that overheard someone—*you*—talking about the conspiracy! He was telling the truth!"

"How do you know?" she asked angrily, accusingly.

"Because he told me! *Because he fucking told me himself!* That's how I know! It came right out of his own fucking mouth! He wasn't lying at all! Don't you see? Victor—or somebody—heard you saying the fix was in and put one and one together! Do they know down there at the Russian Club that you won all that money? Did you tell them or did they find out from somewhere?"

"Well…."

"Aw, Christ! We're going to fucking jail," Jack wailed.

"I'm friends with Victor, he wouldn't turn me in!"

"Don't you fucking understand?? He *did* turn you in! He already did! Or he told somebody at the very least, and *they* dimed you out to the cops! Fuck! Goddamn it! That whole fucking place is in on it now! Good fucking God, how could you be so fucking stupid?! You are fucking stupid, do you know that?!"

"I just did what you told me! And Victor wouldn't do anything to hurt me! Not on purpose, that's for certain!"

"It doesn't matter what his motives were," explained Jack slowly, hearing the hurt in Aleksandra's voice. "Wait, the locals from the club sometimes place bets with Victor, right? He still runs that bookmaking operation of his, right?"

"Yes."

"Oh, my God," said Jack in a hollow voice.

"Now what's wrong?"

"Detective Dietrich said street-level bookies were refusing to pay out on the daily number from that night because there were rumors it was fixed."

"How could street bookies know what we did?"

"I'll bet anything Victor refused to pay out on the numbers because he knew the drawing was fixed. Or maybe Victor placed bets on the number himself other bookies. Maybe he hedged his bets and did both, I can't be sure. That's how Dietrich knew...."

"How do you know?"

"Because Victor's a bookie, remember? That's what he does."

"I'm sure—"

"You fucking people are going to do us in," said Jack with blank, flat despair. "You people couldn't keep your goddamned mouths shut," he said in quiet, but stern rebuke.

"We didn't do anything on purpose," Aleksandra protested quietly. She wasn't in tears or hysterical, but she was softly defiant, feeling Jack had planned the whole thing, every step, and now that there was a problem, he was backing away from the ownership of the plan he'd conceived and so tightly controlled.

"OK, OK," said Jack, regrouping, "no need to panic. If we stick to our story, law enforcement still can't prove anything. Not a thing." Aleksandra was silent. "You with me?"

"Yes," she said, but without conviction, unlike before.

"It is very, very, very important we stick to this, Aleksandra, OK?" he said calmly, but almost begging.

"OK."

"If Detective Dietrich or any other law enforcement or lottery agency official or reporter or anybody else approaches you, it is vital—*vital*—that you stick to your story. And here is the crucial thing: if they talk to you for more than five minutes, you have to say you want a lawyer, OK?"

"OK," she answered. Jack thought she would have more to say, but she didn't. No questions or going over 'what if?' scenarios. Her voice was flat, emotionless, haughty.

"OK, then," said Jack, recomposed. "They aren't likely to call you tonight—cops like their quiet nights at home away from the office just like anybody else, so we can talk more tomorrow, OK?"

"Yes."

"Whenever they contact you, remember what I said, stick to your story, and if it goes on for longer than five minutes, say you want a lawyer and don't want to talk any more, but stick with stout denial the entire time, got it?"

"Yes."

"Great, OK," said Jack, breathing a momentary sigh of relief. He felt he might be able to get a handle on this crisis after all. "Then we'll talk tomorrow, sweetie?"

"Yes," said the frigid voice of Aleksandra.

"Talk to you then," Jack said. "And remember what I said." They both hung up and Jack leaned against his car in the suddenly silent garage. Aleksandra was clearly pissed at him, that much was obvious. She loved him dearly, he knew, but she was angry with him. She didn't like that he'd yelled at her. He'd never really raised his voice to her or any other woman before, but then again, no other woman was ever going to land him in prison before. "Oh well," he thought to himself, "she's mad now, but tomorrow, when we get together and talk things over, I'll be able to sooth those hard feelings easily enough." He could work that stuff out later. He always worked things out.

Still, in the back of his mind, dark doubts gnawed at all his thoughts. If law enforcement or the station or somebody else found out Aleksandra was related to Georgi, stout denials might not be strong enough. At the very least she'd probably have to give back the $2.1 million they'd won because station relatives were ineligible to win jackpots, and Jack would be out the ten thousand dollars he fronted to buy the tickets in the first place. "Well," he told himself, "that's a small price for freedom."

He heaved a sigh, wondered how things had gotten so complicated. "How did it get like this?" he asked himself, vaguely seeing himself as the victim. It had all started out so good—his career, his marriage to Jeanine, his affair with Aleksandra—it was all so perfect, and now his whole way of life was under threat. Then he noticed Jeanine's car pulling into the driveway. She'd wonder what he was doing standing in the garage for no apparent reason, so he hurried back inside and hoped against all odds that she would be in a good mood. She'd promised to be gone for a while but instead had returned quickly. That meant she was probably spoiling for a fight. A good mood on her part seemed ludicrously unlikely, and Jack braced for a battle....

For her part, Aleksandra remained seated in the same spot after she hung up the phone, seething with rage at Jack. She had barely moved a muscle. A passionate and impulsive person, she bristled at the blame Jack had placed at her feet. She was furious beyond words at the way he'd yelled at her—who did he think he was talking to her that way?? No man ever called her a stupid fucking bitch! No man was *going* to call her a stupid fucking bitch!

Haughty and full of pride, Aleksandra got up and started pacing back and forth, furious at Jack. He'd blamed her for everything! And it was *his* damned plan in the first place! She'd been basically dragged along at his insistence! And poor Uncle Georgi, too! They'd both been little more than pawns in Jack's game! And why? Because he was married to that psycho bitch, that's why! Because he was too greedy to dump his wife and take up with her like he should have done a long time ago!

Here was Jack, Aleksandra thought to herself, banging her on the side, keeping her hidden like a little whore-secret! He probably got a good laugh out it, too, that serpent, as he slept with his wife!

Aleksandra continued to silently rage as she got up and paced around her kitchen.

She reached into a cabinet drawer, pulled out a vial and laid out a line of cocaine on her kitchen table. It reminded her of Jack and she became even more angry, and with a swipe of her hand, dashed the powder all over the floor and threw herself down on a kitchen chair in a stifled fury.

Call her a stupid fucking bitch?! That asshole! Keeping her on the side like a dirty secret? Snake! Worm! Then her face grew soft and concerned. And what about Uncle Georgi? He was very much like a father to her, the only person she could truly count on. What if Jack was right and this all went south? They'd both go down with him. That sneaky asshole Jack Webster had drafted them both for his plot. How dare he act that way, and put Uncle Georgi at risk with his lunatic schemes?!

Jack was such a sneak, Aleksandra considered, he'd probably try and pin in on *them*! Maybe he was telling her to keep quiet in the face of police questioning just so he'd have first crack at talking to the cops and cutting a deal for himself?

Impulsive and stinging from insulted pride, Aleksandra hesitated no longer. She picked up the phone, calling a variety of different numbers in her search. Eventually being directed to the number she was looking for by a switchboard operator, she was put through to her destination. If Jack was going to act like this, she would show him. She was not going to be pushed around by the likes of a rat of his kind.

The phone operator on the other end picked up.

"Boston Police Department, Area B," the operator announced.

"Hello," started Aleksandra. "This is Aleksandra Maragos. I won the lottery a few weeks ago. I need to talk to Detective Dietrich." She paused and listened to the response. "Well, if he's not in, you need to get him on phone from home—right now. This is very important. It cannot wait." There was another pause as she listened. "Oh, don't worry, tell him my name. I am certain he's been waiting to talk to me, he'll know who I am. I have a very interesting story to tell him about an asshole of a snake."

*

It was nine months later, and Jack stood, looking down at the floor, chastened, his hands clasped behind his back, his face a mixture of shame and regret, almost all of it for the benefit of the judge in front of him. He was on the fifth floor of the courthouse in Cambridge, Massachusetts, just a few miles from the WKTD studios and his stomping grounds.

His case had become news—big news, national news, but especially monumental in and around Boston. Beloved local television icon Jack Webster had been arrested for fixing the daily lottery. The Triple Six Fix, they were calling it. For a while, you couldn't get away from the story, but it unfolded quickly and soon all the details emerged concerning Jack's guilt, though his motivations and the story behind the conspiracy remained a total mystery, as Jack refused to speak to anybody about what had occurred and everybody else associated with the case was silenced by order of the court. Aleksandra's phone call to Detective Dietrich led to a meeting with the law officer within twelve hours. Within twenty-four hours, all of the details of the plan had been spilled to law enforcement like a trash container emptied onto a desktop.

To Jack, the nine months after Aleksandra blew the whistle on their conspiracy seemed both at once a lifetime and also the blink of an eye. Given how red-handed he'd been caught—two co-conspirators talking freely to police left little wiggle room—it was almost a surprise it took nine months to reach a plea deal, but that's how long a good lawyer will take, and Jack had a good lawyer.

He glanced over at his lawyer, who was standing next to him, in front of Judge Williamson as he prepared to read his sentence. Jack's lawyer, Robert Curtis, esquire, was a highly compensated and well-known attorney. Even when on trial, with his freedom at stake, Jack couldn't resist going for an attention-grabbing name when selecting an attorney. Jack was grateful toward his lawyer for all his efforts. He'd even been able to refer Jack to a great divorce lawyer, which of course became necessary when the story broke and all the media outlets in town blared that beloved sportscaster Jack Webster—an icon at WKTD and the voice of the local NHL hockey team on the radio—was involved in the lottery scam with his mistress and her uncle. Jeanine was not about to sit idly by with *that,* and promptly filed for divorce. So Jack got his divorce after all, but of course, by then Aleksandra was long gone....

Jack looked over his shoulder and in the courtroom gallery sat Jeanine, there to see him sentenced. They made eye contact.

Jack silently mouthed the words, "I love you!" to her. Jeanine responded by contorting her face in anger and flipping her middle finger up at him. "Fuck you!" she mouthed back.

With equanimity, Jack turned back around. "Win some, lose some," he mumbled to himself.

The judge started talking, throwing out various legal terms and charges, but Jack didn't pay attention to most of it. He'd long since become numb the whole process. There were too many terms, too many charges, too many violations and he soon stopped trying to follow the proceedings and quickly became desensitized to the machinations of justice. He'd made his plea deal, and hearing his lawyer counsel him about various legal terms had ceased being of interest to him, he just wanted the bottom line.

"...Criminal mischief, criminal conspiracy, rigging a public contest, theft by deception...," droned the judge.

Jack glanced at his lawyer and for some reason, cracked a crooked grin. *Can you fucking believe this?* he seemed to be asking without words.

Jack actually felt quite indebted to his attorney. The agreement with law enforcement would be a seven-year sentence. His lawyer probably got a fair sentence cut in half. He could have gotten double that amount of time easily, but his attorney had argued—and more importantly, negotiated—tirelessly on his behalf. He'd kept Jack up to speed every step of the way and presented options to him at every juncture, but Jack had became deadened to it all quickly, as non-lawyers do once caught up in the dicey machinery of the law.

Because the lottery tickets had been purchased all over the Commonwealth of Massachusetts, there was confusion about jurisdiction, and that there was some confusion was an opening Jack's negotiator skillfully exploited. Was the legal apparatus about justice or about negotiating? Clearly, it was about cutting a deal. Luckily for Jack, his local celebrity loomed over all the negotiations, as there was always a chance that if the case went to trial, some locals on the jury who liked him would take his side and let him walk entirely. Even when losing his freedom, Jack's popularity and charisma helped him.

The judge said that even though it was a seven year sentence, Jack would be eligible to walk free in three years if he stayed out of trouble. Jack was no hard-core, life-long criminal and he was virtually certain to fulfill that criteria. As his sentence was being read, suddenly Jack could barely process the words of the judge as his freedom slipped away with every passing phrase out of the justice's mouth. It was all too overwhelming to concentrate on. *But I have tickets to a concert this month. I was going to get my pilot's license next year*, his mind silently protested. *And the hockey season will be coming up before you know it, I have to be there!*

Three years of his life—minimum—were disappearing right before his eyes. Jack had become resigned to this loss of freedom for some time. Indeed, when his lawyer told him he thought he could get a deal whereby he could walk in a mere three years (he'd been told to prepare for the possibility of an entire decade) Jack had been wordlessly relieved. But now that the moment had come, there was a suddenly paralyzing avalanche of emotion all over again. Three years in the abstract was one thing, but three years beginning *today* was quite another.

Aleksandra and her Uncle Georgi were nowhere to be seen in the courtroom. Because Aleksandra dropped the dime on her own accord and without any prodding had sung so freely, she was given a suspended sentence in exchange for all her cooperation. She did twenty-four hours in prison as a token punishment and then was sent on her way, with the only proviso being that she stay out of trouble. Since it was unlikely she would be fixing any more lotteries, she essentially went unpunished. Since Georgi also freely and enthusiastically (or, with as much enthusiasm as the sullen old Russian could summon) cooperated with authorities and confirmed every word of Aleksandra's story, thus making a much more perfect case for prosecutors, he also spent twenty-four hours behind bars and was set free.

Jack was pleased about one aspect at least: He had been correct in his calculation that the family bond between Aleksandra and Georgi made them a pair inseparable and incapable of turning on each other. Unfortunately for him, he'd been tragically wrong in figuring that his romance with Aleksandra made them inseparable as well. It turned out the almost-father-daughter bond Aleksandra shared with Georgi proved stronger than the married-man-and-mistress bond Jack had with her. In the end Georgi and Aleksandra had indeed proved perfect conspirators, but only for each other.

It was the staggering ease with which Aleksandra turned on him that shocked Jack. Theirs had been a deep, romantic attachment, their love mutually stated and agreed upon as a near-perfect bonding of souls. Jack had known her to be proud, but he'd been fighting so hard and so long and so much worse with his wife, he never realized the mere angry words he had directed at Aleksandra at the unraveling of their conspiracy would be so much taken to heart, for Aleksandra's motivation for blowing the whistle was not, in fact, an urge to cut a good deal for herself, but instead a desire to show her displeasure at Jack's tone and attitude towards her.

That she soon regretted her rash phone call to the authorities was lost on Jack, of course. In fact, once it became impractical to regret anything, Aleksandra had entirely disassociated herself with any feelings of remorse and went on with the practical business of cutting a deal and putting her lover away into prison. She'd loved Jack, but hell, she'd find love again, of this she was sure. Despite the fact she truly had loved him, Aleksandra had turned the page, cooperated with authorities, and when this was done, she simply moved on, never looked back and barely gave Jack another thought….

Jack realized the judge was finishing up his almost endlessly wordy and melancholy preaching of how Jack had let everyone down, along with the accompanying sentence. He said something about Jack's popularity and how people all across the entire state had liked him, looked up to him and trusted him, but Jack didn't pay a bit of attention. He didn't care about any of that stuff.

"Do you have anything to say, Mr. Webster?" asked the judge in a voice intended to convey his own somber disappointment, for he was clearly a sports fan himself.

"No," said Jack bluntly. He had intended to launch into a long, contrite, apologetic soliloquy, but he decided against it at the last second. *Screw them*, he thought to himself, vibrant with self-pity. If they all really liked him so much, why were they putting him away? *Damned phonies*, he said to himself.

"Don't worry," whispered Jack's attorney, Mr. Curtis, "you'll be free in three years," he said with a victorious optimism that Jack felt was misplaced under the circumstances.

The bailiffs who had chummed around with Jack endlessly during his stay in the courthouse—they being delighted to have a beloved, famous, local, likeable celebrity in their midst—sadly and with regret came over and silently led Jack away to his long, dark, lonely fate....

Chapter Thirteen

(October 2nd, 2010)

Jack sat at a table at the Earthpeace conference room, half slumped over, his eyes lazily half shut, his breathing soft. He felt in constant need of a breather these days and took advantage of any opportunity to sit down and rest for a moment.

The room Earthpeace was renting to serve as an office wasn't truly a conference room like what would be found in the shiny, metallic confines of a high-rise modern business building. This was a Spartan setting. There were no cushy chairs or screens for PowerPoint presentations or anything of the like. There were also none of the boxes of donuts, elaborately diced fruits or other edible fixtures of business meetings, which suited Jack just fine in light of his hunger strike. Being an ecology-minded public interest group, the only thing left around for the Earthpeacers to eat was a bowl of trail mix, but—given how he was racked with hunger these days—Jack had trouble ignoring even that modest offering. He never would have guessed there would be a time in his life where he yearned for trail mix. He was a few weeks into his now-famous hunger strike and didn't want any reminders of food, as each morsel stabbed and gnawed at his consciousness.

His hunger strike had started as a gag, from a throw-away line that Jack had sarcastically tossed out to Billy Bowman at WKTD, but it wasn't a gag or scam anymore. Jack's hunger strike had become a major news story. Because of his fame in fixing the lottery and his subsequent imprisonment, Jack's hunger strike made the wire services and had become a regularly updated and commented upon item on local news outlets, especially WKTD.

If any of this success with the media brought Jack enthusiasm or excitement, it was not evident at the moment, however, as he sat still and unmoving, seemingly untouched by the frenzied world around him.

Jack was alone in the Earthpeace room for the moment, listless and lethargic with fatigue, an empty liter bottle of water sitting at his side next to a new, full bottle of water. He was distracted and bewildered by his continuing thirst and he finally gave in and took a deep drink.

Jack was waiting for a few updates on what was going on with the Earthpeace campaign. He had become the entire center of the Earthpeace operation over the past few weeks, and the whole project had become entirely energized under his leadership. His own energy seemed to constantly flag, but then he'd rally himself to complete whichever task he was working on, and then fall back again a bit further than before, only to repeat the process all over again.

Larry, the old hippie Director, had gladly faded into the background and let Jack take charge. Jack would give lessons on how to talk to media outlets, "This is what he's going to ask you," he'd tell the Earthpeacers, "and this is the angle he'll respond to, this is what he'll see as being good to use in his story," Jack would counsel, he having been around the news business long enough to have an eye and ear for what it was reporters were looking, and what would be a useful narrative for media consumption. Jack got all the volunteers and staff for Earthpeace participating and kept tabs on what everyone was doing, so everybody felt involved and enthused.

Jack also advised some of the young college kids on various topics not associated with the airport campaign, even going so far as to promise to write letters of recommendation for them for when they applied to graduate school and reluctantly advise them on relationships, family advice or other worldly troubles, urging them to remain calm and mentally focused. "Your mind constantly churns out endless speculation and random thoughts," he'd tell people, "don't pay any attention to it, just concentrate on what you're doing right now." He kept the membership motivated when they faced rejection and gave them direction when assignments or concerns came along. "The best way to clear up muddy water is to leave it alone," he'd counseled someone who approached him in a state of frenzied distraction.

In every way, since he'd decided to do the infamous WKTD interview, Jack had become the center of the

---

Stephen Brown

storm for the local chapter, truly their guide and guru. Before he'd been faking it, but now he actually took on the role with sincerity.

All this and his celebrity hunger strike had worn him down. He was endlessly thirsty and even he noticed he'd dropped more weight than he'd expected. Jack was surprised to see his once powerful frame in the mirror these days, so meager and emaciated had it become compared to his old, robust glory days.

As he sat at the conference table, Jack was glad to have a few moments alone to rest a bit, as his labors had entirely sapped his strength.

His respite was ended, however, by a pleasant sight, as Ava came in to see him. She had become something of an unofficial assistant to him in his unofficial leadership role, and he was glad for it, as he needed the help. The media campaign had taken off and he no longer seemed to have time for even half of the details that needed attention.

"Jack—" Ava stopped short upon catching a good look at him. She hadn't seen him in person in a few days after having only talked to him over the phone, and she was surprised at what she saw. "Jeez, Jack, are you OK?" she asked with concern as she slowly approached and sat next to him.

"Huh? What do you mean?"

"You look awful."

"Yeah, I guess I do. I'm just tired."

"You look all… gaunt."

Jack looked down at himself as he sat.

"Yeah, I guess you're right. I *am* on a hunger strike, you know," he pointed out with fatigued light-heartedness.

274

He found himself saying this a lot to concerned on-lookers lately.

"Are you sure you're all right with the hunger strike? It's getting us huge publicity, but you look kind of weak," she asked, expressing some misgiving.

"Oh, sure," Jack assured her listlessly, "I'm just worn out. I'm very, very tired."

"You look it."

"I'm tired—and incredibly thirsty," he said, taking another drink of water. "I guess it's true that we get most of our water from what we eat."

"Maybe it's time for you to eat a little?" hinted Ava.

"Oh, no, no. I'm just tired from all the work that the hunger strike is bringing in."

"Well, if you need to, you're going to eat."

"I'll be OK."

"Well," said Ava, trying to convince herself everything was fine, "at least it's for a good cause."

"Yeah, it's working out better than I could have expected. I'm getting calls from all over the place. Turns out the lottery scandal was a good way to bring in attention about the hunger strike, which is a good way to bring attention to the airport. If it weren't for the lottery, I don't think anybody would have any interest in it. I guess if you go on a hunger strike for a good cause but you *aren't* a crook, nobody cares," he joked sardonically.

"You know, Jack," Ava started in a serious tone, "at first, some people thought you were just hanging around here to, you know, for other reasons."

"It's hard to blame anybody for thinking that," Jack commented with fairness.

"But now, the way you've taken over around here—organizing, getting media attention—you've done more since you've shown up than everybody else in this Earthpeace chapter combined ."

"Well, I don't think Greg is so happy about it," Jack said, to which they both chuckled, knowing Greg wanted a leadership role in order to lead a charge against an entrenched police phalanx.

"He'll be happy in the end," Ava predicted.

"Yeah, I hope so. Now, as far as the October 9th speech at Slocumb Airport I'm going to give, did you do like I told you?"

"Yup. I leaked it to Gary Gibson that you were going to drop a bombshell, and not just read a simple statement, when you give your address on behalf of Earthpeace and the people of Norton at the airport just before Senator Shea arrives."

"Good. Gary will tell Billy Bowman, who I'm quite certain is telling everything to Rudy Baxter, Senator Shea's chief of staff, in order to stay in Shea's good graces. Senator Shea will have us evicted from the airbase, just like he did when you guys tried to protest outside his compound last year, but not before I get to read my statement. That will be a powerful television image when we get ejected. We're guaranteed a lot of coverage for this. At some point, state officials are going to have to deal with the public attention at having this project shoved down Norton's throat," Jack commented, "and once I get up there and talk about Senator Shea's influence in having it placed in Norton, I think something'll happen."

"I think so, too," said Ava.

Jack took another long drink and heaved a sigh and with an effort, dragged himself up to stand.

"Today is October 2nd, so it's a week away. We have to put the finishing touches on the protest plans and we'll be all set. I'm incredibly tired—all this hunger striking really *must* be wearing me down—so if you'll excuse me, if we're done here, I think I'll run home and take a little catnap."

*

It was October 9th and the sun was successfully breaking out from behind rolling gray autumn clouds, giving a bright illumination to the day. Off in the distance, however, dark clouds gathered ominously like menacing charcoal boulders, as if they were pensively waiting for the right moment to break free and charge across the sky and bring ruin.

The trees were falling prey to the inevitable process of losing their lush summer vitality as the leaves turned bright colors, became exhausted, and fell silently from their warm weather perches to the indifferent earth below. Autumn had brought strong periodic rains and the ground seemed moist, cold and unfriendly. The grass was becoming yellow and worn as everywhere life began to fade and die. The world prepared for its dark winter's hibernation and all summer's life and vibrancy seemed in full retreat before a remorseless, creeping onslaught of cold and shadow.

Everything had a hint of wetness to the touch and the wind seemed to blow colder than it had in a long time. It was cool enough to require a light jacket as protection against the moist, occasionally hissing wind, which brought with it a permeating chill. The day had a touch of unmistakable, unavoidable rawness despite the sunlight. A few stray leaves blew along the ground, heralding the coming dark season. It was not winter, but it was unseasonably cool and the warmth of summer would soon be gone entirely.

It was also the day of the planned protest at Slocumb Airport where Jack would read a prepared statement to the assembled media about the behind-the-scene influences guiding the expansion to Slocumb as Senator Shea arrived at the base.

Jack, who had not yet arrived, was scheduled to take to the podium at 11:00 AM. A large assemblage of activists and media people were gathered at the base, waiting for Jack's statement and Shea's simultaneous arrival. There were over a hundred activists milling around, holding signs and showing support. And there was a huge number of media people as well, for Jack's hunger strike had become an ever-growing story. There were TV news vans with dishes on the roof parked here and there with live shots being done and set up and other media "stringers" hanging around as well, putting together newspaper and wire service stories. Word that not only was the hunger-striking Jack Webster going to read an official statement, but that the statement was concerning Senator Shea, made the event a big deal, with perhaps national implications given Senator Shea's stature, were some sort of corruption implied.

Most of the people at the gathering had been there for hours and as the anticipation grew, the tension became palpable.

There was a bank of microphones set up in front of a little platform that the Earthpeacers had set up, where Jack was going to stand when reading his text. The Earthpeacers walked around hoping to be asked to talk by somebody in the media, but mostly, all those assembled there sensed an odd edge in the air, which left everyone feeling preoccupied and distracted.

With a furrowed brow, Greg, the hothead who agitated for confrontation, milled about nervously among his entourage of like-minded radicals anxious for action of some kind. It was noted by some that he was surrounded by people nobody had seen around before, and some surmised he'd put out a call to kindred allies on his own volition.

Gary Gibson, the anchor at WKTD who was Jack's old friend and main media contact, had made a rare foray out into the field to cover the event, signifying the story's importance. Gary—because of the closeness with which he had been following the Earthpeace story, and more specifically, the famous disgraced local celebrity leading it, Jack Webster—had wanted to be there if something big happened. He was waiting for Jack to arrive and was told by several people that Jack, who he hadn't seen in person in some time, wasn't feeling too great—what with the hunger strike—and was going to show up only when it was time for him to speak in order to conserve his strength.

Finally, after a long wait, a little hybrid economy car pulled down the street, virtually unnoticed. Earthpeace had set up a tent on the side of the road behind the platform of microphones that would serve as a base, out of which they could duck in and out in order to have a place free from the cold wind as they prepared for the news conference. The hybrid car quietly and unobtrusively pulled in behind the tent, completely unheeded by the crowd. Jack was the passenger inside the car. He wanted privacy before he went out to speak to the assembled media, as he needed to gather his fading energy.

The hybrid car was Ava's. She was acting as Jack's chauffeur. Ava put the car in park and shut off the engine.

The inside of the car served as a quiet cocoon of stillness and silence against the buzz of activity outside. Ava turned to him with a look of worry.

"Jack," she whispered to the frail, emaciated figure next to her, "we're here."

Jack, who had been sitting in perfect stillness in his seat, gazing closed-eyed towards the floor, slowly looked up and opened his eyes.

"Already?" he asked in a weak, barely audible, husky voice.

"*Yes*," Ava answered softly.

To those who hadn't seen him in even the past week, Jack's appearance was shocking. Just a week before, in the Earthpeace conference room, Jack had been hearing constant expressions of worry about his health. Now, a mere week later, he had deteriorated noticeably. He took yet another long drink of water.

"Do you need more water?" asked Ava gently, helping him hold up the bottle, feeling almost like a nurse. "I've got some more water in the back seat that I brought along. I know you're always thirsty these days."

"Yeah, I'm thirsty," said Jack in a hoarse whisper, his eyes drowsily half shut. "More water might be good to bring along."

Ava opened another bottle and practically helped him drink from it, keeping her hand underneath the bottle. Her eyes were narrowed and her face contorted with concern.

"Jack, I'm worried about you," stated Ava, almost pleadingly.

"Why's that?" he asked with effort.

"You look terrible," she asserted, and he did. "You're wasting away." Jack's face was sunk and ashen and his clothes hung off him, his powerful, athletic frame from his TV days now long gone. He drank water almost constantly and even though he was exhausted, he pushed himself on.

"It's just the hunger strike, that's all," Jack said aimlessly, by rote. "I'll be O.K. Let's get outside." With two hands and a great effort, he shoved opened the door of the car.

Ava got out and hurried around to the passenger side by the time Jack had, with considerable exertion, dragged himself out of the passenger seat. They stood next to the car, but away from any prying eyes, completely unnoticed and in total privacy, shielded by the tent from the crowd of people waiting for them, people who weren't even aware yet that Jack had arrived.

"I think it's more than just the hunger strike," said Ava, worry all over her face. "You're more fragile than you should be. You shouldn't be *this* weak. Just a week ago you looked bad, but not this bad. You need to start eating or something."

"I *am* eating. I'm drinking those FastSlim shakes for nutrition. That's eating. Now come on, we need to go see the media people and get this show on the road."

They started to walk, but after just one step, Jack seemed to lose strength and slumped halfway to the ground, almost collapsing entirely.

"Jack!" Ava yelped with panic, grabbing him and helping him pull himself up.

"I'll be OK, I'll be OK," he said, his words drifting off as he leaned against the car for support.

"Jack, you've lost a ton of weight, you are *not* well."

"I'll double up on my nutritional shakes, then," he retorted sardonically.

"Stop it. Couldn't you just cheat and eat once in a while? Nobody will know."

"No!" Jack asserted firmly in a fleeting flash of strength, his eyes wild in resistance. "No cheating."

"Why not?" begged Ava.

"Because it's time for me to get it right," Jack blurted out stubbornly, looking away.

"Why?"

Jack, struggling to gather himself and catch his breath, scowled in defiance.

"Why?" he repeated rhetorically, having never verbalized his thoughts on the subject before. "Because... I've cheated at everything. I've always cheated—even when I wasn't cheating, I was cheating... cheating in *some* way. I've always been a fraud, a scam artist. I lied, even to myself. No more."

"So *what*?" pleaded Ava. "This is different."

"You're right, it *is* different. It *will* be different."

"Jack, look at yourself. You've done a ton already and you can still do a ton more without a hunger strike. I don't understand."

"I know you don't." Jack took a deep breath as he looked at the ground. He kept a hand on Ava's shoulder to steady himself for fear that he couldn't support himself.

"Jack, the airport expansion isn't worth it. The Blue-Bottled Finches aren't worth it. Are you risking yourself for them?"

Jack shook his head.

"No. It's not about the airport. Or the Finches. It's not about any of that stuff. Not really, anyway." Jack felt his knees almost giving way, but he caught himself. He took another deep breath and gathered himself. "It isn't about causes, even good causes."

"You care about those causes, don't you?"

"Sure…but it's not about that."

"But, Jack—"

"See," struggled Jack, not so much physically, but searching for a way to explain himself, still not looking at her, almost talking to himself, "this whole thing, this is the first time I've done something that…isn't for me…. It's the first time in my whole, entire life I'm not being selfish, not just indulging my desires, not obsessed with my own self. It's the first time I'm doing something right. It's the first time I'm not being… being a creep. And I don't want to let anybody down. I don't want to let myself down. I won't fail."

Ava looked at him intently.

"Are you serious?" she asked.

Jack paused and looked back at her.

"Dead serious."

Larry, the director of the local Earthpeace chapter, poked his head around the corner. He'd been searching for them.

"Hey, guys, there you are—Senator Shea's plane has landed," he announced.

Jack suddenly felt a bit stronger and stood on his own, pulling himself upright and fully erect. Ava looked at him with worry.

"OK," he said, "let's go."

The ever-shifting clouds parted again after having briefly taken control of the sky, and through the cold, moist breeze the sun was shining brightly in Jack's eyes as he walked to the makeshift podium. He was moving slowly, but he had managed to rally himself and move unaided. Ava was stunned to see him tap a hidden reservoir of strength and carry himself to the gathering. For his part, Jack was surprised at how many media members were there crowding around the stage.

"Wow," commented Ava, leading a meandering Jack slightly by pulling at his elbow, "look at this crowd. Are you going to be nervous talking in front of all of these people?" she asked teasingly, hoping to buck him up.

"Hey, in my old life I used to be on TV, remember?" he kidded back in a weak voice and a grin.

"Yeah….Hey, Jack," said Ava with a look of sudden astonishment on her face, "do you know what today's date is?"

"The 9th," said Jack languidly, through a fog of fatigue.

"It's October 9th!"

"And?"

"It's the anniversary of your lottery drawing!"

Jack thought about it. She was right. The rigged lottery was drawn on October 9th. He briefly threw his mind back to that night.

"You're right. An inauspicious anniversary!" he said as they shared a smile.

Jack slowly and with great effort scuffled up behind the bank of microphones and gently took out his prepared statement. He looked out over the crowd, and to his surprise, he noticed Rudy Baxter among the assembled throng, standing slightly off to the side. They locked eyes for a moment as Jack recalled Baxter's threats at defying Senator Shea and how Baxter promised that Jack would regret crossing him. Baxter looked cocky.

Jack absently brushed his hair back into place a couple of times as the chilling wind picked up.

"Thanks for coming everybody," started Jack quietly, feeling weak. He took mental note that he felt weaker than he had even a few hours ago. He started to wonder if he could even get through reading his statement.

Jack paused to slowly take a drink of water from his ever-present bottle, and as he did, looking beyond the edge of his raised bottle, he saw several state police cruisers rapidly descending on the scene, their lights silently flashing. He lowered his water bottle and silently watched the troopers get out of their cars and hurriedly approach the podium where he stood.

The cops pushed their way through the crowd and approached Jack, looking stern and official. Before he knew it, one of them grabbed his arm.

"What's going on?" demanded the old hippie director, standing next to Jack.

"You're being detained," stated one of the cops without emotion, addressing Jack.

"What?" called out Ava. "Why?"

"This man is on government property and is trespassing."

"Trespassing?" asked Jack with quiet alarm. "That's a formal criminal charge, not just a request to leave. That's a violation of my condition of release from prison," he said in a low tone to nobody in particular. He immediately looked at Rudy Baxter, who was wearing a smug look of satisfaction on his face as he stood, arms crossed. Baxter had warned that the Senator had powerful friends all over state government. This was the payback of which he'd warned.

"They'll put Jack back in jail!" cried out Greg, the hothead, and Jack knew he was right. Senator Shea had many friends indeed, and half the government officials in the state felt obliged to him in one way or another. It must have been child's play to call in a favor and have him sent back to prison, Jack well knew. Earthpeace had expected law enforcement to evict them, but charges of trespassing were different. Even if the trumped up charges didn't stick, Jack realized, it would still be a violation of his release and meant a trip back to prison. Senator Shea had easily manipulated state authority to do his bidding.

The Earthpeace people were suddenly surging around, hurling invectives towards the authorities, who were holding up their hands to tell them to back away. Hostility filled the air.

Jack, his energy spent, was now feeling so weak he was no longer sure how long he could support himself, put up his hands.

"No, no," he said quietly, but as loudly as he could, to the Earthpeace people, "I'll go along, everybody just sit still. We can sort it out later."

Greg, his longed-for confrontation finally at hand, was heard yelling. He and his bused-in cronies started shoving back and forth with the police, and all the other Earthpeace people joined in, though Jack, feeling increasingly drained, had troubling noticing exactly what was going on.

"Settle down, everyone," he mumbled weakly, though nobody heard him over the growing din.

His strength wavering, the edges of Jack's vision started getting black.

Jack was aware that there was now a great commotion going all around him, and the jostling started bumping him, the cops and the people around him back and forth, but he found it hard to concentrate on the details. People—he wasn't sure who—started tugging at him from every direction, pulling him this way and that.

There was a great upheaval now, with yelling and screaming all around. Jack realized a melee had broken out, though he felt oddly removed from it. He wasn't sure exactly what was going on, but was vaguely aware of a cop subduing somebody off on the edges of his vision as a baton swung freely, but Jack's consciousness had taken on a dreamy quality as he started to wonder if he was passing out. It was now total chaos all around him, he was pretty sure.

Unable to stand any longer and unwilling to try, through hazy eyes and darkening vision, Jack saw nothing but blue sky as he felt his head hit the moist turf, though he wasn't sure if he'd landed hard or softly. He didn't care so much any longer about what was happening to him, and the tumult all around him now seemed otherworldly and distant. He wanted to urge everyone to calm down, that there was no need to violently resist, that it would only cause more problems, that under these conditions, non-action was the best course, but somehow the words only remained in his head as his mind swam.

Time seemed distorted. He was no longer aware of how much time had passed. Was everything happening quickly or slowly? Had his head hit the grass a second ago or half an hour before? He couldn't tell. Jack was aware of great strife and chaos swirling all around him, people hovering over him, looking down on him with concern, disappearing, others appearing in their place. He wasn't sure what was happening. Noises seemed present, but it as if he was removed from them. Speech was out of the question.

There were sirens and his vision kept getting darker, his thoughts more vague. He heard the words "weight loss," and "Type One" among the yelling, but he let the words pass over him without mental comment. Somebody said "in shock." One voice said something about taking blood pressure and Jack thought he was being strapped down.

He wasn't sure if there was still a violent conflict going on, but people in uniforms of differing kinds hovered all about him and he thought his body got lifted, then jerked, in which direction he could not tell. Then, oddly, he suddenly remembered he never did get to read his statement to the crowd and he wondered if he'd get to see the opening exhibit of Ava's sculpting she had had been so excited about and that he'd promised to attend.

Jack felt a tremendous headache, but he also felt totally removed from his time and place, and even from his own consciousness. Words seemed pointless to him. He felt totally at ease, despite the chaos and conflict surrounding him, even as his vision grew darker still. He was no longer certain how long things had been swirling around him, and he grew more and more removed. He no longer felt thirsty, but he did feel an odd contentment that he'd done what he needed to do. He'd thrown off his old self and attachments. Though his face was serene and almost expressionless, he had an inward, contented smile. His vision got darker and darker until everything went totally black, and his eyes never opened again.